T0029585

The
MIDNIGHT
GARDEN

The
MIDNIGHT
GARDEN

a
novel

ELAINE ROTH

LAKE UNION
PUBLISHING

This is a work of fiction. Names, characters, organizations, places, events, and incidents are either products of the author's imagination or are used fictitiously. Otherwise, any resemblance to actual persons, living or dead, is purely coincidental.

Text copyright © 2023 by Elaine Roth
All rights reserved.

No part of this book may be reproduced, or stored in a retrieval system, or transmitted in any form or by any means, electronic, mechanical, photocopying, recording, or otherwise, without express written permission of the publisher.

Published by Lake Union Publishing, Seattle

www.apub.com

Amazon, the Amazon logo, and Lake Union Publishing are trademarks of Amazon.com, Inc., or its affiliates.

ISBN-13: 9781662513039 (paperback)
ISBN-13: 9781662513022 (digital)

Cover design by Shasti O'Leary Soudant
Cover image: © harmonia_green / Shutterstock;
© seksan wangkeeree / Shutterstock; © Balazs Kovacs / ArcAngel

Printed in the United States of America

To Matt,
my first love, my biggest cheerleader, my reason for
believing in magic

To Gabrielle and Henry,
my why

1

HOPE

This is the part I was dreading. Worse than sitting through the vows, the promises of forever, the "till death do us part," is this: the tribute to Brandon.

A slideshow plays on the big screen as Logan speaks to the guests. His voice begins to crack, and his new bride grips his free hand with both of hers. He tells a story about Brandon as a gangly nine-year-old capturing frogs and keeping them as pets. Everyone laughs, and for a heartbeat, I'm nine again, ankle deep in frigid pond water with Brandon.

Logan shares another story—about a time when Brandon was sixteen and their mom caught him sneaking in a girl to play spin the bottle. Just like that, I'm sitting cross-legged on Brandon's floor, leaning in to kiss the boy next door who I always knew I'd marry.

Logan's eyes, lined with tears, lock on mine. I nod, giving him silent permission to continue. It's his day, his wedding. Brandon was mine, but also his. Even though their age gap meant Brandon spent half Logan's life treating him like a nuisance, in the years before he died, they were as close as brothers could be. Logan needs to feel like Brandon is a part of his day. He *should* be a part of today.

But Brandon's been gone over two years now, and it's still hard to hear his name in the past tense.

The memories continue to rush forward, separate from Logan's stories.

Now I'm eighteen. At prom. Brandon's wearing a baby-blue tie to match my dress. Then I'm twenty-one, standing in front of family and friends, whispering vows for only Brandon to hear.

I'm twenty-three, broken, bruised, battered, and barely breathing as Brandon's coffin is lowered into the ground.

Around the ballroom of the Kingsette Inn, a few hundred sets of eyes shift toward me as Logan tears up mentioning how much I'm like a sister to him, how much it means to him and his new bride, Tanya, that I came tonight. Each gaze is a prick of heat along my spine.

"Are you okay?" Tessa twists in her seat and grabs two flutes of champagne from the passing waiter. She hands one to me. It's my third or fourth . . . maybe fifth. But it's a wedding, and weddings are fun, so—who's counting?

"I'm fine," I tell her, accepting the glass. Bubbles sparkle around the quartered strawberry lounging at the bottom of the glass. "Thanks for being my plus-one."

"Unlimited champagne and a night away from the kids? You're doing me the favor," Tessa whispers as the people at our table begin to clap.

Logan leans down and kisses Tanya. They're so happy, so in love. So unaware that it's all so painfully fragile. I raise my glass to the happy couple along with everyone else, and down the champagne. The bubbles fizzle in the back of my throat.

Tessa frowns. "Let me get you some water. We haven't even made it through salads yet."

I flash her a warning look. "You promised you wouldn't do that."

"Do what?" she asks, taking a sip of champagne. "I'm not playing the overprotective sister role tonight. I'm just trying to make sure we both stay hydrated, so we make it to the cake."

I roll my eyes, but she has a point. My body feels looser than it should so early in the night. "Don't worry. I'll slow down. I don't want to be the clichéd drunk widow crying in the bathroom at the wedding."

A mischievous smile pulls up Tessa's lips, which are lined and glossed to pink perfection. "At least not again."

The corners of my mouth twitch up, too, and some of the jagged places that splintered during Logan's speech smooth over. I take a steadying breath. I can do this. It's just a wedding. Only one night.

"In my defense," I say, scanning the room for Brandon's cousin Selena, who hasn't spoken to me since her wedding last year, when, admittedly, I did make a small scene, "I told her I wasn't ready to go to a wedding. And she used our wedding song. Who does that?"

Within moments, I spot the petite former bride across the room in a conversation with my tenth-grade chemistry teacher and her wife, the veterinarian who sold her practice to Logan last year.

Selena's hands rest atop the swell of her stomach.

When Tessa sees what I see, her shoulders sag. "Ugh, Hope. I'm sorry."

"Nothing to be sorry about. That's what happens. You get married. You have babies. You live happily ever after." I breathe through the flash of what might have been playing across my thoughts.

Tessa covers my hand with hers; the weight is anchoring.

She keeps it there as the band returns to the stage and begins an off-key cover of a pop song. Tanya's bridesmaids swarm the dance floor in a flurry of cream-colored tulle.

"Speaking of getting married," Tessa starts, her voice reaching an all-too-familiar pitch. "Did you notice that Bailey Walters is here alone? I heard she broke off her engagement with Rory Lefner."

"That's awful," I say, easily spotting the pink-haired bridesmaid leading a conga line on the dance floor. Her face is transformed from the last time I saw her—a few months ago, curled up on Logan and Tanya's couch, crying about Rory. "And none of our business."

"I heard she's moving away. Art school in New York." Tessa leans in the way she does when she's been privy to a particularly juicy piece of gossip. "Maeve Winters talked her into it."

I slide another glance toward Bailey, who seems oblivious to the way half the room is watching her, the same way they watched me moments ago.

"Who's Maeve Winters?"

"Hope, seriously?" Tessa looks at me as if I've been living under a rock. "Maeve. The woman who moved into the abandoned cottage by Lake Olam. The one hosting parties under full moons and pretending to be too good for running water."

When I don't react, Tessa rolls her eyes. "Literally everyone has been talking about her nonstop for the last three months. You know, it hasn't rained since the day she arrived in town. She's bad news and creepy AF, if you ask me."

"She's new in town—that doesn't instantly make her creepy. Maybe she helped Bailey figure out what she really wanted. Would you want to marry Rory Lefner?"

Tessa fights a smile. "He's not that bad."

We both know he is.

"This town needs a hobby. Preferably one that doesn't involve rumors and other people's love lives."

"No, what this town needs is a new coffee place."

Logan's wedding is not the setting for Tessa's twenty-minute-long Kingsette-needs-another-coffee-place tirade. "Have you ever gone to the lake to meet Maeve for yourself?"

"No!" Heads turn in our direction, and Tessa lowers her voice. "And you aren't either. Anyone going down to the lake to see Maeve is a fool. The last thing you need is—"

The sound of her phone trilling interrupts her.

Tessa reaches into her purse and shows me the screen. She furrows her brow, glancing from me to the phone and back to me. She makes no move to answer or to silence the sound, though a muscle twitches in her jaw with each ring. After a few tense seconds, the phone stops. Almost instantly, it starts again. Her knuckles go white around the phone. "I'm sorry. He wasn't supposed to call unless it was an emergency with one of the girls."

"You're my plus-one, not my babysitter. Go answer your husband."

She's standing, then walking away from the table and lifting the phone to her ear before I finish giving my permission. For the first time all night, I'm alone. The three couples Tessa and I were seated with are all immersed in conversation with each other. I make a halfhearted attempt to join in. The couple on my right is talking about Bailey, and the couple across from me is discussing Maeve, and—at least I tried.

I lift my glass, only to find that it's already empty. The memories Logan's speech stirred up, along with others that I keep locked away, stalk the edges of my consciousness, demanding release or relief.

The choice is easy—no crying widow in the bathroom this time.

There's just enough space for me at the bar beside Logan's high school friends who've been parked there since before speeches. They call out for another round, their collective voices slurred. The bartender barely hides his irritation as he pours another round of shots for the raucous group and faces me.

"What can I get you?" He fixes dark, soulful eyes on me. The kind of eyes that might get another woman in trouble. Luckily, I'm immune to good looks, charm, and—Tessa would add—fun.

"A chardonnay. I mean charpagne. I mean—" I groan. "Champagne. It's been a long night."

His expression softens. He pours a generous serving and slides the flute across the bar. "You're not driving, right?"

The band kicks up a snappy rendition of "We Are Family" and mutes all other sound.

I shake my head, and he scowls at the crowd pressing in behind me, calling out orders. He leans over the bar. "I'll have the waiter bring another glass in about thirty minutes. Table ten, right?"

"You have a good eye," I say, leaning closer to speak over the music.

"Not really. Certain people just catch my attention," he says and turns to serve the woman shouldering in behind me.

My face flushes. I'm immune, but not oblivious.

Before I can come up with a response, the crowd pushes me away from the bar and spits me out onto the dance floor. I register the strobe lights a moment before my blood turns to ice. I freeze. Even before I became this town's tragic young widow, I had no business walking onto a dance floor. Rhythm and I are not well acquainted. Everyone still talks about how bruised Brandon's big toe was after our wedding dance.

One of the groomsmen crooks his finger, summoning me. Obviously a masochist. I duck my head and beeline to the relative safety of a table full of couples—what a night, when that feels like the lesser of two evils.

I make it three short steps.

"Hope, honey." A shrill voice interrupts my getaway. "I'm so glad to see you. It's been too long." A familiar waft of musky perfume laced with the smell of peppermint hard candy curls up my nose.

A second passes. I cast my gaze around the ballroom, seeking a graceful exit. Too many familiar faces swarm my vision, hampering any chance of a smooth escape. Another second passes. A pudgy hand settles on my shoulder. "Hope?"

I plaster on a smile and turn toward Brandon's aunt Joanne. Concealer collects in the creases beneath her eyes, which are lined with a deep, eighties-inspired blue eyeliner.

"When Logan told me you were coming, I didn't believe it. We haven't seen you in ages." She smiles at me, and I take just a little too much joy in noticing the lipstick smeared on her teeth.

"I've been working." I sip the champagne. *Where the hell is Tessa?*

"I heard you were transferred to the ICU. I just can't imagine how you can stand being there after—"

"I asked to be transferred," I say. "I like knowing I'm helping people during one of the scariest times of their lives."

"Oh, honey," she says, head tilting to the side in that way that's supposed to convey sympathy, but only makes me want to scream. "You always did have a good heart. And I suppose the memories are everywhere, anyway. Brandon would be proud."

"I hope so." The smile I practiced in the mirror for conversations like this feels tight across my face. "I should go find Tessa."

"Oh yes, tell her hello from us. It's so sweet that you two chose to wear matching dresses tonight. Like twins. But older."

"We didn't plan—"

"Will you be moving in with Tessa now that Logan and Tanya are married? Living with newlyweds is just . . . well, you know how I personally feel about being a third wheel. Although I suppose you'll be a third wheel at Tessa's too. You know, my friend is a Realtor, and I'm sure she'd love to work with you."

Air puffs out of me. "We haven't talked about it."

Joanne purses her lips and leans in. "Still have money troubles, dear? It happens to the best of us. I'm sure you heard my mother got swindled by someone on the internet claiming to be a Nigerian prince. Some people are just too trusting. But don't you worry, honey—my Realtor friend works with all budgets. She'd be happy to help you."

By the bar, Logan's friends continue to throw back shots. They slam down their glasses and chant for more. I catch the bartender's eye, and his help-me expression mirrors mine.

Joanne clocks the exchange. "How about dating? Are you seeing anyone? There are apps you can go on now. All the men in Rhode Island, right there on your phone."

My mouth forms the answer I'd rehearsed in the mirror. "No. No dating for me at the moment."

Despite my practice, my voice catches.

She leans in, doubling down on the intrusion. "It can be hard. After my divorce I thought I'd never find love again. Then I met my husband, and look at us now." She gestures across the room with her chin to a balding man with a beer belly as he high-fives the high school principal, another balding man with a beer belly.

The dress Tessa encouraged me to squeeze into shrinks two sizes, and I strain to breathe. "You both look very happy," I say.

"Brandon would want you to be happy, you know."

"I know." The lie leaves a bitter taste in my mouth.

"And you're what—not even thirty? You're young and so pretty. You'll find someone new."

The temperature in the room spikes. Heat, champagne, and bitter lies are a potent combination. A crucial filter between my brain and mouth dissolves.

"Oh, someone new? Like a replacement? Maybe one who's a touch taller and makes more money? Maybe I'll just pop into the husband store and pick out a new model. Or, even better, I'll just hop onto one of those dating apps you mentioned and swipe until I find the perfect new Brandon. What do you think?" My teeth clamp down too late.

Her mouth opens and closes, a fish stranded on land. "Hope, that's a terrible thing to say. You know that's not what I meant. You deserve happily ever after, that's all."

"Maybe I don't want happily ever after." Tears burn behind my eyes.

I was wrong. I can't do this.

A handful of guests stop dancing to gawk. The band begins an upbeat dance song. The crush of attention and sound makes my vision swim. The ballroom blurs, and I barely make out a sign with the word ROOF-DECK.

It's better than a bathroom.

By the time I return, the story will have circulated around the ballroom. Brandon's pathetic widow. Poor heartbroken Hope.

The worst part is, I should be relieved it's the only story that'll circulate.

There are worse stories that could be told. Ones that are known only to Brandon and me. Ones about just how guilty I am.

2

WILL

"That's not how you make a cosmo, dude." Adam, one of the new hires, brushes past me, peering at the gin in my hand. "You need vodka."

I glance down at the bottle. It is, in fact, gin. Not even the good gin. "Who moved the vodka?"

"Not me." He pours another shot for the group of displaced frat boys and leans in to take the drink order of an attractive woman flashing him a flirty smile. Her dark eyes and high cheekbones remind me a little bit of the ex I broke up with last year, and I almost warn him to stay away. I don't. He'll have to learn the hard way like the rest of us.

I put down the gin and grab the vodka, which is where the rum always was. The woman I'm making the drink for has crossed her arms over her chest. She's glaring at me like she's going to ask to speak to my manager. I almost hope she does—it'll be the highlight of my night to see her expression when I tell her I'm the manager.

Manager, proprietor, owner of the Kingsette Inn . . . all thanks to a late-night phone call from my mother's lawyer.

I finish the cosmo and slide the martini glass across the bar. The woman takes it with a muttered "finally," and I remember why I specifically hate tending bar at weddings. Everyone expects the night to be made of true love and magic. But it's so rarely that. Usually, it's just cheesy music and gin where the vodka should be. Inevitably, guests are disappointed—and cranky.

I scan the ballroom for the woman who looked as desperate to flee as I am. She could probably use another drink by now.

She's not at her table, and the older woman who ambushed her has now cornered a pregnant woman.

"Hey, Will." Another of the new hires, whose name I can't remember, appears in the doorway leading from the kitchen. "There's . . . uh . . . a situation in here. We need you to come."

I blow out a sigh and glance at the line forming by the bar. "Can it wait?"

"Not really," he says, glancing behind him as if the *situation* back there might soon come up here.

"Sure, I'll be right there. Just give me a second."

Adam sighs with relief when I tell him I'm stepping away. I follow the new guy into the kitchen, trying to decide why Adam's reaction bothers me. It shouldn't.

It won't, I decide, *once I'm back in LA.*

My brother's slurred words reach me before I turn the corner into the kitchen. The new hire—Jeremy? Jarred?—glances over his shoulder with a sheepish grimace. "We asked him to leave, but he insisted he wouldn't until he spoke to you. I'm so sorry."

"No worries. I'll handle him." I brush past Jeremy-slash-Jarred and head into the kitchen, where the staff has stopped working and is staring at Darren as if he's walked in with a bomb strapped to his chest.

"Darren," I say, and the brother I haven't seen in ten years stops pacing, raises his gaze to me. "What are you doing here?"

When we were growing up, people who didn't know us thought we were twins—same jet-black hair, same hawkish nose, same dark-brown eyes. By the time I was twelve, we were the same height, and even teachers began to confuse us.

No one would confuse us now. Darren's complexion is sallow. There's a nasty bruise on his cheek, and his lip is split. The skin on his arms is paper thin. He looks like the future I escaped when I left Kingsette the first time.

"The prodigal son returns," Darren says, an unfamiliar viciousness deepening his voice. The kitchen staff shifts its attention toward me as one. Spectators at a tennis match, though neither Darren nor I is worthy of a fan base.

"Let's go chat in the office. Let these people get back to work."

Darren sucks his teeth, considering. The silence is interrupted only by the pasta boiling over. One of the cooks mutters a curse under his breath and lowers the flame.

"Nah, let's talk here. If you wanted privacy, you would have answered my calls. You left me no choice."

"Fair enough," I say, putting my hands up like a cop on TV proving he's unarmed. "But these people need to get entrées out to the ballroom, or the guests are going to start getting fussy."

Darren lifts one shoulder. "Not really my problem, little brother." His voice rises. He stumbles toward me, and the alcohol on his breath makes my vision hazy. "You're the one they called to save the day. Not me."

"I didn't ask to be called." Instantly, I'm sure it's the wrong thing to say.

His nostrils flare. "No, you don't have to ask for anything, do you? Things happen to you, right?"

Heat flushes up my neck. "Yes, and if you'd be less of a screwup, maybe things wouldn't have to happen to me all the time."

The tension in his muscles vanishes, a balloon deflating. He shakes his head. "You always go straight for the jugular."

"Darren, I'm sorry. You—there's a lot of people celebrating in the ballroom right now, and it's not a good time." I glance around at the kitchen staff. They busy themselves with work—or some version of pretending to work.

"What do you need?"

"Just some money and I'll get out of your way." Darren's focus is somewhere just left of where it should be. His pupils devour the irises. This isn't the big brother who once told me if he ever caught me smoking, he'd lock me in a room with a bear.

11

"No, can't do that. Something else."

"A place to crash," he says, automatically. "We can stay in Mom's spare room."

"I'm not staying in Mom's house. I'm sleeping on the couch in the office. I don't—"

He snorts. "Yeah, I get it. It's fine. I'll figure it out like I always do." He pivots and disappears out the back door. A whoosh of cool spring air chases away his lingering smell.

All eyes turn back toward me. I point to the sous-chef. "Most people turn the salt upside down to shake it out."

He jolts, noticing his mistake, and upends the salt.

"Show's over." I clap my hands, not quite sure when I became the kind of guy who claps his hands at people. "Let's get back to work."

The kitchen dissolves into a blur of activity as they all resume their work—for real this time.

I start toward the ballroom and pause just in sight of the crowd by the bar. The groom has joined the shot takers. Jeremy-slash-Jarred is shaking up a martini beside Adam, who's still chatting up the dark-haired woman. No one appears impatient or underserved.

I grab a wine bottle off the bar cart waiting to be brought into the ballroom, push open the door to the stairwell, and head toward the roof-deck—the only place I'm guaranteed to be alone.

I'm not alone. The door to the roof-deck slams closed behind me, sending a waft of thick, drought-dry air my way. A woman standing in a pool of moonlight spins around. "Who's there?"

There's an edge to her voice, but without seeing her face, I can't tell if she's afraid or annoyed by my arrival. She leans into the shadows, and I step forward into the moonlight to meet her.

Recognition registers on her face at the same moment I feel a tiny thrill roll through me. Every bit of my strength goes into extinguishing it. Downstairs, she was a kindred spirit. Up here, she's an interruption.

"Oh," she breathes, relaxing into the word. "I'm sorry. I just needed some air. It's . . . stuffy down there."

Stuffy is one word. *Suffocating* is a better one.

"Unfortunately, we don't allow guests up here," I say. "There's a gazebo to the left of the parking lot. If you go out the front, it's on your—"

She wraps her arms around herself. "Can I just stay here? I really can't go back in there." Her voice dips low.

"It's against hotel rules." My hand grows clammy around the bottle. I don't want to be the guy who sends this woman back to whatever she ran from. Especially not after I was the guy who sent his brother packing. But this town has a way of bringing out the worst in me.

The lines of her body go rigid, that soft exterior hardening into something with sharp edges. "Is it also against hotel rules to abandon your bartending post and get wasted on your guests' alcohol?"

I suppress a smile. "Technically, yes."

"Then I guess we both should go." She lifts her chin, daring me to walk down those stairs, return to that demanding crowd.

"I guess so," I say, drawing out the word and studying the determined set of her jaw. "Or . . . we could both stay. I won't tell if you won't."

She taps her nose with her finger. "I like the way you think."

"And I like the way you let me believe you were giving me a choice."

One side of her mouth tilts up. "It's the least I can do after your generous pour earlier."

"Beautiful women never have to thank me for that." I instantly want to take back the words. Because for one—spoken out loud, the words sound creepy. And two—mentioning that I'm giving out generous pours to every pretty girl at the wedding—which I'm not—isn't a stellar flirting technique.

Not that I'm trying to flirt. I'm done with women.

Or at least, on a self-imposed sabbatical from women as I try to get my life together.

She flashes me an uneasy smile, which is more than I deserve, and turns her back to me. Dark hair is pulled up in an intricate updo, revealing a long neck and slim shoulders. The dress she's wearing hugs her hips and shows off lean legs.

Despite my better judgment, and maybe because I just denied my own brother any kind of help and want to feel less like an ass, I lift the bottle. "If you're going to trespass, you might as well have a drink."

She whirls on me. "You're the one—"

I throw my hands up in the air. "I'm joking. I just . . . I had a crappy night too."

A shift in cloud cover allows me to make out the features that caught my attention in the ballroom. She's a blend of angles and soft lines, high cheekbones and full lips. Wide eyes full of indecision consider me.

"Is it that obvious?"

"You're on the roof alone in the middle of a wedding . . ." I walk toward the bench Darren had started building right after our dad died. It was supposed to be the start of a memorial garden, but Darren never got around to finishing it. "And I saw you get cornered earlier by that woman. Let me guess—mother nagging you about grandkids."

She barks a laugh that could mean a thousand things. "God, no."

"Much older sister trying to set you up with that bald groomsman?"

"Nope. He's married."

"Aunt asking why you're not married yet?"

A pained expression dashes across her features, replaced immediately by a smile that looks more rehearsed than natural. "Close enough. You're good."

"In another life I was a writer for TV dramas. One of the job requirements is being able to read people, hear what they aren't saying." *See what they aren't showing,* I think, as an irresponsible part of me notes the empty ring finger.

"Aah," she says.

An awkward silence shivers between us. I twist the cap off the wine and drink. It's impossibly sour while also being sickly sweet, and my mouth puckers. I must be making a face because she breathes a laugh.

"Good wine?"

I cough. "One of the finest bottles of twist-off red wine blend you can find on this side of the Atlantic coast."

Her mouth quirks up. "Let me see."

She approaches and takes the bottle from me. Her nose crinkles as she studies the label.

"Are you a wine expert or something?"

"I did bartend through nursing school, but no. I just want to remember which wine to stay away from if I make it back downstairs."

"If?"

She grins, something abashed creeping into her expression as if she's just admitted something she shouldn't. "I meant when. When I get back."

She lifts the bottle, drinks, and shudders. "Oh, that'll wake you up. Even Dionysus would turn down that bottle."

"Dionysus?" No ring doesn't mean unattached. "Personal friend of yours?"

The mischief tracing her smile makes my heart skip a beat. "Greek god of wine."

She sits, and the air becomes infused with the smell of something light and floral. As far as unwanted company goes, she's not the worst choice.

She drinks again and wipes her mouth with the back of her hand.

"Sorry, I didn't bring glasses. Didn't know there'd be trespassers here."

"Desperate times call for desperate measures and all that, right?" She glances at the closed roof-deck door. "Won't your boss wonder where you went?"

"Nah, my boss is a pushover. He lets me get away with whatever I want."

She arches an eyebrow. "Even stealing the finest red wine blend on this side of the Atlantic?"

The challenge in her words is met with the distant sound of Kingsette's only train rumbling out of town.

"Even that."

A cloud drifts in front of the moon, and the little light between us dims. The familiarity between us blinks out, too, as if it were just a trick of the light. She hands me back the bottle without drinking and starts to stand.

My stomach seizes. I thought I wanted to be alone, but now the idea of sitting on this bench with only my thoughts seems absurd.

"I'm Will, by the way. Thought you should know my name since we've shared germs now."

She sits, melting back onto the bench like she wasn't ready to leave me yet either. "Nice to meet you, Will. I'm Hope."

"Will and Hope. Funny, our parents had the same idea when they named us."

She tilts her head, and I don't blame her for being confused. Bad wine on an empty stomach is a recipe for unfortunate wordplay.

"We were both named after vague, indefinable concepts," I explain.

Her eyebrows draw together. "You really are a writer."

"No. I *was* a writer. Now I'm a bartender. It's a long story."

"I get it. I know a thing or two about long stories."

That low dip in her voice again, the one that sounds like heartbreak, makes my chest tighten. "Is your long story the reason you're hiding up here?"

"Yep," she says, popping the *p*, marking the end of this line of questioning.

"Oh," I breathe, and she stops me with a look.

"Don't you dare say, 'I'm sorry.'" Temper flares to life, as stunning and surprising as a crackle of fire streaking against a midnight sky. "If those words come out of your mouth, I'm stealing your wine and heading to that gazebo."

I put my hands up. "You're the boss."

"Good."

We pass the wine bottle back and forth to the sound of an owl hooting in the distance. Flickers of a bonfire near Lake Kingsette are just barely visible to our far right. On our left, the only strip of light belongs to the few bars that make up Kingsette's nightlife. It's a far cry from the lights and fast pace of LA, which already feels like a distant memory.

I point to a star. "That bright star? Did you know that it's fifteen hundred light-years away? A hundred times farther than any other star you can see. When I lived in LA, we could barely see the stars. But in Kingsette, we can see fifteen hundred light-years away."

The weird thing about Kingsette is that you can see stars that are light-years away, but you can't see a future until you leave.

"Fifteen hundred light-years, huh?" She leans back to look up. Truly look. Most people don't take the time to do that. "How do you know that?" she asks.

I shrug. "I met an astronomer once in a small town outside of Dublin. He gave me a lesson one night."

She purses her lips.

"You don't believe me?"

"I think there's more to the story than you're sharing."

She's right.

I lower my voice. "Maybe I just like to collect facts to impress distressed women escaping weddings on roof-decks."

She tenses, as if just remembering something terrible.

"I'm sorry. I shouldn't have joked about that."

"No saying 'I'm sorry,' remember?" Her voice leaves no room for debate.

"Why do you hate 'I'm sorry'?"

"I don't know. I've heard 'I'm sorry' enough to last a lifetime, I guess. It's a throwaway." She slides a glance my way, and a glint of something playful in her eyes makes my breath catch. "Anyway, it's boring. If you're going to say something, say something interesting."

"Oof. No pressure, huh?" My hand rubs my chin, exaggerating my thinking process. I gamble with a line that will either make her smile or completely send her running. "So . . . why aren't you married yet?"

It sparks a laugh that is at once husky and light. "Will," she says, a note of warning in her voice. My entire chest fills with lightness at the way she says my name.

It's a sign that I need to end this conversation and go. But I don't. I lean closer, feel the heat vibrating off her skin. "What? That grandmother type can ask you, but I can't? We've shared wine."

"Are you always this nosy?"

If it weren't for the glimmer of delight in her eyes, I'd think I overstepped my bounds.

"Can't help it. Stories are my thing. *Were* my thing," I correct and angle myself to see whether her expression fills with pity. Only empathy stares back. Empathy, and an ember of that flare of temper she'd shown. It's sexy as hell.

Hope clears her throat. "I should get back to the party. My sister's probably worried about me." She stands and holds the bottle out to me. "Thanks for the drink. I . . . uh . . . promise I don't have cooties or anything."

"If I wake up with the flu, at least now I know a nurse who can take care of me."

The smile that line earns me is a sad ghost of what I saw earlier.

I reach for the bottle, and our hands connect. Electricity sparks in my fingertips and sweeps through every nerve ending. She holds the bottle. For a heartbeat, we're frozen, our eyes locked. Hers have shades of green that look luminescent in the moonlight.

Laughter filters up from the parking lot. Hope releases the bottle, and it's somehow heavier than it was before. Another cascade of laughter ripples up, and Hope steps back, into the roof-deck's shadows, which embrace her with eagerness. She heads toward the door. Without turning back, she pulls it open and disappears into the dark hallway.

The door slams, bringing with it a rush of air and good sense.

The last thing I need is a relationship to complicate my life.

No relationships. No complications. No extra ties to Kingsette.

3

HOPE

Fog tumbles down from the mountains in the distance and crawls in my direction. A thin line of gold is just visible over the horizon, a slow-moving turn to day, as if the sun would have rather stayed in bed too. As if, like me, it's trying to make itself scarce so the newlyweds can enjoy a bit of privacy their first morning back home after their wedding weekend.

They want you there. They've said as much. Together and separately.

I push my legs faster up the trail, which I navigate by muscle memory. Tessa and I found this trail as kids, but Brandon and I made it our own. We hiked it more times than I can remember. At the top, there's a small clearing where you can see the entire town. Where you feel like you've escaped. Even if only for a little while.

It's where Brandon proposed.

Where he handed me the listing for the house that was going to be our forever home.

Where he promised we would never need anything but each other.

The muted-brown cottage that comes into view tamps down the swell of memories. The low-pitched roof and covered front porch blend into the tree line, though the vibrant-red flowerpots ensure that anyone walking by would see it. So does the smoldering bonfire and slightly sour herbal smell coming from it.

The cottage by the lake.

Everyone who grows up in Kingsette knows about this place. My grandmother's generation called it Ahava Cottage, after the original owner. Or more accurately after the original owner's daughter, who had become so well known for her ability to heal children that mothers started traveling great distances to see her. When it became obvious that she needed her own space, she insisted on being near Lake Olam, which she believed had healing properties.

She died three days before the cottage was completed.

Some say Ahava haunts the cottage. They say on stormy nights they can hear the cries of the mothers whose children didn't survive.

I never believed those stories. Someone who dedicates their life to healing wouldn't spend their death destroying.

It takes a few minutes for my tired brain to dredge up the name Tessa mentioned at the wedding.

Maeve Winters.

The woman who convinced Bailey to end her engagement with Rory.

A shiver runs down my spine as I study the rickety dock leading into the lake and the single gray dress swinging on a clothesline stretching from the house. Tessa's "creepy" was more on the mark than I thought.

Why would someone live all the way out here?

And how?

There's no electricity or running water this far from town. She could have a generator hidden around back, but it's at least a mile to the nearest gas station.

Only someone desperate to flee would live like this.

Someone who'd already lost everything.

Someone not all that different from me.

But would I ever go to these lengths to run away from my life? Could I?

Whatever the answer, the last thing Maeve needs is someone standing over her passing judgment. Especially someone like me, who has made more than her fair share of questionable choices.

My awareness returns to the trail, and I'm greeted by an unfamiliar landscape. When had I stepped off my usual route?

I pivot and retrace my steps to figure out where I missed the trail.

Ten minutes later, sweat pools at the small of my back, and I'm almost ready to admit that I can't find the path.

The thought sends a warning crack through the fragile parts of my heart.

Not finding the trail isn't an option.

A hot wind whips up the drought-dry dirt, adding a layer of discomfort rather than relief. I take a steadying breath, and then another. Sunlight streams in through the treetops, and the glare is so bright, the leaves in the trees look black.

Black leaves, three trees, stay on the opposite side of the breeze.

The silly rhyme Tessa and I made up when we first learned these woods returns to me on another hot gust of wind.

It's my best bet.

A blur of blue at the base of a large magnolia tree catches my eye when I turn my back to the wind.

A closer look reveals that the desperate flutter of feathers is clearly a bluebird trying to fly with only one wing. The other is tucked protectively to its side.

The bluebird hops and fails to take flight. It tries again. Then again. Leaves float down from the tree, blanketing the ground, the bird.

It needs help. It needs—

"Oh, that poor bird." A figure rushes past me and falls to her knees beside the injured bird. A tote bag hanging from her shoulder falls to the ground, and rolls of toilet paper, bags of gummy bears, and a box of toothpaste spill out.

"What happened?" She scoops it up and brings it close to her face as a gust of wind whips between us. The bird chirps, the sound pained.

An awkward moment stretches between us before I realize the question was for me. "I—I don't know. He was like this when I found him."

"Hmm," she says. The woman examines the bird's seemingly healthy wing as she whispers to the animal. "He'll be okay."

"Do you know . . . birds?" She's speaking too low for me to hear, but I could swear she's chirping.

"Of course." She rises with the bluebird cupped in her hands. "I spent an entire year living at the Kuala Lumpur Bird Park in Malaysia. Could you help me?"

Her question registers at half speed as I pull my thoughts back from where they snagged on her casual mention of Malaysia. As if living in Malaysia were no different than living in Vermont or New Hampshire. As if it were that easy to just live somewhere else and then be in Kingsette.

I collect the assortment of items she dropped and stand. She's four inches shorter than me, with eyes nearly the same gray-white color of her hair, which is knotted into a messy bun on top of her head. An orange bathing suit peeks out from beneath a white dress. A sleeve of tattoos culminating in a butterfly backlit by a sunburst on her right bicep completes her California surfer blended with bohemian punk look.

The effect is dizzying.

"I'm Maeve, by the way."

Another gust of wind pulls leaves off the trees. They fall around us like the rain Kingsette so desperately needs.

"Yeah, I know." My cheeks flush. "I mean, I guessed. We don't often get newcomers here. It's a small town . . ."

Her lips curl in a small smile. "And I have a big reputation." She pauses, and a heartbeat later I realize she's waiting for me to hand her the bag, which I do.

My phone buzzes, and I glance down at the message.

Can you cover for me today? Please. I'll owe you forever.

"I suppose you should answer that," Maeve says. "It was nice to meet you, Hope."

The hair on the back of my neck rises. "How did you know my name?"

"Small town." She raises her eyebrows.

The bird makes a small pained sound. Maeve chirps and whistles in response. "I should get this little guy home. Are you coming?"

"Me? No." Tessa's warning twists around my thoughts, but Maeve is more quirky than creepy. "I mean, I can't. I have to get to work." I hold up my phone as proof.

"Of course." She takes a step backward.

Black leaves fall faster between us, blanketing the ground, making the space between us seem impassable.

"He'll be okay, though?"

"I'll do all I can for him, but most of his healing will be up to him." Maeve holds my gaze. "You're welcome to check in on him anytime, Hope. You know where to find us."

4

WILL

A bluebird. A fucking bluebird.

I swing at the squawking bird with the broom I found stuffed in the janitor's closet. The bird takes a sharp left, and its wings beat faster, a hysterical rhythm that's beginning to match the tempo of my pulse.

How did a bluebird get into room 3? The guest staying in this room called down to the front desk, blubbering about the bird and the mess, swearing that she hadn't left the window open while she'd been out. Fine. It doesn't matter how the bird got in. All that matters is I have to deal with it.

I swing the broom again. The bristles graze the bottom of the bird, which pitches to the right and nose-dives toward me. I duck, protecting my head with my hands, and drop flat to the floor.

I scan the room for something to use to catch the intruder, but there's nothing besides the antique lamps on either side of the bed and the frilly decorative pillows my mom is so fond of. The curtains might be useful, but my mother would kill me if I ruined her custom-made window dressings. The silk trim and gold tassels were special ordered around the time I was born to match the floral wallpaper in the parlor.

The comforter is my best bet. I pull it off and use it as a shield as I step onto the bed. I wait until the bird circles around, and then I jump, head, belly, and heart first. And damn me if I haven't turned into a walking, talking metaphor for my life right now.

The comforter catches nothing but air as the bird swings right. I hit the floor with a crack, and pain vibrates through every bone in my body. The bird takes advantage of the reprieve and settles on the headboard. A boxing match opponent resting for round two.

The tension in my body fizzles as I right myself. Blood leaks from my nose onto the comforter. Each drop is a reason I shouldn't be here.

"You win," I say and exit the room, closing the door behind myself. The Inn is short-staffed, but there's got to be someone better equipped to deal with this than me. I hate birds.

Two guests seated on my mother's favorite gold-trimmed chaise longue look up as I enter the parlor, their card game momentarily forgotten. A third, who is curled onto a love seat speaking intently into her cell phone, goes silent. Their intense attention is a reminder that privacy doesn't exist in Kingsette.

Even the visitors are somehow dialed into the gossip network. Another reason to leave.

Rather than make eye contact, I head straight for the porch.

Delilah Stoddard answers on the first ring.

My mother's lawyer waves wildly as I pull open the door to the Friendly Bean. Most of the customers ignore her—used to her enthusiastic greetings—but a few people closest to her look up. I recoil at the recognition in their faces, the quick typing into their phones that follows.

Kingsette loves a good story, and I can't help but think Delilah had that in mind when she chose to meet here. Or she likes to see me squirm.

"Will Reynard, in the flesh and blood." Delilah stands and wraps her arms around me as if I haven't been the only member of my family to decline her invitation to Thanksgiving every year for the last decade. "I cannot believe you're really here. Let me look at you."

She pulls away and studies me. Her brow furrows as she takes in my nose, which feels tender and swollen. "What happened to you?"

"I got in a fight with a bluebird. And I lost."

"Yes, I've heard that bluebirds can be bullies." She smiles at me, soft lines creasing around her mouth. "Well, I'm glad you're okay. Aside from the nose, you look good."

"It's good to see you," I say, and I mean it. Growing up, Delilah was the closest thing to an aunt that I had. She, my mother, and Annette Martina, the Friendly Bean's fearless leader, grew up together. They were as good as sisters for most of my life. "I like the glasses."

She touches her hand to the purple cat-eye frame, which complements her dark skin. "Well, apparently I'm old enough to need bifocals." She blows out a sigh. "Don't get old. It's awful."

She pats the seat beside her on the couch. "Annette's in the back. I'm sure she'll be out soon, though."

I sit with my back to the restaurant and pull my hat lower. "She's not going to be happy to see me here. We couldn't meet anywhere else?"

Delilah studies me over the rim of a mug. Steam curls up and fogs her glasses. "I'm here every Monday for book club." Delilah glances toward the door. "Which starts in just a few minutes, so . . . what did you need to talk about, kid?"

No one has called me "kid" with that amount of affection in too long. Probably since I walked away from Kingsette the first time. "I need to get in touch with my mom. I can't run the Inn."

Delilah tilts her head in a way that's eerily similar to room 3's triumphant bluebird. "Why not?"

"It's not . . . I don't know what I'm doing. That place needs a real manager, with experience. Like Terry." Terry was the one who was supposed to run the Inn while my mother went off grid to "reconnect with nature and get in touch with her true self." Or at least that's what she'd said on the rushed voice mail she'd left me.

A family emergency caused Terry to quit less than a week after my mother had left, and in a state of desperation, Delilah called me.

Clearly, I chose the wrong time to actually answer my phone.

"So, hire someone. Did you read through the candidates for the position?" Delilah's phone pings. She checks the lit screen and smiles at the message.

"You know none of them were qualified." If they were, Delilah wouldn't have called me.

The first three were barely out of high school; they managed a Wendy's and a few stores at the mall. The Inn—my family's inn—is a thousand times more complicated to run.

She unlocks her phone and begins typing. "By your own admission, you're not qualified either."

"Exactly." I throw my hands up, and a few heads swivel in my direction. I lower my voice. "That's why I called you, Delilah. My mom has to come back. She can't just run away from her life and her responsibilities."

Under Delilah's withering gaze, I'm suddenly ten years old again, in trouble for freeing the rabbits from Ms. Lemmings's pet shop. "Oh, she can't? But you can."

"That was different. My welcome had been rescinded." My op-ed in the local paper accusing the town's revered basketball team of grade fixing did not go over well. League officials took it seriously, and Kingsette was disqualified from the championship game. A few kids lost scholarships because of me. Folks were so mad they would cross the street when they saw me coming. It was a lesson—if I wanted to write the truth, I had to embed it in fiction. LA seemed the best place to do that.

Delilah winces. "I know. I'm sorry. You were only eighteen. It's not fair to put that on you, but Will, you need to understand that lately, well . . . I'm not sure Helen felt especially welcome in the weeks before she left."

Her admission makes the rapid-fire speed of my thoughts come to a screeching halt. "Wait, what? What happened?"

"Once Maeve got into your mother's ear . . . it was like I didn't recognize her anymore."

The door opens, and two men and three women walk into the coffee shop carrying copies of the new Danielle Steel novel. Delilah brightens and waves at them. "Sorry, Will. I saved these seats for book club."

"Wait . . . just . . . who's Maeve?"

Delilah heaves a long-suffering sigh. "You haven't heard about Maeve yet?"

I've been in town for a week. I've hardly had a chance to pay the electric bill, let alone get acquainted with town gossip.

"Maeve is—" She presses her lips together and glances over her shoulder at the members of her book club who are making their way toward us. "Why don't you ask Annette? She'll be able to tell you more than me, anyway."

As if on cue, Annette Martina emerges from the back office. She slices a glare in my direction, and the scowl that pulls down her pink-painted lips makes my flight reflex kick into high gear.

I'm twenty-eight. I've lived in Los Angeles, written for a sitcom with famous actors, and hobnobbed with producers who set the tone of the entertainment landscape, and still, no one has intimidated me more than Annette Martina.

Even before I started dating her daughter in high school, I'd try to stay out of her way. She had strong opinions that she believed were facts. Too many nights I heard her expounding on those opinions until my mother would agree with whatever she'd said just to get some peace.

After her daughter and I had started dating, I had a bull's-eye on my forehead. She'd known all along that I would break her daughter's heart. She told both of us as much when our friendship turned romantic.

I never meant to hurt Natalie. Or anyone.

Delilah studies my face and lifts her gaze to the ceiling. "Come on, I'll walk you over."

"You don't have to . . ." The rest of my halfhearted protest fades as she turns on her heel and heads toward Annette.

Annette watches our approach. She's two inches shorter than me, but still manages to glare down her nose at me. She sets her phone down on top of a stack of flyers. "Delilah, it's so nice to see you. We missed you at Garden Club yesterday. One more absence and we might have to revoke your membership." Annette's tone is light, but the edge in it triggers a long untouched nerve at the base of my spine.

Delilah laughs off the veiled threat, the way my mother used to. "Once my dad's new nursing aide is settled at my house, I'll be the first one there. You know that." She glances toward me. "More importantly, look who's finally come back home."

"Hi, Annette," I say. She places her hands on her hips, widens her stance, and keeps her gaze firmly fixed on Delilah. "I mean Ms. Martina. It's been a long time."

"Oh yes, I noticed Will was back when he avoided me at the Gold wedding. I thought he forgot all about me now that he was Mr. West Coast," she says, her voice flat. A message alert pings on her phone. A succession of others follows.

"No, I was . . . I'm the temporary manager at the Inn while my mom is away. It was hectic."

Annette lifts her phone and begins typing.

"Annette, Will needs to talk to you about a few things."

"Mm-hmm." It seems impossible for one word to house that much scorn and skepticism.

Delilah nudges me to take over, then slips away while Annette's focus is preoccupied. If I were less selfish, I'd be happy for her easy escape.

"I wanted to ask . . . ," I say and clear my throat. Annette puts her phone down and looks up. The razor-sharp tip of her attention is especially cutting after the blunt edge of her disregard. "Delilah said you might know how to get in touch with my mom."

Annette exchanges a look with a woman in a flower-print dress, who's been standing like a loyal sentry beside Annette.

"I don't, actually." Annette's never had a good poker face.

"If you know where she is, you need to let me know. What if something's happened to her? Is she alone? She could be—"

"Helen is fine. She sent me a postcard last week telling me as much, apologizing for worrying us, and asking me to respect her need for space."

"Did she write anything else? Where did the postcard come from?"

"I don't know. I threw it away. Recently your mother was confiding in other people." Annette emphasizes *other people* so there's no mistaking her opinion of those people.

It takes a heartbeat too long for the puzzle pieces to connect. "Delilah mentioned a woman named Maeve. My mother got close with her, right? Is she the one my mother was confiding in?"

Annette's raised chin is my answer.

"Who is she?"

Annette and her friend exchange another long look. "She's a con artist and a predator who is staying down at the Ahava Cottage—illegally, I'm sure. I've complained about her to the sheriff multiple times, but he hasn't done a thing about it. I can't fathom why not."

My mind dredges up a decade-old image of Sheriff Wilson. He lost his husband a few years before my dad died and has always been kind to my mom, even looked the other way a few times when Darren was young. "I'm sure if there was a reason for the police to be involved, they'd be on top of it."

"Did you know she took advantage of Linda's daughter—persuaded her to cancel her engagement and go to art school?" She makes a face like she just tasted something awful. "In New York. Bailey's just a child. She can't make that kind of decision for herself."

The woman who must be Linda brings a tissue to her glistening eyes. Annette covers the woman's hand with her own plump palm. The whole scene feels staged, and I should go, but an abrupt exit would cause an even bigger scene. Maybe that's what Annette's hoping for.

"Don't worry," Annette says, the sincerity in her voice belied by the shrewd sweep of her gaze across the restaurant. "Bailey's a sensible girl. She'll come around."

Linda sniffs. "I'm not so sure. She drained the money from her savings account for this nonsense. Canceled the ballroom at the Inn, despite a nonrefundable deposit. It's awful."

"Did Maeve talk my mother into going . . . off grid? Is that why she left?" At Linda's hardened expression, I realize my mistake and arrange my face into a sympathetic expression, murmur reassurances, and promise to refund the deposit. Once Linda's properly mollified, I ask again.

"Like I said, your mother was confiding in *other* people. All I know is that good, responsible people don't just walk away from perfectly good lives." The implication in her words would sting if I expected any less from Annette. "Anyway, I'm sure you have bigger things to worry about now that you're running the Inn. Running a business is a bit harder than daydreaming at a desk all day. And I suppose you'll have to start repairing burned bridges."

The bell above the Friendly Bean's door chimes, and Annette calls out a "goodbye" to a departing customer. Her plastered smile deteriorates as she turns back to me. "Speaking of, Natalie's fine. Happily married with two kids. Not that you even bothered to ask."

"I'm glad to hear that." I'm not surprised. Natalie and I were over long before we—I—ended things. She knew that too. Though she would never have admitted it. If I hadn't walked away, we would have been unhappily married with three kids and a golden retriever by now.

"I hear you've got your sights set on Hope Gold now." Annette's eyes narrow, ready to see what I'm not saying.

I suck my teeth. "You've heard wrong this time."

Annette purses her lips. "You two spent quite a bit of time alone on the roof-deck."

"And that means something?" I ask. Kingsette needs more than one coffee place. Then maybe gossip wouldn't travel so fast.

"You be careful with her." Everything she thinks of me is undisguised in her expression. "That girl has been through enough trauma to last a lifetime. She doesn't need someone else to come into her life if he's just going to disappear without a trace."

"Trauma?" Instantly, I wish I hadn't asked.

No complications. No ties to Kingsette.

Annette leans closer, always willing to put aside personal grievances for gossip. "Her husband died. Terrible car accident. He was so young and handsome. They were deeply in love. It was all very tragic."

An image of my mother holding my hand at my father's funeral flits into my thoughts. When she lost her husband, everything changed. The way she ran the Inn, the way she spoke, even the way she laughed.

"She hasn't been the same since," Annette adds, as if reading my mind.

"I should go." I tap my knuckles on the counter. "Thanks for your help, Annette."

"Of course." Annette's cool gaze captures mine. A beat of silence snaps taut between us. "Despite what you may believe, Will, I'll always help one of Kingsette's own."

5

HOPE

The ICU is laid out like an upside-down *U* with ten glass-walled patient rooms anchored to the nurse's station at the center. Beeping and hissing underscore the voices of nurses speaking in hushed, urgent tones, and the forced hot air hums through the vents like an elegy. Doctors shuffle between rooms, and the smell of antiseptic lingers on walls and hands. It's a place of few happy endings.

It's impossible this world exists in the same reality that Logan's wedding did, separated by just a few days.

The first room I enter is dark and smells of sleep and sickness. The patient—a thirty-four-year-old mother of two with a brain tumor—needs a miracle.

She stirs only once as I take her vitals, and my throat tightens. One of the first things I learned when I started working was to keep an emotional distance between my patients and me. For reasons I can't understand, that's becoming impossible.

"She's dying, isn't she?" The question billows through the hollow quiet of the room, catching me off guard.

I turn to find Mr. Matthews, my patient's husband, standing in the doorway, his expression stripped of everything but worry. Thick, black-rimmed glasses make his watery eyes seem too large for his face. The hospital-cafeteria coffee cup in his hand tips to one side, the liquid threatening to spill over. He rights the cup and hugs an oversize tote bag to his chest with his free hand.

"Dr. Welsh is one of the best brain surgeons in the area."

The machine monitoring the patient's blood pressure releases a deep sigh. Wires escape from beneath a thin white blanket and disappear behind handmade cards that her husband taped to the wall.

He swallows hard. "What if she doesn't make it tomorrow? How will I—I can't live without her."

His eyes lock on mine. I inhale, but my chest still feels empty.

"You will. You'll live. You'll wake up and you'll breathe. And by muscle memory and reflex, you'll live. Then you'll go to bed and wake up and do it all again the next day—and the day after and the day after that."

His eyes shine, and I wish I could deliver a happy ending. But I can't promise he'll be okay—that it will be okay. The universe isn't safe. Bad things happen to good people. Words get said, and they can't be unsaid.

A yip escapes from his bag. His eyes widen as his gaze darts from me to the bag and back to me. He hugs it tighter to his chest.

"You can't have a dog in here," I say. Lydia, the nurse manager, is not only a stickler for rules, but severely allergic. "It's against the rules."

A furry snout appears from inside the bag. Color flushes Mr. Matthews's cheeks. The dog hiding in the tote bag yips again, and the woman in the bed stirs. She makes a small noise, sounding more alert than she has in days.

"Please," he says, something caged and desperate haunting his features. "Just once. I'll only stay for a few minutes."

I bite my lip and glance back at the patient. Another stir at the dog's yipping. She's someone's mother, someone's wife—the keeper of someone's whole heart.

It shouldn't matter, but it does.

"He's her good luck charm."

Automatically, my hand goes to the hollow of my throat, where the locket Brandon gave me—my good luck charm, which has been missing since he died—should be. Good luck is only the beginning of what they need.

"I know what I'm asking is crazy. But I need a miracle and whatever luck and magic I can get." Heartache chases his words, and it unravels every part of me except the part that would have done the same for Brandon.

"Okay," I say, fixing a stern look on my face. "Two minutes and then he doesn't come back."

"Yes. Absolutely. He doesn't come back."

The dog yips, and from the corner of my eye, I see my patient stir again as I walk out of the room.

Two nights ago, I trespassed on a roof-deck. Today, I'm breaking hospital rules. One more infraction and I'm officially on a spree. Which would bring my lifetime spree count up to . . . one.

"Hope. There you are." Lydia's raspy voice stops me in my tracks just feet from the Matthewses' closed curtain.

My heart plummets.

She heard the dog. Of course she did—Lydia Ritter knows everything happening in the ICU at all times, often before it happens.

She marches toward me, her usually kind face pinched together with unfamiliar anger. Useless excuses prickle on my tongue.

"You're on again?" Lydia's wearing gray scrubs and gray Crocs, and if it weren't for the spots of red on her cheeks, she'd blend into the gray walls. "I thought you were taking a few days off after the wedding."

"Rosalie called in sick."

"You mean Rosalie called in lazy. I'm on my last stitch of patience with that girl. I swear Gen Z, or whatever they're calling themselves now, is going to be the death of me."

"She sounded sick."

Lydia shakes her head. "You're too trusting. She's taking advantage of you."

Tessa accused me of something similar when she picked me up outside a bodega on a Manhattan street corner. Considering I'd just spent my last two dollars on a rock-hard bagel, I wasn't in a position to argue with her.

"Or maybe she's actually sick." In my mind, the words are snarky and strong. In my mouth, they're lame.

"Don't get mad. I'm just looking out for you." Lydia sighs. "If Rosalie calls you again tomorrow, do not answer. I don't want to see you back here for at least three days. No. A week. You're no good to me if you're burned out. In fact, you should use the time to finish your application. I just spoke to my friend who works in admissions for the University of Rhode Island's nursing master's degree program. He received my letter of recommendation but hasn't received your application. He wanted to make sure it didn't get lost in the mail." Lydia crosses her arms over her chest. "Did it get lost in the mail?"

"Oh," I breathe, an entirely new set of excuses stinging against my lips. "No, I missed the deadline."

Tension dissolves from her face. She tilts her head and flattens her mouth. "This is the third time you've missed the deadline."

"I know. Time got away from me."

"Hope, you are an incredible nurse. You could be doing so much more with your career. One day, you could have my job. But you need to want it."

"I do," I say, the pitchiness in my voice just high enough to cover the faint yip from down the hall.

Lydia's phone buzzes, alerting her to an incoming patient. A shadow crosses her features, telling me all I need to know. Car-accident victim.

"What do you need?"

The corners of Lydia's mouth turn down. "I'll get someone else to help. You've got your hands full."

"I can handle it."

"I know you can. This time, someone else will." Lydia turns down the hall and pauses. "By the way, watch out for patient 4A's husband. He's been trying to sneak a dog in all morning."

Two hours later, my first shift break arrives with a splatter of vomit, courtesy of a patient who failed to alert us that he gets nauseated at the sight of blood. After I change into freshly laundered scrubs, I take my coffee, my headache, and my phone to the courtyard.

Late-afternoon shadows lengthen across the outdoor space, which was once green, but is now the color of burnt toast, thanks to the extended drought. It makes it seem as if Kingsette is living under a sepia filter.

Three months of no rain is a record. If it continues, our town, which prides itself on its unwavering commitment to staying the same, might have to change. Permanently.

I find the little sunlight left in the day and stretch my legs into the space.

Two missed calls from my mother. Three from Tessa, along with twelve text messages asking where I am.

Lucky number thirteen vibrates as I take my first sip of coffee. It's burnt and unsatisfying.

Tessa: Please tell me you did not go to work. You promised you'd take a few days off.

Me: They were in a bind. Rosalie had car trouble, I respond, which is half-true.

Three dots appear on my screen. They disappear a moment later. Thirty seconds after that, they're back.

Tessa: Rosalie's car worked fine when I saw her this morning at the Friendly Bean. She told me she took the day off to go to Newport.

Serves me right for serving up a half truth.

"Don't bother." Tessa's disembodied voice startles the coffee out of my hand. It drops, and grainy liquid pools around the legs of the bench. It's that kind of day.

She appears a heartbeat later, wearing the twin braided pink head-band to the one in my hair and holding two coffee cups from the Friendly Bean. She hands one to me. "Extra milk. Extra sweetener. Basically an artificially sweetened milkshake—just like you like it."

"One, you're an angel. Two, what are you doing here?"

"I came to check on you. Mom said you seemed off last night at dinner." She looks me up and down with a sly grin. "I mean, more off than usual."

"Family game night isn't the same without my nieces there to distract Mom. She spent the first half of the night showing me pictures from her and Peter's trip to Paris and the second half of the night reminding me what a great hospital Newport has, in case I was looking for a change. You know, wink, wink, change, leave Kingsette, wink, wink."

Tessa laughs. "Mom's subtle like that. Did she show you the guest room too? I think she even painted it the same color as your childhood bedroom."

"Maybe we should get her a dog to take care of. Then she'll stop worrying about what I'm doing." Tessa's mouth turns down, and that's my cue to stop reminding her that she's worried about me too. "More importantly, how's Emma?"

"She's fine. She's on a steroid for croup, but already tearing up the house." A critical gaze travels the length of my scrubs. She's only eighteen months older than me, but sometimes, like now, it seems as if those eighteen months have stretched into eighteen years. "Is it even legal to work this much?"

"Of course it is," I say, and it's not a lie if it's an honest guess. "Besides, you're not allowed to give me a hard time today. You ditched me at Logan's wedding. I get a pass."

Tessa frowns. "I didn't ditch you. My daughter was sick, and I tried to call you. You disappeared on me," she says, but her expression is already softening, and I know I've been forgiven. One of the small perks of Tessa's obsessive overprotectiveness since Brandon's death is that she won't stay angry at me—no matter what I do. Sometimes I miss the Tessa who would just tell me what she thinks, without worrying I'll shatter like some fragile doll. Right now, though, I don't. "Did you really say 'husband store'?"

I suck in a breath through my teeth. "You heard?"

"Do you see where my coffee is from?" She lifts the cup so that the name of the only coffee place in town is eye level. The Friendly Bean is the heart of Kingsette—where everyone goes to eat, drink, and get their fill on what's happening where and to whom.

It's gossip central, ruled by Kingsette's gossip queen: Annette Martina.

"She compared her divorce to Brandon's death."

Tessa cringes.

"And she asked me about dating."

"That's—"

"That's not anyone's business." A rush of temper flares through me. The same temper I showed Will up on the roof-deck.

My stomach does a backflip at the memory. I'm usually—always—composed with strangers. I don't get angry. The idea that he saw me lose control like that, even for a second—it would be less mortifying if he'd just walked in on me completely naked.

A bluebird settles on a neighboring bench. It sets its beady eyes on me, as if calling my bluff.

Fine, him walking in on me naked would be worse. In my defense, I haven't been naked with anyone but Brandon ever.

"We just love you," Tessa says, pulling me back to the courtyard. "We want you to be happy." Tessa's casual use of the word *we* makes me wince. Her life is full of *we*: She and Noah are *we*; she and her girls are *we*. Even Tessa's part of the gossip chain makes her a *we*. I didn't realize the joy of *we* until I became just *me*.

"I am happy."

"Yeah, tell me again how many hours you worked last month and exactly how big the room is you rent from your late husband's brother, who—in case you forgot—is now a newlywed. Three was a crowd when they were dating and engaged. Now they're married. Married couples want privacy, not roommates." Tessa's observation traces a familiar path of frayed nerves down my spine. My room, with its abundance of sunlight and closet space, would make a great nursery.

"Which is it? I'm either working too much or intruding on their privacy."

"You know, Mom's not the only one with a spare room. And mine wouldn't require you to start over at a new hospital."

Memories strain against the dark box where they're buried. "You know why I can't live with you."

"You can't avoid that corner forever, Hope."

"We're going to have to agree to disagree on that one." There's only one way to get from Tessa's house to the hospital, but at least five ways to get there from Logan and Tanya's.

"Did you call the therapist I found for you?"

"No, because I told you I don't need a therapist. Been there, done that." An alarm on my phone shrieks into the space between us. I stand, my feet already cramping at the idea of walking for another six hours after spending a night in heels. "I have to get back."

"Wait." Tessa sits up taller. "I need your help."

The dark circles under her eyes take on pronounced meaning. My knees buckle, and I drop back to the bench. "What's wrong? Is Mom okay? Noah?"

"I got a date."

"A date? Are you serious?" My alarm shrieks again. "I have to go."

"Not for you. For me. Or for Noah, actually. For his fortieth birthday party. Since Bailey canceled her wedding, the ballroom at the Inn was available last minute. I already paid the deposit. But I need your help. You have to be the point person. I can't have Will calling my phone, or Noah will find out. This is the year I'm surprising him."

My phone rings, and Lydia's name appears on the screen. "I really have to go."

"Okay, okay, but—Helen Griffin's son Will has your number. I told him you'd call to coordinate everything." Tessa's excitement shifts.

Whatever she's spooling up to say makes my phone's insistent ringing lose urgency.

"It's a good thing you two met the other night, because you'll be working pretty close together to pull this thing off in such a short time."

I shake my head, replaying the night in my mind. "I didn't meet him."

"Oh, no? That's odd. Because I heard you two were spotted heading to the roof-deck together."

Between the champagne and the emotional maelstrom Brandon's aunt kicked off, parts of the night are blurry. But not that blurry. "Heading to the roof-deck? I went up there alone. There was some bartender there, but he—"

"He answered to the name Will?"

"Yeah, but . . . Will . . ." Vague wisps of memory come back to me of a lanky boy with deep-set brown eyes. I try to square that memory with the broad-shouldered man I met on the roof. That man seemed like a surrender. The Will I remember was a wildfire waiting for a match. Which he found when he published an op-ed in the *Kingsette Gazette* accusing the high school administration and the basketball team's coaches of grade fixing. Kingsette's reputation hasn't recovered, and most of the town still blames him for the difficulty we have getting Division I recruiters to come to our games. Somehow, through the magic of small-town politics and an unfair universe, it's Will's fault Kingsette's kids aren't all scholarship athletes at top schools.

Kingsette has a way of blaming the wrong people.

I never faulted him for taking off without telling anyone.

And now he's back.

He must be miserable.

"I can't work with Will. He's—" A lump in my throat prevents the rest of the sentence from coming out.

Tessa's beaming like she's just won homecoming queen again. "You can. You're allowed to find another man attractive, Hope."

"How do you know I think he's attractive?" My voice rises to a telltale pitch.

Tessa snorts a laugh, which manages to sound more affectionate than mocking. "Because I know you—and I'm not blind."

"I'm sure Noah will be thrilled to hear that."

"Don't change the subject." Tessa's voice softens, threatens to penetrate the wall I'm desperately trying to construct to keep back the swell of emotion rising in my chest. Her hand covers mine. "You're allowed to move on and live. Brandon would want that."

Another shrill ring pierces the air. The sound reverberates against my spine. "You don't know what Brandon would want."

"Then, what do *you* want?"

"I want—" To breathe without guilt. To sleep without nightmares. To say I'm sorry to the only person who deserves to hear it. "I want impossible things."

"Oh, Hope. You know . . ."

Her words dissolve into the effort it takes to keep locked memories chained away. I peer past the courtyard, to the street, at the routines of daily life playing out the way they have every day since Brandon died. The bluebird rises as my attention sweeps toward it, hovers as if waiting for a cue, and then takes off as if it knows exactly where it's supposed to go.

6

WILL

Two days after the bluebird incident, my face looks like I went two rounds in a boxing ring instead of ten. Luckily, the only in-person meeting I have to schedule this week is with Hope—and as long as I keep reminding myself that I don't want her to care about my face, I'll be fine.

As if the universe is calling my bluff, a headache pulses along the back of my skull. It's equal parts physical pain and frustration.

Though I hate to admit it, Annette was partially right. Running a business is harder than daydreaming—at least for me. The last few days poring over the Inn's books have made two things abundantly clear: the Inn's in major financial trouble, and I have no idea how to fix it.

Maybe . . . maybe . . . the Inn can stay afloat for another few months, but based on the projected income versus the expenses, it won't be treading water by this time next year.

It makes zero sense that my mother would let things get so bad. The Helen I knew—at least after my father's death—was prudent and penny pinching. She paid cash and avoided anything that charged interest. She was deliberate and cautious and subscribed to the belief that days off were a luxury, not a necessity.

She'd never let things get so dire. And she certainly wouldn't do anything that jeopardized the Inn. Her whole life is wrapped up in this place.

I plop into the office chair and search my mother's Rolodex—because God forbid she computerize her contacts.

Terry, the only person who might know what the hell is going on, answers after the fifth ring. His hello is tinged with wariness.

"Hi, Terry. It's Will—Helen Griffin's son." I tune into my best good guy, no-hard-feelings voice. "Delilah told me you left abruptly. I wanted to check on things."

"Yeah, yeah. Family emergency. Sorry to leave you guys. Is Helen back?"

"Nope." The word is traced with bitterness, which probably isn't going to help warm Terry up for my request. "She's still . . . away. But I'm here."

"Oh."

In that "oh" I hear ten years of hurt. Terry was one of the people I should have taken the time to say goodbye to before I took off. He always stepped up after my dad died, when most people stepped away.

"Listen, I'm—" A dog barks in the background. A woman calls his name.

"Is that Lacey?" A memory of a little girl in oversize glasses filters into my thoughts. Lacey followed Darren around like a lovesick puppy.

A pain in the back of my throat trails the memory. Now is not the time to think about a long-gone version of Darren.

"Will, I gotta go." Terry's voice catches. "Thanks for checking in. Your family has always been good to me like that."

"Wait—I . . . uh . . . I was calling for another reason too." I push back the office chair and pace the area behind the desk the same way I saw my mother pace a thousand times before, pausing in front of a black-and-white photo of the Inn. Back then, the imposing Victorian house had been surrounded by farmland and a horse stable, and my great-grandmother had allowed ivy to grow up the walls. The farmland is now a gazebo and tennis court, and my grandmother had cut back the ivy to show off the house's scalloped shingles.

"I need your help. The Inn's in financial trouble, and I'm way out of my comfort zone here."

"That's not necessarily a bad thing, Will." It's not the response I expected.

Terry hesitates. I imagine him massaging the bridge of his nose, the way he always did when my mom began to pace. His stillness balanced her anxious energy. "Unfortunately, I'm not surprised things are falling apart over there. Your mother wasn't herself before she left. She stopped coming in regularly, and when she did show up, she spent the entire time talking about adding meditation spaces and salt rooms."

"Please." Begging for help feels like being punched in the stomach.

"I wish I could help. It's just not a good time."

"There's money missing." Saying the words out loud makes my cortisol levels spike.

"What?"

"I noticed . . . there are some odd payments to vendors but no proof of service or delivery. When I started digging . . . I don't know. One of my mom's personal retirement accounts is closed too."

"Have you asked your brother?" The edge in his voice could cut glass.

"Darren?"

"It wouldn't be the first time he's stolen from your mother."

My brain struggles to make sense of the words Terry's just said. Darren wouldn't steal. He'd—

My stomach knots.

He'd show up three sheets to the wind and demand cash. If that demand was rejected . . . is it that much of a leap to imagine Darren stealing? His name is on the Inn's accounts—it wouldn't be hard.

After ten years of minimal contact, can I even presume to know what my brother would do?

Terry promises to be in touch, and it takes all my willpower to hang up without begging further. He's given enough to the Inn.

I lean my head back in my mother's office chair and rub my temples. The air blowing from the vents slides across my skin, and I attempt to breathe through the pounding in my head. I need Tylenol. Or coffee. Or a plane ticket.

7

HOPE

What are your professional goals?

The cursor blinks expectantly, waiting for my fingers to find the keys that will make an answer appear on the screen.

My professional goals are . . .

No. Delete.

Goals are funny things . . .

Absolutely not.

It's hard to have goals when everything could be ripped away without warning.

Hard pass.

The admissions board does not need a thesis on my feelings about grief and the instability of the universe.

"This is awful," I say to a framed photo of a smiling, oblivious Brandon.

"What's awful?"

I startle at the man's voice coming from behind me, and Logan chuckles. "Sorry, didn't mean to scare you. Tanya and I needed your opinion. We were calling you, but I guess you didn't hear."

"No, I guess not." I shut the laptop screen before Logan can read what I'm working on. "What's up?"

"We need you to settle a debate for us."

I follow Logan into the living room, where Tanya's staring at the mantel. A photo of the three of us at the July 4 carnival sits in a gilded frame that certainly didn't come off the registry.

The photo is from a lifetime ago—though it's only a year old. A year since Logan offered me space in his home after my bad choices left me broke. A year that was only supposed to be a few months.

"What do you think?" Logan crosses his arms over his chest. Sunlight dings off the wedding band he picked to match the one Brandon used to wear. "Tanya wants to return it. Get something that matches our decor. I kind of like it. Gives the mantel some character."

"I really hope you're just trying to antagonize me." Tanya shoots Logan a glare and turns to me. Though the wedding was almost a week ago, her dark curls still sparkle, thanks to the ill-advised dance floor glitter bomb. "Please talk some sense into him."

I put my hands up in mock surrender. "Oh no. I'm not getting in the middle of this."

"Lame," Logan mutters as Tanya's expression softens. A smirk appears a heartbeat later—and I'm struck, for the millionth time, by the knowledge that Brandon would have loved her if he'd gotten a chance to know her.

"Would it change your mind if I told you it was from Logan's aunt who accosted you at the wedding?" she asks.

"Oh." I pretend to reconsider the tacky frame with gemstones carved to look like hearts. "Actually . . ."

Logan throws up his hands. "Fine. I'll make you a deal. We return this and put the cash in the honeymoon fund."

"Deal," Tanya says, extending a hand to shake.

Instead of shaking her hand, Logan lifts her knuckles to his lips. I turn away, and my gaze snags on the tub of mint–chocolate chip ice cream melting on the coffee table. Memories tumble forward, and a lump climbs my throat as my stomach sinks. The simultaneous rising and falling makes my head spin.

Tanya notes the focus of my attention. "Sorry about the ice cream. I'll buy more next time I'm in the store. This tub was going bad soon anyway."

I fight against the knot in my throat to force out the words. "Of course. Don't worry about it."

Tanya looks pained. The edges of her voice soften with tenderness. "I really am sorry, Hope. I thought I'd have a chance to run to the store before you got home."

Home.

The word sounds like a mirage, the way it did when I was ten and spent more nights at Brandon's house than mine to avoid my parents' arguing.

"It's really not a big deal." I brighten my voice and will my thoughts away from the direction they're heading. "I need a favor, actually."

Logan's spine straightens. "Everything okay?"

"Tessa asked me to plan Noah's surprise party. He's into the local music scene, and I thought, since you two just planned a wedding, you might have some suggestions."

"Oh, totally." Logan ticks off some of the bands whose posters hang at the Friendly Bean. "Oh, Ian Summers's new band, obviously. If you can get him. We heard him sing at Maeve's a few weeks ago. His voice is insane."

The name sends a jolt through me. "You went to Maeve's? For one of those midnight meditations?"

"Once with Bailey." Tanya glances guiltily at Logan for confirmation.

"What happens? I assume she's not casting spells and sacrificing baby bunnies." Other rumors I heard over the past few days included naked dancing, summoning water demons, and performing blood rituals. Tessa was right—literally everyone is talking about Maeve. Somehow I was too caught up in my own world to hear it, until now.

Logan scoffs. "No. Some chanting. Sometimes she'll hand out little packets of leaves and tell people it'll help with aches. I think she gave Tanya an amethyst crystal." Logan's gaze slides to Tanya.

"To help calm my mind during wedding planning," Tanya says, standing up straighter. She holds Logan's gaze and raises an eyebrow. "She does more than packets of leaves and crystals."

"Like what?"

Logan swallows. "Nothing really. On full moons, she does a thing with flowers and then pretends to commune with spirits. Or something. We—I—didn't want to tell you after . . . everything that happened with . . ."

"Yeah, I get it." Heat pools in my cheeks as my thoughts turn to the medium I went to see last summer in New York City. She'd come highly recommended on grief message boards. Thousands of dollars later, all I had was a mortgage I couldn't afford on a single income for a house Brandon and I had bought with the entirety of both our savings, and a disconnected number saved in my phone for a woman who made promises she couldn't keep. "What was it like?"

They exchange a private look.

"Don't worry. I'm not planning to go. I promised Tessa no more mediums." Promising to stay away from mediums, psychics, and tarot-card readers was easy while in the throes of a shame spiral with the Manhattan skyline in our rearview. Keeping the promise has been mostly easy too.

Only two slips. Once, at a carnival—something about the old woman in medieval costume sparked hope. Probably because I'd just finished reading *The Night Circus*. And once because a medium who'd been featured in a Netflix documentary was in Newport. Neither asked me for money, besides the agreed-upon rate. Neither actually connected with Brandon either.

They told me he loved me, he missed me, he was always with me. But the things I needed to know remained unsaid.

"Logan," I say, crossing my arms over my chest and glaring at him the way his mother used to when he'd talk back to her. "Tell me."

"It was strange, mostly," Logan says, relenting. "She made it seem like Bailey's grandmother was with us, or something. She told Bailey to go to art school. Bailey ate it all up too. I'm sure you heard she broke off her engagement?"

"It's the right thing for Bailey. She's been unhappy for a long time," Tanya pipes in, adding the frustrated sigh of someone who's tired of defending her friend's choices to people who have no business passing judgment. "Also, she said Bailey's grandmother would send a sign in the form of a feather—you saw the feather Bailey posted on Facebook. It landed on her acceptance letter."

Hope flickers in the pit of my stomach. It's quickly tamped down when Logan turns his stony expression from Tanya to me.

"Please. It was a coincidence. That's it."

"Maeve knew things about Bailey she couldn't have guessed."

"Everything she said was generic. Haven't you ever heard of the Barnum effect?"

Tanya and I exchange a look.

He rolls his eyes. "It's the idea that some of us have a tendency to believe things like horoscopes or fortune tellers are accurate, even though they're so vague they could apply to anyone ever."

"Some of us, huh?" Tanya's hands go to her hips.

My phone rings, rescuing us all from the awkward tension seeping into the room. The caller ID displays the name "Kingsette Inn."

Heat rushes into my cheeks.

A rational part of me knows I have no right to be angry. He didn't owe me his life story. God knows I was happy not to share mine. But . . . Will should have told me who he was.

I consider letting his call go to voice mail. If I do that, then I'll have to call back—again. Tessa didn't ask me to play phone tag with Will; she asked me to coordinate Noah's party with him. A small request compared to all the things she's done for me in the last few years.

Another shrill ring and Logan angles to better see whose call I'm purposefully ignoring. He can be as overprotective as Tessa. And as infuriating.

I excuse myself and head back to my room, closing the door behind myself.

"Hope Gold."

"Hey, Hope, it's . . . uh . . . Will. From the other night on the roof-deck."

My heart does a strange flutter-sink-twist thing at the sound of his voice.

"I remember." My voice is colder than I mean for it to be. I sit on my bed. "The bartender who is actually not a bartender, right?"

"I *was* a bartender that night. I'm also the owner. Or temporary manager, you could say." He sounds amused at that, as if it's a joke.

"You lied to me."

"I didn't."

"You said your boss was a pushover, that he lets you get away with whatever."

"There's some truth in there," he says. "Why does it matter, anyway?"

It doesn't matter. Or it shouldn't matter. "A lie by omission is still a lie," I say.

"In that case, we're even."

"What do you mean?"

"You didn't tell me about your husband." His voice goes soft on the word *husband*.

"That's different. We both admitted to long stories." I stand, too agitated to sit, and pace my room.

"Whether I'm married or not, widowed or not, shouldn't change how you act toward me. Whether you're the damn owner of the Inn—"

"You're right. I should have told you who I was." The sound of floorboards creaking punctuates his confession. "I guess I liked the anonymity. It's hard to come back to your hometown, where half the folks never wanted to see you again and the other half feel vindicated because they always knew you'd come back with your tail between your legs."

I'm silent for a long moment as the truth of what he just admitted settles between us. "I can understand that—the anonymity part, at least. Kingsette has its charm and its starry nights, but also its strong opinions and gossip."

"That it does . . ." He clears his throat.

I search for a way to fill the silence, but my thoughts are stuck on that roof-deck, when for a little while, I wasn't Hope-the-pathetic-widow. I was anonymous, like Will. The symmetry is a salve to my anger.

"Speaking of stars . . . your sister mentioned a theme? Starry night?" He sounds stiff, like he's trying to hold back judgment.

I laugh because their theme is worthy of every eye roll it gets. "It was the theme of their senior prom. Supposedly it's sweet."

"Aah, well. What the customer wants, the customer gets." His voice takes on a professional tone. He shuffles papers, and I try to picture the man I met on the roof-deck sitting behind a desk.

We iron out a few of the details over the phone, but because Tessa was very specific about the table and dance floor layout, we plan to meet to go over the space.

"Sounds good. I'll see you then," I say.

"You got it. And Hope—I really am sorry about your husband." He hangs up. I pull the phone away from my ear and stare at it as my earlier agitation begins to make sense. Will was the only person who didn't know about Brandon, who didn't see me as the young widow who needed pity.

Now that's gone.

My phone lights up with a new text. It's Tanya.

It takes me three reads to understand.

Maeve's the real deal. I'm sure. Please don't tell Logan I told you.

8

WILL

Darren's phone is disconnected. Given the state he was in the other day, that's not entirely surprising. It does, however, make finding him difficult.

The first two bars I try in town haven't seen Darren in months. The third, owned by Chase Marshall, one of Darren's former varsity-basketball teammates and one of the few guys I didn't make the mistake of mentioning by name in my widely read and poorly received op-ed, directs me to an apartment building that's typically reserved for community college kids who still go home to do their laundry.

He's not there, either, though one girl confirms he used to hang around the building.

"Maybe he was selling weed. I'm not really sure," she says flippantly, as if Darren wasn't once the poster child for straitlaced living—up at 5:00 a.m. for a run, breakfast smoothie, honors classes, and then an afternoon on whatever sport the season dictated.

Thinking about that Darren, broad shouldered and full of future, hollows out my stomach the way thinking about my dad hollows out my chest. The difference is I could have helped Darren.

If I stayed. I had seen the direction my brother was heading, and I left anyway.

Would he really steal from Mom?

No.

Maybe.

My next step is the downtown section of Kingsette. Aside from the 7-Eleven on the corner, it looks exactly as it did a decade ago. Saloons and pubs housed in brick buildings proudly bearing the dates they were established advertise karaoke on Friday nights and ladies' night on Tuesdays. Happy hour is still from 5:00 to 7:00, because Kingsette gets to make its own rules about what an hour means. Just like it gets to make its own rules about what passes for nightlife.

LA was supposed to be different. It was supposed to be bigger and brighter and significant. It was at first. But then, it wasn't. Something was missing. The pockets of glamour and glitz hid the fact that LA was identical to everywhere else—just a little too small, too dull, too insignificant.

Or maybe it's just me. Maybe I'm hoping to find something that doesn't exist.

The restless feeling that defined my last year of high school creeps into my legs like muscle memory.

When the strip of shops ends and no sign of Darren appears, I head toward the sound of the ice cream truck idling in Kingsette Park.

The foolish spark of hope that guided me here is snuffed out as quickly as it flared. Darren's not here, not ordering a Spider-Man popsicle, because he's not ten anymore. I buy myself a mint–chocolate chip ice cream sandwich and head into the park for shade and a new plan.

On the far right, a group of women argue about how best to decorate the gazebo for the town's upcoming bicentennial celebration. Delilah and Annette round out the circle.

I pull my hat down over my eyes as I veer left, and nearly crash into a girl wearing a bright-red beret and matching paint-splattered apron. A rainbow-colored feather is threaded through the loop of her overalls. She looks vaguely familiar, though I'm sure I would remember the shock of pink hair she's sporting.

"I know you," she says, as I recover my balance and clumsily sidestep the picnic blanket and cooler she's laid out for herself. "You're the reason half the town stopped gossiping about me."

I shake my head. "I think you have me confused—"

"Will Reynard. I remember when you left. It was all anyone could talk about. Taking bets on how long until you came crawling back." She shrugs and sips from a travel mug. "You did better than people expected. But they're still talking about you."

I tilt my head to study the unapologetically blunt girl. "Have we met?"

"Nope. I'm Bailey Walters."

The name tugs on something in my subconscious, and a moment later, the memory is there. "Oh," I say, and she beams, as if proud of her infamy.

"I'm sorry about your engagement."

"If you knew Rory, you'd be congratulating me."

"That bad?" I ask.

"Worse." She reaches into the cooler and refills her travel mug from a large thermos. Flower petals in a pink-purple liquid pour out.

She catches me staring and holds the thermos out to me. "Want some? It's ginseng, rosemary, and a few colorful-looking flowers with names I can't pronounce. It's supposed to get your creative juices flowing. It tastes good too. Kind of like bubble gum mixed with tree bark."

My nose wrinkles, and she laughs. "Yep, that was my first reaction when Maeve made it for me. But—it works. I painted the piece I submitted with my art-school application after I drank this stuff for a week. They *called* me to offer me a spot. That's unheard of, by the way."

"Congratulations," I say, feeling the heat of Annette's glare find the back of my neck. My cue to go.

"Thanks. It's a dream come true, right? I mean, not the expense—jeez, they could have offered me a scholarship with that phone call. But at least Maeve is helping with that."

The hair on the back of my neck rises. "She's helping with the expense? Like paying your tuition?"

Bailey snorts a laugh. "God, no. Maeve doesn't have any money. She's got some investor friend who owes her a favor. He's going to see what he can do. I wasn't sure, but she got me this far, so why not."

"Wait. You gave her money?"

"All of the money I'd put aside for my wedding," Bailey says, oblivious to how incredibly naive she sounds. "No risk, no reward, right?"

I take a breath, which does nothing to lower my rising blood pressure. It's not my place to tell Bailey she's made a huge mistake. Besides, what's done is done.

"I hope it all works out for you."

"Thanks." She considers me. "You know, I get why you left like you did. Trying to do the right thing and give people here notice—just gives them more time to judge my life choices."

Like I just was.

Behind me, an argument breaks out over whether Kingsette's colors are green and gold or gold and green. Bailey rolls her eyes, and I feel her exasperation on a kindred spirit level.

My mouth opens against my brain's better judgment. "You know, I have some friends who moved to New York from LA. I can put you in touch, if you need a place to stay."

"Really? That'd be great!" Her voice rises in a way that sounds staged. She glances around, as if seeking an audience, the way Annette does. "I just rented a place in Alphabet City with two guys I met at orientation. Rory would have killed me if he and I were still a thing. I totally trust them, though. But it'd be nice if I had a friend in town."

"My friend might be able to set you up with a job too. If you need. I know how hard it was for me when I left town. Stepping into the wider world outside of Kingsette is jarring—a little bit of support from home would go a long way."

She beams. "That's really sweet of you. You know, you really don't deserve all the stuff everyone's saying about you."

Bailey's backhanded compliment—or was that a subtle insult?—makes me grit my teeth. "This town always needs someone to talk about."

We fall silent, and Bailey fidgets with a crystal pendant hanging from her neck. She dips her brush into a dab of blue paint on her palette and lifts it to the canvas.

"Welp, I didn't mean to hijack your walk," she says. "And your ice cream's melting."

My feet don't take the cue. "Bailey, can I ask you a question."

She answers me with an eyebrow raise.

"When you were with Maeve, was my mother there?"

"Oh yeah. She was always there. She held my hand when Maeve spoke to my grandmother."

"Your grandmother went to Maeve too?"

Bailey laughs. The sound reveals notes of the young and impressionable girl behind the pink hair and big-city aspirations. "No, she died three years ago."

At the horrified look on my face, Bailey winces. "Sorry, that must have sounded crazy. Or callous." She pulls a face. "Maeve's kind of like a medium, but she doesn't call herself that. She's just . . . like . . . this messenger for our lost loved ones. It's strange. Have you met her yet? She's staying on the lake, at the Ahava Cottage."

I shake my head. I never believed the stories people told about that cottage, but I've always been unnerved by it. Something just feels off about that place, like if you stay too long or look too closely, you'll see the pieces don't quite fit.

"You should. Especially if you want a sign from your dad. She really connected with him, and I know it meant a lot to your mom."

The scabbed edges of an old wound prickle. "My dad?"

"Oh yeah. Maeve felt his energy all the time. He was so into the idea of your mom taking a trip somewhere exotic." Bailey assesses me with an artist's scrutiny. "You should go see her. I bet she'd like to meet you."

"I don't really believe in all that messages-from-the-beyond stuff."

"You will . . . after you go."

9

HOPE

After my first full shift back at the hospital, all I want is mint–chocolate chip ice cream—and Kingsette is out. Both the 7-Eleven, which created a loud but short-lived uproar when it appeared in town, and the ice cream truck always parked in Kingsette Park are sold out. My last hope was the Kingsette Mart, which is owned by the Jones family and is second only to the Friendly Bean in volume of gossip exchanged. That hope is dashed after a quick scan of the freezer section.

What kind of town runs out of mint–chocolate chip ice cream?

Not for the first time, I wish Kingsette had more . . . of everything.

"With all the hullabaloo about the bicentennial, which I'm sure you've heard we're sponsoring, we've gotten so behind on ordering things. I'll make sure we order more in the next shipment." Mrs. Jones emerges from behind the snack foods and blocks my path out of the freezer section. She blinks up at me from behind thick lenses, her dark eyes magnified.

"You don't have to do that for me," I say, eyeing the space to her right.

As if she read my mind, her hands come to her hips, her elbows blocking me from escape. Cold air from the freezer at my back makes the skin on my arms prickle.

Mrs. Jones tilts her head. "I remember how often you and Brandon came in here for mint–chocolate chip ice cream." Her hand flutters up to her heart. "I don't know how you manage it, Hope. I really don't."

My nerves are too frayed from the last forty-eight hours to respond with anything other than murmurs about one day at a time and the power of community. Mrs. Jones seems satisfied, and I step forward, expecting to be released. Instead, her stance widens.

"How's your mother?" Mrs. Jones's nostrils flare with the simmering heat of a thirty-year-old rivalry between her and my mother. "I haven't seen her car at your sister's in over a month."

"She's . . ." I debate the best way to phrase the truth—that after she was publicly snubbed by Annette Martina at Selena's wedding, she refuses to set foot in Kingsette. That's she's tired of apologizing for being happier after her divorce. It's why she didn't come to Logan's wedding, even though he promised her a table far from the Martinas.

The door chime announces the arrival of a new customer, and Mrs. Jones steps to the side to see who's entered. I slip into the space she's ceded and navigate toward the door without looking up. No eye contact means no chance of another awkward encounter—or at least less of a chance.

"I thought I told you I'd prefer you didn't shop here. It's making my customers uncomfortable." Mrs. Jones's voice takes on an unfamiliar edge.

It's enough to make me glance up to see who's on the receiving end of her harshness.

Maeve.

"I just came here to drop off the tea we talked about the other night," Maeve says. Her smooth voice has the same calm cadence it did the day I met her in the woods. It's as soothing as it is hypnotizing.

She produces a mason jar from her tote bag. It's a deep-purple color. Flower petals and twigs float near the top. "Add boiling water, and let it sit overnight. Drink half of this tomorrow and the other half in three days."

Mrs. Jones shoots me an alarmed look. "I don't know what you're talking about."

She backs away from Maeve, her eyes still on me. Her face has turned a shade of purple red that matches the mason jar and would cause a hospital alarm to shriek. "I didn't ask you for . . ." She gestures loosely in Maeve's direction. "Whatever that is."

Maeve smiles, unflustered by the pitch of Mrs. Jones's voice. "You already paid for it. Take it. Hope won't tell anyone. Right?"

I shake my head. "No, of course not. It's . . . it's none of my business. I just—I was just leaving anyway."

Outside, the shift from artificial light to intense sunshine makes my eyes water. The air, thick and dusty, doesn't help. It's better than being caught in the middle of . . . whatever that was.

I reach the corner and freeze. Left leads to the hospital—where I can't go because Lydia will lose it if she sees me back so soon. Right leads to Logan's house—where I can't go because I'm on a mission to give him and Tanya as much privacy as possible—or Tessa's house, where I don't want to go because she'll want to talk about nursing school and her spare room and about a dozen other topics that make me feel like I'm slowly being pulled under by quicksand.

That leaves only forward. Or back.

"Or you can come with me." Maeve's smooth voice startles me out of my brooding, and I spin around to find her standing behind me, a bag of gummy bears in her hand. "Want one?"

I shake my head no. "How did you know what I—"

Maeve shrugs. "The light's turned green twice, and you haven't moved. I know a thing or two about figuring out where to go next." She brightens. "I might be able to help you with that, actually."

"I doubt that."

"Galileo once said, 'Doubt is the father of creation.'" She scrunches up her face. "Or maybe invention. I get them confused all the time. Nevertheless, you're welcome to come with me. The midnight blooms don't open for another few hours, but in the meantime, you can fill me in on what's making your energy vibrate like that."

"My energy?"

"I find grief vibrates at a much lower frequency than most would expect, but you . . ." She tilts her head to study me. "No, there's something more. Is it . . . guilt?" She turns her gray-eyed gaze on me.

Too trusting. Lydia's earlier criticism plays in my mind with Tessa's voice singing backup. Even my subconscious doesn't trust my judgment.

"Oh, Hope." Her mouth purses. "That was . . . I have a bad habit of speaking before thinking."

I inhale, letting the breath fill in the cracks splintering along my rib cage. "I should go."

Left. I'll go toward the hospital. Maybe inspiration will strike, and I'll get my essay done.

Maeve sighs. "I understand. Please tell Tessa I said hello, and that I'm happy to continue discussing the thing we were discussing whenever she's ready."

My body goes cold, then hot. Then cold again. "You spoke to Tessa?"

"Only briefly. She came to a meditation once."

"Oh," I say. It's all I can manage as a white-hot heat explodes down my spine, making sentences impossible. Tessa called Maeve bad news. She said anyone who goes to a midnight meditation is a fool.

What she meant was Maeve is bad news *for me.*

That *I'd* be a fool if I went.

"Are you okay? You look overheated." Maeve touches a hand to my shoulder, her face clouded with concern.

I shake off her hand. "I don't need help, if that's what you're thinking. And I have no money."

"Oh, dear, I believe you do need help. And I don't need your money. There are some things money can't buy."

A scoff slips past my lips. "And yet, I've tried to buy them."

"I'm sorry you had that experience."

"Don't say 'I'm sorry.'" My back teeth hurt from grinding together.

"Hmm, yes I suppose those words belong to someone else." Her gaze holds mine as her eyes blacken, as if she's seeing all the things I keep in the dark. "To Brandon, right?"

My mouth goes dry.

Maeve nods, as if I've confirmed something she already knew. The light turns green, and she turns to leave. Her foot steps off the sidewalk.

Tanya's text flashes through my mind. *Real deal.* What if Maeve is telling the truth? What if this is the chance I've been waiting for?

"Wait."

My command stops Maeve midstep. She holds the pose, balanced on one leg, with a ballerina's grace. She spins and returns to the sidewalk, eyebrow raised.

"You know? About Brandon? About—"

"Yes, Hope." The heartbreak in her voice makes my pulse jump. She knows.

"How? No one . . . it's impossible."

"Impossible isn't the roadblock you think it is," she says. "If you'd like, I can show you."

I squeeze my eyes and try to tamp down the hope igniting in my chest. "I shouldn't."

"That's probably true. But what do you want?"

"Can you . . . can you give him a message for me?" My voice is so thick with tears I hardly recognize myself.

She shakes her head. "That's not how it works exactly."

"Then how does it work?"

Across the street, a group of teenagers emerges from an arcade. Their laughter arcs between us, and my vision clears. My sense of time and place returns with a rush.

"I'm happy to talk here, but I imagine there will be consequences for you if we continue." Maeve heads toward the lake.

I hesitate only for another moment before I hurry after Maeve— marking the third time I've broken my promise to Tessa.

As they say—third time's the charm.

10
WILL

A line of sweat slips down the middle of my back and collects at the base of my spine. Desert-dry leaves, twigs, and stems crinkle and crack as I hike to the place Bailey told me about. My breath comes in heaving, embarrassing puffs as I finally reach the top of the trail, where it splits. One way leads up to a cliff with a killer view. The other, to the right, is a steep descent to the lake that I'm already dreading scaling after this—whatever this is—is over.

Bailey was cryptic about what to expect, describing which trail to take and confirming three times that I'd go at dusk. "That's when the magic really happens," she said.

The trails are familiar at least. Darren used to run them every morning. I loved when he invited me to come. He'd tell me about his plans to visit Europe, his idea to settle down in Montana. I'd teased him—because who purposefully moves to Montana? But the idea of wide-open skies had caught his attention early on, and he'd never once wavered on that plan.

Until our dad died. Until free mornings on the trail were replaced by hours helping our mom at the Inn. Until Darren turned to alcohol to deal with his grief.

Until I realized if I didn't leave fast, I'd never leave at all.

A slash of firelight streaking toward the sky reminds me why I'm trekking through the woods at sunset.

As I crest the hill, the lake and the source of the firelight come into view. A bonfire on a small stretch of beach surrounded by trees is irresponsible on a normal day. During the height of a monthslong drought? Even a hint of an ember could cause everything to burn up.

Beyond the bonfire and just past an old, gnarled crab apple tree, a long and lean cottage sits at the entrance to the woods. The fire roaring to the side of the property illuminates the paint peeling from the porch in long, curling admissions of neglect. Dusty windows outlined with the shape of missing shutters complete the front-facing facade. A weatherworn dock stretches into the lake.

My steps slow as I approach. I don't know exactly what I was expecting. Flowing white robes and floral headdresses, maybe. Definitely weird chanting and a ritual dance. But the scene before me is—ordinary. A bunch of adults ranging in age from late twenties to early sixties dressed in anything from sundresses to khakis. One man wearing a navy-blue suit, his tie hanging undone from his neck, looks as if he just walked out of the boardroom. I'd sooner believe I walked in on a PTA meeting or the after-party of a librarians' convention.

A woman in a Hawaiian shirt and cutoff shorts with silvery-blonde hair down to her waist emerges from the ramshackle cottage carrying a bushel of sticks. She's trailed by a woman wearing jeans and Converse sneakers, who looks as beautiful as she did in a body-skimming dress.

"Come on down. All are welcome." The woman with the silver hair, who I guess must be the infamous Maeve, throws her arms open. From the corner of my eye, I see recognition and something else I can't read registering on Hope's face.

"Will?" Hope squints against the fading light.

At the base of my spine, my flight instinct buzzes. My teeth grit in an effort to silence it.

"Looks like we could have carpooled." I grimace at the hokey tone and then manage to trip over a tree root. All eyes are on me as I recover and approach the bonfire.

Maeve's lips twitch up, the smirk of a mean girl spotting fresh prey in the school cafeteria.

"I . . . uh . . . I didn't know if I should call first or . . ."

"You two know each other," Maeve says, looking between Hope and me.

"Not really. We met a few nights ago. At a wedding."

"We're working together to plan my brother-in-law's surprise party." Hope sounds unsure.

"I didn't know Hope would be here," I say.

Maeve winks, as if she can see the layer beneath the layer I'm showing her. The skin around her eyes is only just beginning to crease, but something about her reminds me of someone much, much older. That blend of youth and age is disorienting.

"Any friend of Hope's is a friend of mine. Come on in, Will. We're just about to roast the marshmallows Ashley brought." Maeve pivots and heads to speak to the man in the suit, leaving me standing there, staring at Hope.

"I promise I'm not stalking you or anything," I say, sounding exactly like a man who is stalking someone. I clear my throat to get the catch out.

Hope fixes an unflinching gaze on me. In the fading sunlight, her green eyes are ringed with gold.

"Let me get this straight. First, you follow me up to an abandoned roof-deck, lie about who you are—then you coincidentally show up in the middle of the woods . . ." She sucks in a breath through her teeth. "It's concerning."

She's right. I'm one run-in away from a restraining order. "Oh, God. Hope, I know how it looks—"

Her smile reaches to her eyes, and it's immediately contagious.

"Maybe you're the one stalking me," I tease.

She scoffs. "You should be so lucky."

Her eyes brim with amusement, just as they did the night of the wedding. This time, though, her face isn't cast in shadows, and I note all the ways that lightness brightens her features.

Women sabbatical, I remind myself and force my feet to inch backward.

A bark of laughter erupts from two women standing on the other side of the fire. Hope glances at them, and her expression dims.

"Actually, I'm glad you're here. I didn't realize so many people come to these . . . meditations. I'm not great in groups. It's nice to have a familiar face in my age bracket." Hope steps to the right and gestures meaningfully with her chin to the man sitting on Maeve's porch swing.

Sheriff Wilson's watching the sunset with an intensity that's almost reverent. He looks just like he did in my memory—maybe slightly grayer. Maybe slightly sadder.

"Who are you here to . . . uh . . . connect with?" *Connect* is the word Bailey used. It's probably more appropriate than *be manipulated with.*

Hope's expression shudders, and my question registers in my brain. I'm an idiot.

"Don't answer that," I say. "I wasn't thinking."

"It's okay. I'm not here for that," she says, a sharp edge to her voice. "I just wanted to see what all the fuss is about."

"I'm s—"

"Maeve said some of these flowers only bloom at midnight on a full moon," Hope continues, as if she hasn't heard me. "Have you ever seen anything like that?"

She tells me the little Maeve told her about night-blooming flowers, and suspicion prickles across my skin. Dead grandmothers and magic flowers—how did my mom end up here?

The sun dips beneath the horizon, and an orange sky melts into a deeply purple night. Outdoor lights turn on in the million-dollar homes on the other side of the lake. A matching light leaks from an open window in Maeve's cottage. Maeve's lakeside cottage.

It's certainly not worth millions, but it's worth something, and could be worth more with a few renovations. My mother's newly emptied retirement account would go a long way. So would Bailey's wedding savings.

We meander toward the bonfire, and a woman who introduces herself as Ashley passes us marshmallow-tipped sticks.

"This is my wife, Vicky," she says, pointing to a woman with tan skin and toned arms, who greets us by passing a tray of graham crackers. "Neil's over there in the suit talking to Maeve. And that's Libby, Lisa, and Dylan."

Libby, Lisa, and Dylan shoot us a coordinated wave, as if they're used to being introduced in one breath.

"You don't live in Kingsette," Hope asks, though it's really more of a statement. She twists her hand, expertly maneuvering the flame around the marshmallow.

"Nice technique," I murmur, trying and failing to mimic her grace. My marshmallow is charcoal colored on one side and pure as snow on the other.

"Kingsette? God, no," Ashley says, and Vicky elbows her in the ribs. "Sorry. I didn't mean that. Small towns aren't my thing. We're from Newport. We have a little yoga place downtown."

"We're here for Maeve," Vicky adds. "Friends of ours met her in Tucson last year, and when they heard she was coming up this way, they told us to look her up. We've been coming every Sunday night, but the full moon nights are always best. You're in for a treat." Vicky scans the crowd and frowns. "Wilson ducked out early again. I hope he's okay . . ."

"He was in a deep conversation with Maeve earlier," Ashley says, as if that means anything about whether he's okay.

Maeve claps her hands, and everyone falls silent. I see the moment she notes Hope standing beside me, and her eyes glimmer with something that makes me want to hide Hope away.

"We have two new participants this evening. Hope Gold and Will . . ."

"Reynard," I fill in, grateful that my mother never took my father's last name and I can hold off showing all my cards.

"Reynard," Maeve repeats, and the hair on the back of my neck rises. She glances up at the full moon and then back at the assembled group. The sole trait shared among them is the way they look to Maeve. Like she can heal something broken. Hope's eyes shine with that same worship.

"We're all here for different reasons. Some of us are here because we've lost someone important to us and we're looking for words of love, hope, or absolution. Some of us are here because we want to be a part of the bigger universe, to see beyond what we are told to see. Others of us have come because they've heard things and want to make a decision for themselves." Maeve flicks her gaze to me. Despite the heat from the bonfire, an icy knot forms at the base of my spine.

"Regardless of your reason, I caution all of you to remember three things. One, the veil between worlds is a fickle one. I cannot choose when, or even if, someone from the other side appears. Two, avoid the flowers in the western quarter. And three, whatever you decide about tonight, whatever you choose to share with others, please don't mention the names of those who've gathered beside you. Theirs are not your stories to share."

Maeve pivots and heads toward the garden. The wrought iron gate creaks as she lets herself in. Ashley and Vicky follow. The others aren't far behind. Only Hope hesitates.

"I don't know why I'm nervous," Hope says with a little laugh. "It's just a garden. It's not like I'm afraid of the dark."

"If it helps, I'm terrified of the dark and I don't particularly love flowers."

I feel the heat of Hope's gaze as she weighs my words. "That does help, actually."

We make our way toward the others. They're gathered at the far end of the garden, illuminated by the moon as if a spotlight were being shone on them. The smell of pine and lavender fills my lungs, which expand to take in more sweet-smelling air.

Lisa puts a finger to her lips as we approach and points to the stalks in front of her. After seconds of stillness, one by one, delicate white buds expand under the moonlight, exposing a petal so white it's almost glittering. A light floral scent sweeps in on a breeze.

Hope's breath catches. Her hand comes to her mouth.

Maeve begins to speak, and if I weren't consumed by the feeling that something is completely off about all this, I'd feel validated. I knew there'd be chanting.

"I am light. I am love. I am breath and I am willing. I am ready to receive, to see, and to feel. My heart is open and welcomes abundance."

Maeve repeats her affirmations a second time. All except for Hope and me join in. The sound swells around us, Maeve's voice reaching higher than the others. Her voice has a depth and vibrato that I've heard in professionally trained singers. She moves her mouth with expert precision to form each word. Put together, she seems sincerely moved by what she's doing. Then again, I've seen actors look equally moved until the director yells "cut."

Maeve raises both hands into the air. Moonlight glints off a set of rings on her left hand that she wasn't wearing earlier. The first, on her pointer, is a thick band that looks as if it's set with red gemstones. The second is a stone surrounded by two smaller stones. I know it, even with the firelight distorting its color.

My mother's sapphire ring. She inherited it from my grandmother, who'd gotten it from her mother. My mom was so afraid to lose that ring she kept it in a false bottom in her jewelry box.

She loved that ring.

No. She loves that ring.

"Ashley," Maeve says, the word little more than a ghost of a sound in the hollow moonlight. "Your sister Chloe is here with us tonight. Do you feel her?"

"I do. I—" Ashley's voice quivers. She closes her eyes and turns her face up to the sky. "I think I smell her perfume."

A breeze makes the floral scent explode with notes of maple and lilac.

Hope sucks in a breath.

"She misses you," Maeve says. "So much."

"She said that?"

Maeve shakes her head. "It's in her energy. All of it is encircling you, worrying about you. Wondering why you think you must keep your life small because hers was cut short."

"It's just not fair," Ashley rasps. "She never got to—"

"She's with you. She'll be with you. Look for the pennies. She'll leave them for you."

A choked sob escapes from Ashley. Vicky steps into the moonlight, toward Ashley, and wraps her in a hug.

Hope slides a hand into mine. Her attention is wholly fixed on the scene in front of her. I'm not sure she realizes she's taken my hand in hers. For about a dozen reasons, it's all I can focus on.

"Oh my God," Hope breathes. "She is the real deal."

"Real deal?"

Tears run down her cheeks as she watches the scene between Ashley and Maeve. Maeve—whose eyes are all pupil, black saucers against stark whites—who is saying all the things a grieving sister wants to hear.

The others are as enraptured by the scene as Hope. After a while, Maeve dips her head and starts to chant. She asks us to join, and the others do. Even Hope. They would do anything for Maeve in this moment—do anything, share anything . . . give anything.

That makes Maeve dangerous—more than I could have imagined.

11

HOPE

The events of the night buzz around my mind, too fresh to make sense of. Only one thing is clear as Will and I trail behind the others back to the cars: Maeve is more than the rumors.

"What did you think?" I ask Will once Maeve's cottage is a speck of light behind us.

"It was . . . like nothing I've ever seen before." His voice is just above a whisper, as if he's afraid to speak too loudly and shatter the magic of this night too.

"Have you ever been to a medium before?"

The moonlight gleams off his dark hair as he shakes his head no. "Have you?"

Something about the intimacy of the night we just shared makes lying feel especially wrong, but I have to wade through a deep pool of shame for the truth. At least, it's easier to admit my gullibility in the dark. Or maybe it's easy because Will makes it easy. We've just met, and I've already accidentally shown him some of my worst parts—my temper on the roof-deck, my grief in the tears at Maeve's—and he's still here, and he hasn't tried to fix me once. "Last summer. I heard about this medium from my widows group. I went to see her in New York. Let's just say, thousands of dollars later all I have is bad credit and a reputation for being gullible."

"Oh," Will says, and I brace for the blend of judgment and pity that comes next. "Well, it's better than being a selfish asshat who writes a tell-all and then abandons his family to deal with the fallout while he chases fame and fortune, only to return with his tail between his legs."

A laugh moves through my chest. "Fair enough. Thank you for putting that into perspective."

"It's the least I can do to make up for not telling you who I was."

Silence falls between us, broken only by the sound of animals scurrying through the forest. Moonlight illuminates the dust rising up from the drought-dried ground. My breath matches his, and the calm rhythm is an antidote to the adrenaline of the night.

"You know, you didn't actually abandon your family, right? You were a kid with a dream in a place that doesn't always make space for dreams. You had to go."

"Most people around here would disagree with that retelling."

"Most people around here are shortsighted. Trust me, I know abandonment. My dad walked away from his family and never looked back. He built a life and then walked away from it and didn't care who he hurt. That was his choice, and it was selfish as hell. What you did was different. You were just a kid. You needed to build a life."

Will is silent for long moments, no doubt trying to figure out how to respond to a woman who lectures him about his life when she's not threatening to have him fired at a wedding.

"I shouldn't have said that. It's none of—"

"Thank you for saying that. It . . . I'm not sure I believe it, but it means a lot to know that you do."

Warmth creeps up my spine, and for the first time since we met, I'm speechless around Will.

"Where is everyone?" I ask, suddenly aware that I haven't heard Ashley, Vicky, or any of the others in too many minutes. The light they were using to brighten the path is gone too.

"They're—" Will stops walking and glances around. Without our movement, the forest is eerily, impossibly silent. He turns on his phone's flashlight and floods the space with artificial light. "Where's the path?"

Ahead of us, there's nothing but forest floor. We're surrounded by trees, with no way to tell which is forward or back.

Will makes a full circle with the light. "There's a chance we're lost."

A quiver enters his voice, which he tries to hide by clearing his throat.

"We can't be too far from Maeve's. Let's just turn around and retrace our steps."

"Yeah, that sounds reasonable." His voice rises in pitch. "Which way is back?"

It's my turn to circle around. Though without the benefit of a flashlight or my phone, which is sitting in my car, I'm met with indiscriminate shadows in every direction. For the second time, I'm lost. If this is some message from the universe, it's been received—loud and clear.

A crow caws, and I point to the left. "That way. Downhill."

He lights the way I pointed. "You sure?"

"Do you have a better idea?"

He falls into step beside me.

"Don't worry, my stepdad taught me what to do if we see a bear," I tell him, though *taught* is generous. On his one and only attempt to take Tessa and me out camping like our dad used to, he read aloud about bear attacks from a guidebook: *An Idiot's Guide to Hiking*. Then, he stayed up all night stoking the fire because Tessa told him she was afraid of the dark.

That was the trip he went from "that guy our mom is dating" to "Peter."

Will freezes midstep. "Oh, God. Bears? Actual predators who will eat me? I was scared enough when we were just talking about nebulous shadows."

A snort escapes the back of my throat. "Were you this afraid of things in high school?"

"What? You mean was I afraid of being lost in the woods and eaten by a bear in the middle of the night? Yes, and I think you should be more afraid."

My cheeks hurt from holding in a second snort. "So that tough-guy act was actually just an act?"

"What tough-guy act?" He sounds genuinely confused.

"You know, the 'expose small-town corruption, keep to yourself, never show up at parties' act?"

"Oh," he says in a way that makes me wish I could take back my teasing tone. "That wasn't my tough-guy act. That was my 'working for my widow mom and spending every other free moment making sure I get out of this town' act."

"You hated it here that much?" I clamp down on the impulse to tell him I felt the same way. Back then, I thought there was no fate worse than turning into one of those people who live ten minutes from where they grew up.

"This town shrank after my dad died. I can't explain it. I just couldn't breathe."

"I get it," I say. It's becoming a pattern to reveal too much to Will.

His flashlight catches something dark and fast moving. "We definitely did not pass this stream."

"No, but I see a light over there." I point just over the next grove of trees to a soft outdoor light from the seasonal houses. Somehow we walked to the other side of the lake. "We can cross over to there and call an Uber to bring us to our cars."

"Better than turning around and becoming bear food." Will shoves his phone into his pocket, leaving only the moonlight to see by. He puts the toe of his sneaker on a mostly dry rock in the water's path and reaches for a branch hanging over the other side of the stream. He tests the branch by pulling on it twice, and when he's sure it won't break, he pulls himself to the other side with impressive agility.

He holds on to another branch, leans forward, and extends a hand to me.

"I don't need help," I say.

"I know," he says. "But my mother would eviscerate me if she knew I didn't offer you a hand."

I take his hand. "My mom might eviscerate me for letting you help me. After my dad left, she made sure Tessa and I were completely self-sufficient."

"She did a good job," he says, releasing me. "I'd probably still be walking in circles in the dark if not for you. She must be proud."

"I think she's more worried than proud." Again, it's more than I should admit. "She'd probably try to ground me if she knew I went to Maeve's."

"Well, your secret's safe with me," he says. His breath travels along my cheek, and electricity registers across every nerve ending like it did when our hands touched over that bottle of wine. Like then, the urge to flee drowns out every other thought.

Unlike then, I'm not quite ready to walk away.

12

WILL

Time bends backward as I enter my mother's living room and note the couch against the wall, the bookcase stacked with romance novels kitty-corner by the window, and the photos of a happy family of four on the mantel. It's the house I grew up in—only smaller, shrunken to fit inside an apartment annexed to the Inn.

I make my way toward the bedroom and pause by the guest room, although that's a generous way to describe the alcove my mother made up with a bed and two dressers—one for Darren's clothes and one for mine.

She was always ready to welcome us back. Neither of us bothered to come.

I breathe through the sudden tightness in the back of my throat.

My mother's choices are hers, just as mine are mine.

In the bedroom, my mother's closet doors hang open. Dresses, blazers, and linen pants hang in the closet, which are hopefully a sign that my mother plans to return, even if the number of empty hangers is greater.

A fine layer of dust coats my mother's jewelry box, which rests, as it always has, on top of her dresser. All her costume jewelry is stored inside. Her most special jewelry is safely tucked beneath a false bottom—not exactly high-tech security, but it's Kingsette.

A ballerina springs to life when I open the box. A few cracked notes echo through the abandoned room, and a shiver runs down my spine.

Get it together.

All the recent talk of dead grandmothers and spirits has my wild imagination running in overdrive.

I release a breath I didn't realize I was holding and use the velvet pull to reveal the false bottom. My mother's diamond earrings. A pin I made her for her thirty-first birthday that reads BEST MOM EVER, and my mother's emergency twenty-dollar bill.

The ring should be there. She never wore it. She was too afraid of losing it or damaging it.

My pulse ticks up, even though the rational part of my brain is already listing the reasons the absence of the ring proves nothing except that my mother was not acting like herself.

She was acting like someone who had nothing left to lose.

It's more familiar than I'd like to admit.

A knock cracks on the other side of the office door not five minutes after I sat down at my desk. It's thrown open before I can say, "Come in."

Annette Martina stands in the doorway with two cups of coffee from the Friendly Bean. She's wearing a hot-pink T-shirt that's one size too small and a look of utter delight. It should be a nice change from the harsh welcome I received the other day.

The skin on the back of my neck prickles.

"I hope this is a good time. I would have called first, but . . ." She sweeps an assessing gaze around the room, taking in the clothes spilling out of my suitcase and the toiletries stacked on the desk. She wrinkles her nose. "Does your mother know you're sleeping in the office?"

"To know that she'd have to call me back." It takes all my effort to keep my tone even.

"I suppose that's true." She strides into the room and places one of the coffees in front of me. "Extra bitter. That's still how you like it, right?"

"What are you doing here?"

Annette eases herself into the seat on the opposite side of the desk. It groans under her weight, as if like me, it's too tired to be dealing with her right now.

"We need to chat, and I didn't want to speak in front of everyone at the restaurant." She sniffs delicately, the smell of woodsmoke wafting off my skin heightened by my rising body temperature.

"That's odd. I've never known you to be private."

She purses her lips. "There's no reason to be unkind, especially when I'm here to help you."

The headache that was wrapping around the back of my skull becomes a drill burrowing into various hot spots around my brain. Forget Tylenol and coffee. A plane ticket is the only thing that can help now.

"Help me?" Annette's not leaving this office until she says what she came to say. It's easier if I just sit back and let her.

Annette scrutinizes the office, starting at the framed sailboat photo my mother took after a photography class she'd started—and then quit—a few months after my father died, and ending on the papers scattered across the desk. "Your mother shouldn't have dumped this job on you. It was quite selfish, if you ask me."

"She didn't dump it on me." My voice rises with a defensiveness I'm not even sure my mother deserves. She did dump it on me. It was selfish. But it's not for Annette, or anyone in this chatty town, to judge the choices she made.

A memory long buried deep in my subconscious flares to life. My mother had a rare free night and made a reservation for the three of us at our favorite restaurant. There, we ran into three couples, including Annette and her husband.

My mother chatted with them, her posture rigid, with a smile I knew wasn't her own. She came back distracted, with a look that then I didn't understand but that made me want to punch through a wall.

Not unlike how I feel now.

Annette brings her coffee to her lips. It comes away with a pink lipstick stain on the white lid. "Well, semantics aside. You're here. Your mother's gone, and everyone knows the Inn is in serious financial trouble."

I shake my head. "This town is unbelievable."

Annette places her coffee cup down on a spreadsheet. "There's no reason to be defensive. I'm trying to help."

"By telling me the entire town knows I'm running this place into the ground?"

"By offering to buy this place from you."

A roaring silence in my ears chases her offer. It takes a beat too long to recover from the shock of her words. "What? You want to buy the Inn? It's been in my family for generations."

"Yes, I'm aware. The Kingsette Inn is a fixture of this town. It's part of our legacy, and it belongs to all of us. It—and we—deserve an owner who cares about this place and wants to see it flourish."

"I care about this place."

Annette's cool gaze runs over me. "I'm sure that's true in some fashion . . ."

She clicks her tongue, and as if a veil has been pulled from my eyes, details my attention skimmed over this past week sharpen into focus. I see the office with its water-stained walls and faded carpet the way Annette must see it. Heat flushes up my neck.

"Will, you're not up to this, and you don't want to be the son who lets it fail." Her words hover between us, heavy with the weight of old fears and unrealized expectations. This is the problem with returning home, returning to Kingsette specifically—too many people know too much. They can weaponize your past. "We can discuss terms after you've given it some thought."

"I'm not going to sell. I won't change my mind."

She breathes a laugh. "We both know you will. The only thing that's ever mattered to you about this place is the door. This time, I'm showing you the exit."

13

HOPE

I expected Logan's confused expression when he walked into the waiting area of his veterinary clinic and found me sitting between a cocker spaniel in a cone of shame and a boxer with an injured paw. I did not expect him to answer my question about bird injuries by escorting me through the private door connecting his clinic to Mrs. Lemmings's pet shop.

"You really could have just told me what I needed," I say, as Mrs. Lemmings gives us a narrow-eyed once-over. Two decades ago someone released all the rabbits from her store, and she's watched every customer with hawkish suspicion ever since.

Even me, despite her sobbing on my shoulder at Brandon's funeral and promising to be there for me.

"I needed more details about the bird's injuries." Logan salutes Mrs. Lemmings and breezes past her to the bird supplies. "And I wanted to catch up with you in private. You've been . . . off . . . since the wedding. Tanya and I have barely seen you."

Because you've only been married ten days and I've been giving you and your new wife privacy, I think. Although making myself scarce is going to get much harder soon—Lydia's threatened to have me transferred to labor and delivery if I pick up one more extra shift. As much as I love Logan and Tanya, I'm not willing to risk a run-in with Brandon's pregnant cousin . . . or her mother.

"I'm fine. You shouldn't keep that poor boxer waiting."

Logan shrugs. "Hope, I'm the only vet in town. They'll wait because they have no other choice."

"Logan Gold! When did your head get so big?"

He laughs. "I'm joking. They're here for follow-up. My nurses are taking their vitals, and I'll be right back. Besides, looking out for you is as important a job as anything."

His protective streak is only slightly less annoying than Tessa's. "Does that mean a cone of shame is in my future too?"

"It's not out of the question." He plucks two emergency-bird-care kits off the shelf and studies the contents of each. He hands me the bigger of the two and returns the other to the shelf. "I can bring this to Maeve to save you the trip out there. Better yet, Maeve can bring the bird to the clinic, and we'll care for it here."

"She said she knows what she's doing . . ."

"Do you know what you're doing?" His expression softens, and for a heartbeat time folds in on itself and it's Brandon standing in front of me, waiting for an answer to a question with no good answers. "I liked her when I met her too. Doesn't mean I trust her."

Logan's phone buzzes. "Oh, I should take this," he says, bringing the phone to his ear and turning his back to me. Giving me space to breathe.

Do I know what I'm doing?

No.

But I know what I heard last night was real. Maeve knew so much about Ashley and Chloe. A Google search wouldn't reveal that much. No one who saw what I saw could believe anything other than the truth that Maeve can do incredible, magical, impossible things.

She gave Ashley her sister back—the chance to say what had been left unsaid.

That's all I've wanted. A chance to speak to Brandon, to tell him I'm sorry for what I said. To explain.

Maybe it's crazy to believe Maeve. Maybe it's crazier not to take a chance.

My phone pings.

Still can't get the smell of smoke out of my hair. I'm getting dirty looks from the kitchen staff. Any advice?

Will's text startles a smile onto my face. The answer is no. I have no advice because I rushed out of the house this morning and I'm sporting a smoke-scented ponytail. That's a little too pathetic to admit, though.

I type #letmegooglethatforyou and press send.

His response comes a heartbeat later: Harsh, real harsh.

And then: I thought we decided we were taking care of each other from now on.

My heart goes through a hop-skip-and-jump routine. That's exactly what we decided after our ill-fated hike had turned into hours on the phone, despite the weight of exhaustion pulling me into sleep.

The extended phone call had been Will's doing initially. He wanted to make sure I got home okay after I almost fell asleep in the Uber on the way back to our cars.

Then, we just stayed on the phone. Even as we brushed our teeth. He told me about his life in LA, the celebrities he'd casually brunched with and the ones he'd run into at parties in locales I could barely picture. It made me realize how little I've traveled. Traveling had always been on my list of things to do, but then the rug was ripped out from under me and traveling took a back seat to keeping my head above water.

I reread the message: *I thought we decided we were taking care of each other from now on.*

He's just joking about taking care of each other, just referencing the night before, but . . . there's something intimate in seeing the words typed out.

I type back: This is me taking care of you. I add a kissy face and press send.

And freeze. Tessa and I use the kissy-face emoji to soften sarcastic, obnoxious comments, mostly as a joke. It's a habit to use that emoji, which pops up in my favorites, but—

A kissy face? To Will? Seriously?

This is me taking care of you . . . kissy face?

Oh, God. I barely know Will. He's going to think I'm flirting. He's going to think I'm attracted to him. Which I'm not. I mean, I'm physically attracted to him—but so are half the nurses at the hospital, who can't stop debating if he looks more like a dark-haired Ryan Gosling or an olive-skinned Ryan Reynolds. And obviously I think he's easy to talk to and genuine and charming. But I'm not attracted to him like that.

Heat pools in my cheeks as I consider the best message to send next that won't make it awkward. More awkward.

Just kidding about the kissy face.

My sister and I use the kissy-face emoji all the time, don't read into it.

Ignore that kissy face. It was meant for someone else.

I scan the shelves and find no solution among the bags of birdseed. I'm screwed. Anything I send will make it worse. There should be an unsend feature for texts that works for all phones, not just the latest ones. Or at least a redo button. It's frankly barbaric that there isn't.

"Ugh," I groan out loud. The only option is to throw my ancient iPhone 8 out the window and change my number.

At least he hasn't replied. That's probably a good thing. My best bet is to play it off like it's no big deal too. Because it's not a big deal. It's an emoji, and neither he nor I are tweens who read real adult emotions into emojis.

"Everything okay?" Logan asks, returning to my side. His attention attaches to my phone, and his brow furrows, the way it does when he's disturbed by something.

Did he see Will's name on my screen? Did he see the kissy-face emoji?

My pulse ticks up, and I stuff the phone into my back pocket. The heat of it seeps through my jeans, like a smoking gun.

"I have to get back. Cat emergency." He glances to my now phone-free hand. "Everything good?"

"Yep," I say, popping my *p*.

"And you'll be careful at Maeve's?"

"Yes, I learned my lesson. I'm just there for the bird. Nothing more."

Maeve's lying facedown on a wide branch, etching a new word into the tree, which already bears countless words and names, some that look new, and others that are nearly smoothed over by time.

"A little birdie told me you'd be stopping by," she says, easing herself into a crouch and hopping to the ground with the grace and strength of a panther. She's wearing ripped jean shorts, a vintage Nirvana T-shirt, and a small metal stud in her nose that I didn't notice yesterday. She smiles as I once again try to assemble into a cohesive whole the old-fashioned way she speaks with the punk rock look she presents.

"I wanted to check on him," I say, gesturing to the bird tucked into a makeshift nest balancing on the porch steps. It doesn't look any worse. Although, it doesn't look any better either.

Maybe the bird does need Logan.

"I brought this," I say, extending the emergency bird kit. "Something in this kit might help."

"Perhaps," she says, taking the kit and placing it to the side without another glance. "I'm surprised to see you back here so soon."

"Well, I feel responsible for the bird." At least that part's true.

"Mm," Maeve says, smiling the way my mom used to when I was a teenager insisting Brandon was just a friend.

"Will he be okay?" I lean forward, close enough to share breath with Maeve. I realize and step back.

"Yes. A broken heart simply needs time and a warm place to land while it heals." Maeve pulls a tiny glass vial from her pocket and sprinkles drops around the bluebird's nest. "A little broken heart tonic doesn't hurt either. I'll teach you how to make it if you'd like."

"A broken heart? But his wing looked hurt. He couldn't fly."

"Broken hearts often find it hard to soar, in my experience," Maeve says, and it's not hard to guess she's not talking just about the bird.

"I noticed your roses were wilting. I'm working night shifts the next few days, and I thought maybe I could help you with them in the mornings. My mom wins awards for her roses, and she taught me a bit."

Maeve assesses me, and I wonder if she sees an object of pity, the way Tessa does when she looks at me; or a disappointment, the way Lydia does; or even a person to keep at arm's length as if bad luck and grief are contagious, the way the rest of this town does.

"I'd like that," she says, and I exhale the breath I was holding.

"Roses are the bane of my existence," she continues. "I've lived in hundreds of different places, and even in perfect conditions I can never get them to grow."

"I can't believe you've gotten anything to grow. This is the worst drought Kingsette's ever experienced." Even Tanya's prized vegetable garden stopped producing weeks ago, her tomatoes abandoned nubs on wilting stalks.

"My mother taught me well. She was . . . eccentric. She saw magic in rainstorms and sorrow in rainbows. She taught me everything I know about flowers, how to nurture them, how to heal with them. Of course I wanted nothing to do with her or her flowers. Or the way she saw me."

The way Maeve's talking, her use of the past tense—it's too familiar. "Do you want to tell me about her?"

Maeve lifts her hand to allow a butterfly to light on her finger. Her features soften as she gazes at the delicate creature. "Maybe another time."

The butterfly takes off, and Maeve turns to study me.

"Come, I'll give you the grand tour." Maeve leads me through the garden, stopping by a row of raspberry bushes. She pops a handful of berries into her mouth. "Try one."

My hesitation makes her smile. "They're just berries. You won't be trapped here forever if you eat one."

"Persephone and the pomegranate seeds?"

"You know your Greek mythology," she says, sounding impressed, which is only mildly insulting.

"I majored in ancient-Greek studies my first year in college. I switched to nursing when I realized I needed something more practical." Something that would fit into the spaces Kingsette had for me and Brandon. Nurse for me. Lawyer for him.

"Have you ever been?"

I shake my head. Brandon and I were supposed to go for our honeymoon. Then for our first anniversary. We would have made it there for our tenth anniversary. Probably.

"The years I lived in Greece were the only years I tried to grow olive trees." She scrunches up her features and scrutinizes the garden. "I wonder if I should try to grow those again."

"They'd be the first olive trees to grow in Kingsette ever." I pluck a berry off the vine and almost moan at the flavor, which is the most perfect blend of sweet and citrus I've ever tasted.

Maeve beams. "I knew you'd appreciate those. Come look at these too."

She leads us past the midnight blooms, which remain tightly closed against the sunshine, and points out Amazon lilies, which reach to my knees and smell like pockets of heaven; African violets; Chinese hibiscus; and a variety of other orchids with names I've never heard.

"Over there are the mandrake, nightshade, and hydrangea. Belladonna, of course," she says, pointing to the purple flowers with the dark berries in the western quarter of the garden.

"Why do you grow poison flowers?"

"They're not poison flowers, they're flowers that can be poisonous when used by the wrong person. A touch of belladonna goes a long way when someone comes to me with a broken heart." She considers the flowers, something tender passing over her expression. Something honest. "Of course, they need to be handled with care. Even touching the leaves can irritate your skin. If you have an open wound, it's even worse. Then there's the hydrangea—beautiful flower, but it's quite underestimated."

"Can I speak to Brandon at the next meditation?" The question blurts out of me.

"I thought you came here for the bluebird. And the roses." A hint of a smirk.

"Please. I just—I've seen more mediums than I care to admit. None of them could do what you did last night. I felt the energy you were talking about. A vibration?"

"I never said I was a medium," she says as a breeze kicks a cloud of shimmering dust over the lake.

"Please, Maeve."

She pulls a bag of gummy bears out of her back pocket and pops a red one into her mouth. "I can put out the call for his energy, but whether he comes is out of my control. I don't want you to get your hopes up too high."

"He came to you before, though?" I press.

"Yes," she draws out the word, as if there's more she's not saying.

A butterfly lands on her shoulder; its wings flutter against her cheek.

The same flutter materializes in my chest, only it's a thousand butterfly wings. "Please. Tell me."

She squeezes her eyes shut and blows out a reluctant breath. Her free hand touches the empty space at the hollow of her throat. "The night I met Tessa. I don't know whether she realized how powerfully her energy was calling for him."

Heat blooms across my entire body at the sound of my sister's name, and it takes everything inside me to barricade the wave of emotion. "Did Brandon . . . was there a message for me?"

My breath stalls in my lungs.

"I got the sense that he wanted you to find what you lost. Something that has always been meant for you, though it's been missing for too long. Something that, when you find, will lead you to what you seek."

The edges of my vision blur. Everything in my body goes silent, as if I'm suspended in time. My hand mimics hers and touches the empty space where the locket Brandon gave me should be. It's been lost since the accident.

"My locket? Could that be . . ."

Maeve's silence feels like an answer. She eats more gummy bears, and a pattern is emerging. Red, yellow, green.

After all this time, I assumed it was gone for good. Impossible to find.

But maybe no more impossible than flowers that bloom in moonlight and birds with broken hearts.

"It's worth a try, isn't it?"

"I don't know where to look." My voice is a whisper.

"As they always say, where there's a will, there's a way."

14
WILL

For maybe the hundredth time, I type some version of *Maeve* and *medium* into my web browser and come up with exactly nothing. As far as the internet goes, Maeve does not exist.

Though, how that's possible is a mystery. Because she looms large in real life. It's impossible to get a cup of coffee without hearing a Maeve story. She has something. I can see why people are drawn to her. A lot of celebrities I've met have that same energy. But—ticket sales for bad movies notwithstanding—they don't inspire fans to give up fistfuls of cash and jewelry.

I blow out a breath and open Facebook. I've avoided social media since my show was canceled—the diminishing number of friends and followers is a reminder of the direction my career is going—but desperate times call for desperate measures.

The cliché makes me think of Hope, and my fingers scroll to her page, as if they've got a mind of their own. Her profile picture is of her and a handsome man who I vaguely recognize from high school— Brandon. Their faces are smooshed together, matching mile-wide smiles reaching all the way to their eyes. Brandon is a head taller than Hope, with sandy-brown hair and a jawline my agent would drool over. He's good looking in a boy next door way that matches Hope's gentle spark.

The last album she posted was two months before Brandon died. Photos of Brandon and Hope posing with a SOLD sign in front of a modest house and making faces into the camera populate the screen. Farther down her page, her wedding album. Their joy in every photo is almost audible through the phone.

Something inside me breaks for Hope—to have had that happiness and lost it . . .

No. Hope made it clear she doesn't want my pity.

My mother's page is more current than Hope's, but not much. A photo of Lake Kingsette at sunset, taken just before she disappeared, sits at the top of her timeline. I recognize the tree line a second before I see the two figures in the far-left corner of the photo. They're blurry and half-concealed by a shadow. I zoom in, and their faces become more pixelated. One of the figures is Maeve—silver hair and all.

The next series of photos is in black and white, with an intentional pop of color. A photo of Bailey, her pink hair highlighted among the shades of gray. A red rose in the monotone garden. A photo of Ashley and Vicky seated around the bonfire. It takes a moment to spot the pop of color.

My stomach twists like it did when I spotted my ex kissing her old boyfriend.

The spot of color is a bright-red ring on Ashley's finger. The same ring Maeve wore the other night alongside my mother's ring.

Either everyone's in a giving mood, or Maeve has a way of getting what she wants.

After another round of unsuccessful interviews for the manager's position and an awkward check-in of a single-night guest under an obviously fake name—S. R. Chard should stick to banking rather than adultery, though it's none of my business—I input into Waze the address I googled. Within an hour I'm entering the yoga studio as the class lets out. Ashley is the last to exit the room, bringing with her the smell of eucalyptus and sweaty feet. She does a double take when she sees me.

"Hey. Ashley, right? We met the other night at Maeve's."

Ashley's eyes widen, and she looks around to see if anyone's overheard. The yoga students are on the other side of the reception area, slipping into shoes and chatting about where they're going for dinner.

Hope's teasing "stalker" accusation comes to mind. I should have thought through how it would look to show up here—without even the pretext of taking a class.

"What are you doing here?" she asks, voice clipped.

"Is there some rule against socializing away from the lake?" In my head, the words sounded casual. Out loud, they're a creepy smile away from a restraining order.

She scowls. "No, but some people like to talk more than they should." She glances at the students stuffing yoga mats into tote bags with designer labels. "I'd rather not let my personal activities impact my business."

"Oh," I say. "Well, I didn't mean to intrude. I just wanted to see how you were doing. The other night was pretty intense."

"I'm fine."

"That's . . . good. I'm glad to hear that," I say and lick my lips. My mouth is so dry it feels like rubbing sandpaper over a nail file.

The yoga students call out their thanks as they file out the door. She plasters on a smile as she waves. Once the door's closed, the smile fades. She reaches for a mason jar. The liquid inside is lilac colored. Twigs and shredded leaves thicken the mixture. "Was there something else you needed?"

"Yes. No. I mean . . ." I run a hand through my hair. At the bonfire, Ashley was easy to talk to and gracious. This suspicious and irritable Ashley is setting fire to the mental script I prepared during the drive over.

She sips and makes a face.

"What are you drinking?"

She shudders. "Maeve gave it to me. It's supposed to help with my anxiety. Since Chloe . . . you know . . . I have trouble sleeping."

"Does it work?" Bailey had been drinking a tea, too—for creativity. Another coincidence from a woman who is made up of coincidences and conundrums.

Ashley turns her back to me and straightens a display of yoga mats and towels. "No, but Maeve said to give it time. She has teas for everything."

"How long have you been going to Maeve?"

"Hmm, maybe two months? Maybe longer. Why?"

"Just curious." Framed photos of Ashley and Vicky with various friends hang on the wall behind Ashley. In one photo, Ashley, Vicky, and another couple wear matching I LOVE ARIZONA shirts. "You mentioned friends in Tucson. What did they tell you about Maeve?"

Ashley's towel folding falters. "Honestly, not much. They just said we needed to meet her. That she could help with grief." She begins folding again. "At first, I really just wanted to see her tree."

"Tree? Like a bonsai tree or a houseplant?" I can almost hear Darren's eyes roll. Despite growing up around trees, I know little about them. The outdoors was Darren's first love.

"No. Like a real tree. The one in front of her house that's carved up with all the names. She carries it with her everywhere she goes."

"That's—"

"Impossible. I know. But you saw it there, didn't you?"

I saw a tree carved with names. High schoolers with a blade and too much time on their hands. Or Maeve and a long night spent re-creating a tree she carved up in Tucson. People have done crazier things.

"What about . . ." I bite my lip. Magic trees didn't put Ashley's ring on Maeve's finger. "Did you pay Maeve or . . ."

Ashley whirls around to face me, hands coming to her hips. "Why are you asking?"

"I just heard some strange things."

"The rumors aren't true. She's not a con artist." The desperation in her voice makes it clear I'm not the only one of the two of us she's trying to convince.

"I know. I don't think she is, but—"

"But what?"

"I don't believe what they're saying." My words sound flat even to my own ears, even though I'm telling the truth. Maeve is a con artist, not a witch sacrificing animals during a full moon. "She was wearing your ring. I . . . guess it made me suspicious."

"I think you should go." Ashley moves toward the door.

I trail her to the exit, stepping over the rainbows cast by the assortment of crystals surrounding the window. She flings open the door, and I walk out. Before the door closes in my face, I catch it. "I didn't mean to ambush you. I've just lost a lot of people and a lot of things that were important to me. You have to understand—I don't have much left. I can't take a risk."

Ashley's shoulders ease away from her ears. "I do get that. But one thing you'll learn from Maeve is that sometimes you have to lose what you're holding on to in order to find what else you might need."

She lets the door close and avoids my gaze as she turns the lock. The click echoes in my ears—a long, somber note, a memory.

I'm so lost in my thoughts that I don't see the woman standing by my car until I'm nearly on top of her.

"Fancy meeting you here." She flashes me a lopsided smile.

"Vicky?" I glance behind me. The yoga-studio door is tightly shut, the shades drawn. "What are you doing here?"

"Picking up Ashley. What are you doing here?"

"I—" My words scatter. There's a reason I stuck to writing scenes rather than acting in them. "Just checking on Ashley."

Vicky gives me a discerning look.

"Well, it was nice to see you." I step around her toward the car door.

She holds her ground. "You want to know if it was legit."

"If what was legit?"

"The flowers. Maeve. Chloe. All of it." Vicky raises an eyebrow.

"I do know. She's legit." If this is a test, I'm failing miserably. I barely believe myself.

Vicky breathes a laugh. "Don't worry. I won't tell, and I agree with you."

"You do?"

"Of course. Everything she told Ashley was available somewhere on the internet, if you know how to look."

"So why were you there?"

She looks up at the yoga studio. Tenderness enters her features. "Ashley needed the closure. There's no harm in going if it gives her some peace."

"Yeah . . ." Peace is elusive. The last time I felt truly at peace was before my father died. Since his death, it has felt like the world is constantly rearranging itself and I'm just a step behind. No matter how far and fast I run, I never catch up. "So you don't care that Maeve is manipulating her?"

"I don't know that I'd call it 'manipulating.' Maeve doesn't make any promises. As long as Ashley doesn't run off or decide to break up with me to pursue an art career like some of the others, it's harmless." Vicky breathes the easy laugh of a person who isn't worried that the person who means most to her will disappear.

"What about . . . ?" I lean in the way Annette and Delilah do before exchanging gossip. Vicky seems to be on my wavelength, but we're still strangers, and it would be so easy to disturb the candidness she's demonstrating. "Did Ashley give away her ring?"

Vicky frowns. "It was Chloe's lucky ring. She wore it to every doctor's appointment. Ashley wore it a few times, but she said it was too hard to look at. She gave it to Maeve the other night. She thought maybe Maeve would find someone who could use a little luck."

"Does Maeve always expect jewelry from her . . ." Flock? Clients? Prey? I settle on the least-offensive and least-honest word. "Friends?"

"No, it's not like that. She charges for her teas, obviously, but for the other stuff . . . people tend to give her things." Vicky's brow furrows. "Now that I think about it, I guess that is a little strange."

15

HOPE

Framed photographs, fleece throws, books, candlesticks—all the odds and ends that fill a house, that had created the backdrop of my life with Brandon—lay strewn around my bedroom. The vestiges of my old life are all here, except the locket Maeve told me I need to find.

For maybe the millionth time, I try to remember where I left it. But the morning before the accident, like the days after, is a blur. Only the accident, the moments directly before, during, and after, remains in my memory, jagged edged and unforgiving. Even after all this time.

I close my eyes and try to replicate a breathing pattern the first medium I saw taught me.

Seven counts to breathe in. Four counts to breathe out.

Seven in. Four out.

Seven in, and—

Canned laughter from the sitcom Logan and Tanya are watching in the living room interrupts my thoughts. As if the universe were mocking me for continuing to follow advice from a woman who charged me five figures and then recited Brandon's obituary with a few details from Facebook thrown in.

There's a reason I never mentioned that medium to Tessa, which is something I feel less guilty about now that I know Tessa's lied to me too.

My phone buzzes with an incoming text, and I bolt up, checking the time.

Do you need a ride to Emma's game? We can swing by and pick you up.

Shoot. I forgot Emma's peewee summer soccer league has its first away game today, and I promised I'd go.

I type out a text letting her know I'll be a few minutes late, throw a sweatshirt that says **Soccer Aunt** on over the T-shirt I slept in, and shove my feet into sneakers. A quick glance in the mirror reveals dark circles under my eyes, and a whiff of my hair confirms I smell like the fire Maeve lit in her hearth before I left.

Hopefully I'll air out and Tessa won't question the rest.

My tentative hope is squashed the moment I step onto the field.

Tessa's standing with Noah, Peter, and my mother, who's wearing a bright-red sundress, a wide-brimmed hat, and more bracelets than I own. Tessa spots me and jogs toward me before I can do an about-face.

"I didn't know they were coming," she says, breathless. "I mentioned the game on the phone last night, and that it was an away game and you were coming, and . . . here they are. Mom says you've been avoiding her."

"I'm not avoiding her. I've just been—"

"Working, I know. Although . . ." She gives my outfit a once-over. "Wild night last night?"

"No, regular night. I just . . . overslept this morning."

"You know I can tell when you're lying. Your voice does this weird high-pitched crack thing, and it's a total giveaway." Tessa's expression is the same one she wore when she asked about my first time with Brandon—a blend of sisterly love and nosiness. "Were you on a date?"

"Tessa," I say, and it's warning enough for her to throw up her hands in surrender. "Oh, before I forget. I heard from Noah's cousin. She's coming with all three kids. Have you worked out the table layout yet? I may need to move some things around." Her question sounds neutral, as if she's really asking and not trying to determine whether I spent any more time with Will.

"Not yet."

She jerks her head to look at me. "But you will, right? And you made the appointment with Sunshine Bakers in Newport?"

"I have a meeting tomorrow afternoon." I make a mental note to call the baker. Once I schedule the appointment, my lie becomes truth. "It's under control."

Her body relaxes. "Thank you. I don't mean to be such a micromanaging control freak."

"Uh, yes you do," I tease, and she puts on an outraged look before shrugging and agreeing.

We approach the group, and my mom sweeps her hat off and presses forward to wrap me in a tight hug. Since Brandon died, she always hugs me like this. Like she wants to squeeze the sad out of me. Like she wants to absorb all my heartache.

Peter clears his throat. "Madelyn, the rest of us would like to say hi to Hope too."

She releases me reluctantly, and Peter takes her place. "How you doin', kiddo?"

"I'm good," I say as he pulls away and looks for truth in my words.

His assessment is cut short by two little bodies that barrel into me while screaming my name. Noah catches me before I crash to the ground. "There's probably a nicer way to greet your aunt, don't you think?"

Emma and Macy shout an apology over their shoulders as they race back to the field. My "hi, girls" is lost to the chorus of shrieks their arrival earns.

"Sorry about that," he says. "Grandma brought Fruit Roll-Ups and apple juice as a pregame snack, and they're on a sugar high."

"It's my joy to spoil my grandkids, and I won't be shamed about it." Her gaze gets misty, and I know she's thinking about the grandchildren she'll never get to spoil—the ones that had Brandon's perfect smile and steady calm.

"Hey, Mom. I need to steal Hope away for a minute, but Noah can show you the perfect place to sit so you can yell at the ref during time-outs."

Noah widens his eyes and mouths, "You owe me." Tessa winks and blows him a kiss.

When Noah, Peter, and our mother are out of earshot, Tessa makes a noise that's half sigh, half primal grunt. "If you ever see me guilt-tripping my kids like that, please stop me."

I weave my arm through Tessa's. "Thank you for saving me."

"Don't thank me yet." She gestures, and I follow the line of her gaze to the three women heading toward us. The PTA moms, formerly known as the head cheerleader, the prom queen, and the student council president. "Your turn to save me," she whispers and pulls me forward.

After everyone says their versions of "Hello" and "It's been so long" and "We need to make a plan, for real this time," the conversation shifts to kid topics, and my attention turns to finding an escape hatch out of the conversation for Tessa. She's always despised small talk—and swears it gives her migraines. When we were kids, I'd just throw a temper tantrum, and she'd pretend to be annoyed while she led me away. As adults, it takes a little more finesse.

"I heard the financial problems are so bad the Inn might shut down."

The prom queen's comment jars me out of my scheming. No good sentence in Kingsette ever starts with "I heard." "Financial trouble?"

"I heard they're deep in debt, and that's why Helen left so abruptly— because she had some sort of breakdown from the stress. Apparently she paid Maeve to help her disappear."

My stomach churns at the viciousness of the gossip surrounding Will's mom, though it's not a surprise. This town can be cruel to single women—it villainized my mother, even though it was my dad who'd left, and it's turned my life into fodder, open for discussion, judgment, and opinion.

"I don't think we have the full story," I say and hate how small my voice sounds. I don't just "think" we don't have the full story. "Maybe Helen just needed to get away."

"Or maybe she was brainwashed." The former prom queen leans in to deliver the gossip. "I wouldn't be surprised if some of those rumors about Maeve were actually true. I saw her outside the library leaving crystals and rocks with inspirational quotes written on them. It was weird. My gut says she's bad news. Not like witch-with-magic-powers bad news. Like . . . loony tune bad news."

"Because she left a few rocks?" They can't be serious.

The prom queen shrugs. "If the shoe fits."

"She's not a loony tune just because she doesn't look and act the way you think she should. Just because she wants to live her life her way, and not your way, doesn't mean something is wrong with her. That she's wrong."

"The game's starting." Tessa glances at me, her expression full of concern. I'm supposed to be saving her, but it feels like she's about to save me—again. "Let's go—"

"What do you think?" The former student council president lands her gaze on Tessa.

"I never met her, so I can't say." Tessa's voice does a weird high-pitched crack thing when she's lying too.

The ref blows a whistle, and all the parents turn toward the field. Tessa pulls me away. "What was that about?"

"What?"

"That Team Maeve rant you just went on?" Tessa narrows her eyes. We both inherited our mother's green eyes. Only Tessa inherited our mother's shrewd ability to hear more than what's being said.

"I'm not Team Maeve. It's just that . . . this town is so vicious if you don't fit their mold. The minute I became a young widow and they didn't know what box to put me in, I started getting pressure to fit into some life that didn't fit anymore. They did the same thing to Mom. And it feels like that's what's happening with Maeve."

Tessa tilts her head in that way I hate—the pity tilt. "This is different. Maeve is different. We're just looking out for each other—not malicious, or whatever you think it is."

I bite down on my response. Tessa simply can't understand what it's like because she's not other. She's *we*. "Can we just watch the game? No more Maeve talk."

"Only if you promise to stay away from her."

"I promise," I say and resist wincing at the burning sensation that always follows when I lie to my sister.

After the game, a shower, and an assurance to Logan that I'll be at the house for dinner tonight, I head toward the Inn, like I promised Tessa.

I find Will sitting at the desk cradling his head. There's a tension around his mouth that I haven't seen before. "Everything okay?"

He nods his head. "Yeah. Just the joys of being temporary manager of the family business in a small town that knows all about your past."

"Aah, yes. Can't escape that in a small town." I think of the gossip about Will's mother.

His eyes travel the length of my sweatpants and shirt. Laundry day came and went days ago, and this time, I can't blame the extra shifts at the hospital—because I haven't picked any up.

"Yeah." He blinks, as if waking up. "Let me get your paperwork. I know you have better things to do than listen to me complain."

I take the seat across from him and note the suitcases stacked by the desk, the button-down shirt draped across the top. He swivels in his chair and riffles through a filing cabinet topped with a shaving mirror, toothpaste, and deodorant.

The meaning of "temporary manager" couldn't be clearer.

His face is flushed when he spins toward me. "Still getting organized here."

"I'm sure it's a lot of work. Especially if you're planning to leave soon." There's an edge to my voice. I sound like Tessa when she's fishing for information.

Will pauses.

"Not that it's any of my business," I say quickly, before he can read any more into my question. "Because it's not."

His features soften. "Don't worry, Hope. The whole town knows my mother took off, and I know you won't report back to the Kingsette powers that be that I'm living like a nomad. If you were one of *them*, the whole town would be talking about our roof-deck rendezvous."

I might not be a *we*, but at least I'm not a *them*. As far as consolation prizes go, it's not half-bad.

"Oh, you're out of the loop, buddy. Young widow. Tragic artist. Come on. They're not just talking about it. They're salivating over it."

Will's obliviousness confirms what I suspected: he's further outside the Kingsette gossip loop than I am. Which means, he probably doesn't know what people are saying about his mother and Maeve. It's probably better that way.

Will grimaces. "I'm so—I mean I sincerely apologize you have to deal with that."

I laugh. "Are you trying to bypass my no-sorry rule with a synonym?"

Will opens his eyes in mock innocence. "Never."

"I thought we were past the lying portion of our friendship." My voice climbs a notch and sounds . . . flirty. I clear my throat. I'm supposed to be doing kissy-face-emoji damage control, not . . . whatever I'm doing.

"We are, Hope," he says, his voice low and husky. "Past that part of our friendship, for sure."

Our eyes lock. It feels like he's challenging me to hear what he's not saying. I look away first. "So that's the contract?"

The heat of his gaze remains for a heartbeat longer. Then it's gone, and a shiver vibrates down my spine.

"It is," he says, sounding more composed than I feel. "Just need a head count."

"Aah, easier said than done, actually. Tessa told me she may have more guests than she originally thought. Would that be a problem?"

"Hmm . . . it'll change the layout, but we could make it work." He talks me through floor plans and table settings with the ease of someone who's been doing this his entire life. He gives me copies of everything to show Tessa.

I place them in a binder with information I've gathered about the best florists and bands in a fifty-mile radius.

Will lets out a low whistle. "I didn't realize you were planning the *whole* party."

"Tessa doesn't want anyone calling her phone and ruining the surprise." No doubt she's also thrilled that she's found a way to keep me busy and distracted and directly in Will's line of sight.

"She's lucky to have you."

I shrug. "We're lucky to have each other."

He looks past me, and I remember that he has a sibling too. Darren has been in the emergency room a handful of times over the past few years, though I haven't seen him in a while. Hopefully that's a good sign. "How's Darren?"

"He's . . ." Will blinks. "No one ever asks me about Darren."

"That doesn't mean they shouldn't."

He considers me for a long moment. "He's Darren, I guess. I haven't seen him much since I've been back."

Will's quick glance away belies his indifference, and memories of Will and Darren swoop into the space between us. At the Fourth of July carnival shoving each other in line for cotton candy, at the town-wide Halloween parade dressed as zombie basketball players, at the Memorial Day barbecue in collared shirts splattered with condiments after a food fight gone wrong—or right. In each memory, they're side by side, inseparable.

"Have you talked to Maeve about him? She has—"

"Teas. I know. For creativity. Anxiety. Not—" He exhales, and his entire body sags. "Not for what Darren has. He needs real support, and he has to want it."

A useless "I'm sorry" pushes against the back of my teeth. "I should get going. Thanks for your help with the party."

"Hope, can I ask you something?"

An intensity gathers in his expression, and I force myself to breathe normally. "Of course."

Will glances down at the contract. "I was just wondering. About Maeve. Do you—" His gaze finds mine again. Conflict is etched into each furrow of his brow. "Do you believe she can . . . all that medium stuff?"

"No." My mind takes a beat too long to change gears. Later, I'll have to examine what I thought he was going to ask me, and why I feel so disappointed that he didn't ask it. "Maybe. I don't know. I don't have a great track record in this department."

"But you'll go back?"

I nod and think of the last afternoon I spent with Maeve, surrounded by bright colors and larger-than-life aromas. It felt like a reprieve from reality. "I'm helping her with the garden."

"The garden?"

"She was struggling with the roses, and I love gardening."

"Oh," he says, as if he were expecting another answer.

"Not just the garden," I admit. "She said some things about Brandon. She knew about a locket he gave me. It's lost, but if I find it and bring it to her, she might . . . I don't know. Connect with Brandon? It's worth a try, I guess." My cheeks heat up.

Will's silence makes me wish I could take back every pathetic word I just admitted.

"So . . . if you find a locket lying around . . ." My attempt to defuse the sudden seriousness makes the grooves in Will's forehead deepen. Underneath that conflict, there's something else.

"I'd like to help you look for the locket, if you'll let me."

16

WILL

When Hope leaves, I open Facebook. My heart punches out an anxious beat along my ribs as I scroll to the photo that prompted that impulsive offer.

I find it easily. Anyone with internet access and a Facebook account could.

It's a selfie of Hope, her face raised to the camera as Brandon squishes his lips to her cheek. A locket with a glittering diamond center rests delicately in the hollow of Hope's throat. It looks expensive.

My mother's office chair creaks as I lean back and interlace my fingers over my eyes.

Vicky claimed Ashley gave her ring to Maeve, that Maeve never asked or demanded payment. But if I learned anything from my years in LA, surrounded by people who were always trying to get something from me, there's a lot more to a hustle than what's said out loud.

Getting closer to Hope as she gets closer to Maeve could help me figure out what Maeve's really after. It could help me understand why my mom left—and what might convince her to come back.

It could also blur a line I need to keep bold and defined if my plan is to leave.

I do what I should have done the moment Delilah told me my mother had gone off the grid. I call a private investigator who moved to the East Coast after he got tired of being paid to watch my agent's ex-wife.

He answers just as I'm about to hang up.

"Hey, Will. What's up?"

I look down at the receiver in my hand. The caller ID should have displayed "Kingsette Inn." "How'd you know it was me? I never told you where I'm from."

"Aah, it's my job to know, don't you know?" He makes a clicking sound, like he's pushing a hard candy against his teeth. "I assume this isn't a social call, so . . ."

"Right. I need your help." I explain about my mom, Maeve, and the voice mail claiming she needed to get in touch with herself. "Something's not sitting right."

"So, what's the job? You want me to find your mom or look into Maeve?"

I hoped to have that question answered for myself too. "My mom. She—I just need to know where she went."

"You got it. As long as I get paid, it's all the same to me." Knuckles cracking join the clicking sound his mouth is making. "Send me copies of your last exchanged messages, bank statements, credit card bills, anything like that."

"She hasn't used her credit card since she went off grid."

"What about bank statements? Anything out of the ordinary?"

"Yes, but . . ." My mind trips over the question. "No. There are some discrepancies with the Inn's accounts, but that's not . . . my mother wouldn't take the money for herself like that. Not from the business."

She loved the Inn more than anything. Growing up, it felt like keeping the Inn going was the most important thing in the world. More important than her happiness—our happiness.

"People do strange things when it comes to money. You'd be surprised how many family members steal from each other."

Terry's accusation darts into my thoughts, and the instinct to bat it away makes me dizzy. The private investigator asks a few more questions that I distractedly answer, and then he tells me he'll be in touch.

"Wait, before you go . . ." I stand and rub the back of my neck with my hand. "I just wanted to ask your advice."

"Okay," he says, drawing out the *o*. I can almost hear his eyebrows rising.

"Just . . . it's for a new show I'm working on about addicts. What would you . . . ? How would someone, a regular guy, let's say, find someone who's on a bender? What would you do first?"

He breathes a laugh. "A new show, huh?"

"Yeah," I say, pinching the bridge of my nose. "Can't be stuck in small-town life forever."

"I hear that," he says and sighs. "I guess, if I'm a regular guy . . . the first thing I'd do is try local bars, the seedier the better. If not, maybe the police station or hospital."

"Hospital?" My mouth goes dry.

"That's how these stories go, my friend. Unless you're trying to dream up a surprise ending."

My finger hovers over the hospital's phone number lit up on my cell phone.

Press call.

The command from my brain short-circuits before it reaches my finger.

Darren is either in the hospital or he's not. Whether I call to ask if he's there or I don't won't change that.

My screen goes dark. My finger remains frozen.

Press call.

A text lights up my screen. Annette Martina has texted me three times—ever. Once, after the rabbit-freeing incident at Mrs. Lemmings's, to let me know she was keeping my secret for my mother's sake. Once after I started dating her daughter—to confirm we'd be using the stretch limo at prom. And once after I left town to add a PS to the voice mail she'd left.

This text makes four.

Your brother was spotted at the cemetery. I convinced the caretaker to wait an hour before calling the cops. I told you I take care of Kingsette's own.

Her next message pings on my screen before I can respond: Have you considered my offer?

Twenty minutes later, I park beside a beat-up Honda Civic. The hood is more rust colored than red now, and the dent in the rear bumper is new, but it's unmistakably the same car Darren received for his sixteenth birthday.

"You look like shit, little brother," Darren says, barely looking in my direction as I approach. He's sprawled out on a ratty blanket, a half-eaten burger and mostly full carton of fries by his feet. Our father's stone stands like a moss-colored sentry in the center of Darren's downward spiral.

"You don't look much better." Dark circles frame his eyes. The cut on his lip is still swollen, possibly infected.

"Always a competition with you, huh?" He rips off a piece of bun and tosses it at a tree that was a sapling when Dad's stone was placed. Now the pool of shade it casts covers Dad's grave and six others that weren't there a decade ago.

"The Inn's in trouble. I think . . . something shady is going on," I say, shielding my eyes from the sun's glare to peer into the tree. A flock of dark birds peer back. "It's been keeping me up."

Darren breathes a sardonic laugh. "And you're here to confront your number one suspect?"

"I'm here to make sure you're okay. I got a text from Annette."

He hurls another piece of bread at the tree. This time, a handful of birds scatter. "Mission accomplished, little brother."

"Have you been sleeping here?" The sleeping bag amid the crumpled bags of chips and crushed cans of beer answers my question.

"Are you asking because you want me to come stay with you?"

"Do you have to answer every question with a question?"

"Do you?" He stands and dusts off his pants. Dirt clouds around him, and for a moment, time folds in on itself. Darren's fifteen years younger, stumbling around, kicking up dirt, with a bottle of gin in his hand, ranting about the universe and Mom and the "fucking Inn." The pressure of filling Dad's shoes and being trapped.

I drove us home that night—my first time illegally behind the wheel. I put him to bed and then completed the chores Mom had asked him to handle.

It was that day that I realized if I didn't get away, I'd end up like Darren—or Dad. Buried under the pressure of being the man of the house or just buried.

"I didn't steal money from the Inn," Darren says, maintaining eye contact as he places a small stone on our father's grave.

A pain strikes the back of my throat as I count six stones. Two sons, one wife, and seventeen years gone—only six stones to show for it.

"I know," I say, taking the three stones he extends—out of habit or lingering brotherly affection—toward me. I place the largest of them beside his and drop the others into my pocket, vowing to myself that I'll visit again.

He snorts. "But you weren't sure."

"Do you know why Mom left? Did she seem okay to you?"

"Mom gave up on me a long time ago."

"That doesn't actually answer my question."

He raises an eyebrow at my tone, which I belatedly recognize. Ten years away from this town and I can still channel my mother without a thought. "Sorry," I murmur.

"No, I have no idea. She stopped answering my calls around the time she met Maeve. Something about enabling me." He shrugs, but the gesture is less casual than it should be. Darren's feelings have always been too big to contain. Only basketball and alcohol have ever managed to dull them. "Bad timing too. Had some big news to share."

"What's that?"

"It doesn't matter anymore." He shakes his head and kicks the carton of fries.

The birds descend on the loose fries like vultures.

Only, they're not vultures.

They're bluebirds. Dozens and dozens of bluebirds.

17

HOPE

"What time is the appointment with the baker?" Tessa sounds muffled, like she's cupping a hand over the phone to keep from being heard. In the background, dishes clatter and my two nieces argue about who gets to hold the remote. My brother-in-law's voice reveals he's trying, and failing, to act as mediator. "I need to get out of this house. Maybe I'll make an excuse and meet you."

"Meet me?" My voice hits a high note.

"You made the appointment, right? I told you he's only available to meet with new clients the first Saturday of the month. That's today."

"Yes, I did. Of course." The phone number for Rhode Island's most famous bakeshop, which I highlighted and taped to my laptop, stares like an accusation.

"So what time?" Tessa sounds impatient. No, she sounds like she doesn't believe me.

I rub at a sudden tightness around my chest, as if lying to Tessa had a physical consequence.

"It's just that . . . I'm going with Will."

My pulse ticks up, though that's not exactly a lie. I am going with Will. We're just not going to the baker.

"Will? Roof-deck Will? Kingsette Inn Will?" A crash punctuates her question, and guilt screws up my face.

"Yes, that Will. But don't read anything into it. He's just doing his job."

"Mm-hmm. His job is to make sure you have enough tables and chairs in the ballroom. I doubt he goes to bakery appointments for all his clients."

"He's invested in this party. It's the first official event he's overseeing from start to finish."

"Oh, he's invested in something, all right."

"Tessa," I warn, but halfheartedly. For the moment, my nonexistent relationship with Will is safer territory than my nonexistent baker appointment. There will be time later to manage her expectations about Will.

"Okay, okay. But I want details."

"There won't be details, but let's catch up tomorrow." I catch a glimpse of my reflection in the mirror. For the first time in forever, my cheeks have a little color—probably from the extra hikes I've been taking to the lake and the time spent helping Maeve with her garden. As it turns out, I still have a green thumb.

"Fine. Meet me for a run tomorrow. I decided I'm going to do a 5K this fall, and training starts in the morning."

I agree, and Tessa hangs up as the shouts erupt into full-blown shrieks. Once things settle, I'll take the girls for a sleepover and let Tessa and Noah have a night to themselves. Maybe Will would be willing to let me reserve one of the honeymoon suites at the Inn. The girls would love it.

Will's text interrupts my best-aunt-ever daydream: You sure you don't want me to ring your doorbell and come in? I feel obnoxious sitting in my car and texting you to come out.

Nope. Text is fine.

Will: Then . . . I'm here.
Me: I'll be down in two seconds.

A moment later, I add: Wow, I can't believe you're really not even going to ring my doorbell. Chivalry's truly dead, huh?

I stare at my phone with a wide grin, anticipating his response, and watch the three dots appear and disappear twice.

Finally, two messages come in quick succession. First, an angry-face emoji blowing steam out of the sides of his mouth. It's only significant because we haven't exchanged emojis since the never-discussed kissy-face-emoji incident.

Then: You're lucky you're cute.

The tidal wave of heat is swift and stunning. It takes two full breaths for the wave to ebb. When it does, I swallow the last drops of the tea Maeve sent me home with and check my reflection one final time. There's still telltale color in my cheeks. At the last minute, I find a tube of mascara that hasn't yet dried out and sweep it over my lashes to even out the look.

Tanya does a double take when I walk past the kitchen. She sets down her sandwich to give me an exuberant thumbs-up. "Wow, you look beautiful, Hope. I haven't seen you wear makeup in . . . ever, I think."

The wide smile Logan was wearing turns strained as something unfamiliar crosses his expression. The knife he was using to slice tomatoes hovers in midair. "You . . . are you going somewhere?" His voice cracks. His tone is unreadable, but his grief is unmissable.

"I'm just meeting a friend. For an errand." My stomach knots. When did I become a person who has so little trouble spewing half lies?

"Oh," he says. "You look . . . good."

"Thanks." My gaze drops to Logan's shoes—red Nikes, like Brandon always wore. Maybe they are Brandon's.

"Hope, if it's a date—" he starts, and I know what's coming next. To Logan, I'm Brandon's. To be anything else is to remind him that Brandon is gone.

"It's not. I promise." I lift my gaze, letting Logan see the truth. "I should go."

They exchange one of those now-frequent private looks, and I'm out the door before the heartbreak in Logan's expression devolves into something worse.

Mercifully, Will's waiting inside his car, and I hurry in, throwing a glance over my shoulder. Logan and Tanya aren't at the window. It should feel like a relief. Instead, it feels like an indictment.

18
WILL

The passenger door swings open, and Hope drops into the seat. A light floral scent fills the car as she pulls the door closed.

"Hello to you too," I say, shutting down the sudden rush of pleasure rippling across every nerve ending. So much for no complications.

"I didn't mean the slam—hectic morning," she says, blinking rapidly, which usually suggests discomfort or dishonesty. In Hope, though, it's hard to tell what it means. From the moment she challenged me on the roof-deck, she's proven she's not like many other people I've met before.

"Where to?"

"Brandon bought the necklace at a jewelry store in Newport. It had the store's very distinctive emblem on the back. Maybe he brought it there to get it cleaned."

The urge to point out how unlikely it is that a jewelry store would hang on to a necklace for two years melts away as I take in how Hope's stress seems to dissolve with every turn we take out of her neighborhood.

"Do you think I'm crazy? Am I sending us on a fool's errand?" The cautious optimism in her voice makes the urge disappear entirely.

"No, not crazy. We have to start somewhere. What's the address?"

Waze gives us a driving time of forty-four minutes. It's exactly enough time for me to tell her about the show I worked on in LA,

The Burning, and how budget cuts and a new production director who wanted to take the network in a different direction got it taken off air, despite a cult following.

"Tell me more," she insists. "I like hearing your stories. Adventure by association, or something."

"I've been talking about myself for nearly the entire drive. You tell me something interesting, your adventures."

"I haven't really had any adventures." Her gaze slides toward me.

"Why not?"

"Life. Brandon and I planned to adventure together, you know? We figured we'd graduate from high school and then travel. But then, his mom got sick, so we hung around and said we'd go after college. But then he started working for his father's firm, and he couldn't just leave. Years passed and . . ." She inhales deeply. "Then he died, and everything just stopped."

"Do you still want to go on adventures?" My voice is low.

"I do," she says, holding my gaze just long enough for me to confirm her eyes are the most perfect shade of green that has ever existed.

"Then you will. When you're ready." I clear my throat and return my attention to the road.

A silent moment swells between us. Hope punches the button for the radio, and the droning sounds of the AM-news-station reporter dull the sudden impulse to tell her I'll go with her on any adventure she chooses. She punches another button, and the traffic report cuts off midsentence.

I frown at the pop song leaking from my speakers. "Seriously?"

"Yes, seriously. Shotgun gets to choose the music. Don't you know the rules?"

"No way. My car, my listening." I reach for the radio, and she glares at me with an expression that would make my unflappable agent flap. "Fine. You win."

She grins, too wide. "Thank you."

We listen to half a song before my phone rings and an unsaved Rhode Island number lights up the console.

"Convenient," Hope mutters, a smile tugging at her lips, as I answer on Bluetooth.

"Hey, Will. It's Jeremy. From work."

My mind takes a heartbeat too long to connect the name with the bartender who was working by my side the night of Logan Gold's wedding.

"Listen, I . . . I can't work for you anymore." His voice rises, as if he's asking a question, instead of damning the Inn. "I quit."

"No." The word blurts out of me, and Hope flashes me an alarmed look. "I mean. Why? I can pay you more."

I can't, but he's the third person to quit this week. I was already short-staffed. Without him, I'll have to cancel all the upcoming events. I can't afford to cancel more than I can't afford to pay bartenders more.

"It's not the money." Papers crinkle. A door clicks closed. "I'm not supposed to tell you, but . . . Annette Martina came to me. She basically said if I didn't quit, she'd get my fiancée's membership in the Garden Club revoked. It's messed up, but—Bella loves that club."

"Don't say any more. I get it." Annette has a way of getting what she wants in this town. A way of making things miserable for the people who stand in her way. "Thanks for your honesty. I appreciate it."

"Sorry, man," he says, sounding genuinely sorry, which is a kindness, considering I've called him Jarred on at least three occasions.

"She can't do that!" Hope says as soon as Jeremy's off the phone and a shrill song is once again screeching into the silence.

"She can and she did." A pain rushes up my arm, and I release my death grip on the steering wheel. "She wants to buy the Inn. I told her no. I guess driving the Inn into bankruptcy is plan B."

"She's unbelievable." Hope crosses her arms over her chest. "We have to do something."

Something is the last thing I want to do. "Right now all I need to do is find someone to work a retirement party."

"I can help, if you want." She studies my face. "Strike that. I know that face. It's the face I make when I want help but don't know how to admit it. What time do you need me?"

"Am I that easy to read?"

"To me you are." She flashes me a smug grin. "So what time?"

"Eight. On a Thursday night. Are you being serious?"

"Of course. What are friends for?"

We sit in silence as the impact of her words reverberates through the car.

Friends.

So much for no ties to Kingsette.

All I'm missing is a relationship and I've reached the trifecta.

19

HOPE

Emotion crashes through me as we return to Will's car. The owner of the store remembered Brandon, remembered the locket, but no one had returned it to his shop. He promised to keep an eye out for it and took my number. It was the best he could do.

I hadn't really expected the locket to be at the jewelry store. Still, I'd gotten my hopes up higher than I'd realized. It's what Brandon called my fatal character flaw—my hopes were always too high.

"Are you okay?" Will asks, lowering the volume of the NPR broadcaster discussing the pros and cons of interest-rate hikes. "Do you want music?"

"We listened to my music on the way there. It's your turn. That's the rule." I don't realize what I've said until the words are out of my mouth. That's only the rule between Brandon and me, established the moment he'd gotten his driver's license. Shotgun chooses music to. Driver chooses for the way back.

Will changes the station back to the one I chose at the start of our failed mission. A raspy-voiced pop star who's barely older than my niece croons about first love. Will's hand reaches out at the same time as mine to turn down the volume. Our fingers touch, and he yanks back his hand.

"Go ahead," I murmur as the young pop star's voice gives way to Waze letting us know we're going straight for another two miles. Two miles and then another fourteen minutes driving through Kingsette's slow, traffic light–riddled streets in this silence that I have made unbearably awkward.

"Hang on." Will jerks the steering wheel to the right. The car cuts across three highway lanes. A car horn blares.

My hand shoots to the grab handle, and the seat belt tightens around me, preparing for an impact that's haunted all my dreams. I brace myself. Images rise up from that dark place I've buried. Brakes squealing, metal twisting, glass shattering, screaming.

We glide onto the side of the road. The horn fades. In some distant part of my mind, I register Will leaning over me, bringing a hand to my shoulder.

"Oh, God, Hope. I'm sorry. I wasn't thinking how that must . . ."

Brakes. Metal. Glass. The sounds clamor over each other, twining into one awful keening in my mind. I grip the handle tighter. My stomach twists.

"Shit. I'm sorry. I feel like all that at the jewelry store is my fault, and I wanted to . . ."

Brakes. Metal. Glass. Over and over. Somewhere beyond that keening, Will's still speaking in that calm, deep voice.

"I know I said you'll go on an adventure when you're ready, and you will. I don't want to push you, but I thought it might be good to go on a mini adventure now. Call it an adventure trial run? Obviously I should have handled that exit better."

Adventure. The word is a beacon, three clear syllables among the noise, and I hold on to it. Hold on and let it pull me up and above the keening, just high enough that I can push the lid closed over that dark place where those memories have to stay.

Will's fingers brush mine. "I'm so sorry."

I shake my head, command myself to look him in his earnest eyes. I don't need his apology or his pity. Air fills my chest on my inhale, pushing at the walls I've built and fortified over the last two years, testing their strength. I exhale. "Please don't say 'I'm sorry.'"

He regards me. After a long moment, he nods. "One day you'll have to tell me why you hate 'I'm sorry.'"

I open my mouth to deliver my rehearsed answer, but he holds up a finger. "The real answer, Hope. Not the one you give everyone else."

Will's car rocks from the force of passing cars. I wipe the sweat from my palms on my jeans.

"I'll take you home." He secures his seat belt.

The idea of being in my cramped room with all these memories drawn so close to the surface makes me nauseated. "No, don't—" I force a smile onto my face. "I mean, we survived that lane change, might as well make the panic attack worth it, right?"

Will's eyes darken, the conflict he's not saying aloud etched into the thin line formed by his lips. "I don't think that's a good idea. Maybe another time."

"I don't want to miss another adventure I . . . think I'll regret not going." I restore my trauma-nurse expression. It doesn't fit quite right this time, but Will nevertheless sighs at the sight.

"Okay. You're the boss."

He checks the rearview mirror and drives—under the speed limit—for another ten minutes. In that time, my pulse returns to normal, and I feel like myself again. Meanwhile, Will's knuckles have gone white on the steering wheel and his movements are small and jerky.

We park in a dusty lot beside a blue broken-down Toyota Camry and in front of a massive faded sign, the word ADVENTURE just barely legible. It looks like the entrance to an amusement park, though I've never seen one quite so desolate.

"This feels like the beginning of a horror movie. Am I the stupid girl the audience is yelling 'run' at?" I ask Will, hoping to elicit a smile from him.

It doesn't.

Through the rearview mirror, we both watch a flock of birds rise from distant treetops. The sun disappears behind the massive shapeless swarm, and a chill replaces the golden warmth.

"Maybe you were right. We should go home."

He faces me, and the dusting of amber around his dark-brown eyes glints with mischief. "You should know better. Horror is ghosts. If I've lured you here for nefarious reasons, we're in a thriller."

The sun reemerges with new intensity, lighting up every inch of the dashboard. The last bits of the knot in my stomach melt away.

"Well, thank you for clearing that up. I'll make sure Tessa gets the genre right when she brings your photo to the police."

He grins, and I follow him across the cracked asphalt to a rusted ticket booth. Will produces two smooth stones from his pocket. He hands one to me and gingerly places the other one on top of a precarious pile of similar stones.

"Do you always carry rocks in your pocket?" The smooth stone is the baby-blue color of a robin's egg.

"Long story."

"We seem to tiptoe around a lot of those," I say, and his smile confirms he's thinking of the first night we met as strangers on the roofdeck. The way fate has woven us into each other's lives makes that night feel like a memory of a dream.

"It took . . . what . . . about twelve hours for both of our long stories to come out?"

I scrunch my nose. "Ten. Max."

The sound of his laughter echoes through hollow spaces in my chest. I miss this—talking to someone, joking with someone, without subtext or worrying that if I say the wrong thing, I'll get a lecture about moving on with my life.

"In that case . . . you might as well hear it from me. I saw Darren yesterday. At the cemetery. He's . . ." Will shakes his head, and his silence fills in the blanks.

"He gave you rocks?"

"Jewish tradition. Flowers wither. Rocks are forever."

I glance at the rock pyramid. "And this?"

"Our father used to take us here when we were little. Darren and I started coming here on his birthday as a kind of memorial a year after it closed." Will looks out at the amusement park, which has been so thoroughly reclaimed by nature it looks dystopian. "This place gave me my first taste of adventure. Which isn't a surprise, considering it's called Adventure Land."

"I'm not sure there's much adventure left."

"You'd be surprised. Follow me."

We walk past gutted food stands and a rickety barn that once housed a petting zoo. Someone spray-painted the words *Fix Me* across the barn's doors. We pass a rusted teacup ride, a playground with a broken swing, and an old go-kart track outlined by well-preserved tires. Tree roots encircle a merry-go-round like tentacles.

Too quickly, my hair is stuck to the back of my sweaty neck, and I miss my ponytail. "Honestly, if you were going to murder me, I'd think there were easier ways."

He chuckles. "Just trust me, okay?"

"The last time someone asked me to trust them, I ended up at a wedding for Brandon's cousin. Let's just say it didn't end as well as it did the night you and I met."

"Because you didn't meet a dashingly handsome former writer?"

I roll my eyes at Will's back. "Dashingly handsome, huh? Good to know you have a healthy ego."

"Nah," he says, glancing over his shoulder. "Just a healthy ability to cover up insecurity with humor."

"Maybe you could teach me how to do that. Probably would save me a few spins across the rumor mill." The brittleness in my voice shifts the lightness between us into something somber and quiet. "I mean, there are worse things than being at the center of the rumor—"

"Why do you let them get to you?" he asks, his voice low.

"What?" The toe of my shoe snags on a rusted piece of metal, and I stumble forward, closing the space between us. The heat of his body hits me in a rush.

"It's just . . . I remember how hard it was for my mother after my father died. Everyone had an opinion about everything she did. She just . . . let them, even though if they lived an hour in her shoes, they'd see—God, I just wanted her to find her voice, push back, do—" He pivots. The wildness in his expression is impossible to look away from. "I'm sorry. I'm doing the exact same thing."

"You are. You're also right." A thousand moments exactly like the one he described sketch a story of swallowed anger and unspoken retorts. "But you saw what happened at Logan's wedding. I made a scene. I alienated everyone."

"Yes," he says, that wildness sparking. "And you survived."

"No, I ran away. I ended up alone on a roof-deck."

"You weren't alone," he says. "And you won't be alone next time. I won't let you be alone."

"Hard promise to keep." My thoughts turn to the unpacked suitcases in the office. Why would Will trade LA for Kingsette?

"Hard promises are the most important ones." The wildness in his expression recedes, and he's Will—grounded, slightly disheveled from sleeping in his office, Will. "You know, I know a thing or two about alienating. Back when I left, the varsity basketball coach was so pissed that I didn't stay for the summer league, he removed my MVP trophy from the display at town hall."

"What? Where's the trophy?"

"The bottom of the ocean?" His palms turn up in a who-knows gesture.

"That's awful," I say, and he shrugs.

"Nah. I never cared that much about basketball."

We walk another ten feet and stop in front of a Ferris wheel that's about twice the size of every boardwalk Ferris wheel.

"This is it. Ready for the adventure part?" he asks.

"Do you really want me to answer that?"

He pushes a button on the control panel, and a thousand tiny lights burst to life. He pushes another button, and the creak of old gears coming alive echoes across the deserted field. A moment later, the Ferris wheel begins to move. The cars scrape past as if in slow motion. Will turns to me, beaming, and glimmers of the little boy who came here with his dad shine in his expression.

"How is that possible?"

Will flashes a sly grin. "Must be magic. Come on."

"What?"

His hand grips the pole of the passing car, and he throws a leg over to climb in. He extends a hand toward me. "Quick. Before it gets too high. I don't want to ride this thing alone."

"I can't." The refrain is out of my mouth at the same time my hand grabs his, as if my body knows my brain will overthink and miss the moment.

The car lifts into the air. I'm hardly a foot off the ground, but for a single breathtaking moment, I'm suspended in the air, and Will is my only connection to anything sturdy.

"I'm afraid. I'm going to fall." Panic beats against my rib cage as the Ferris wheel takes us higher.

"I won't let you fall. You can trust me." He tightens his grip, muscles straining against the effort. We fly higher. Dusty earth gives way to blue sky as far as I can see.

"You need to pull yourself up," Will urges.

"I'm trying."

"You're going through the motions of trying. You need to use your legs too."

"I can't. I'm going to fall."

"You're going to fall if you're afraid. Use your legs, and stop thinking about what will happen next. Trust me."

I bend my right knee and search for a grip. Will directs me with his words, and I find enough purchase to rise an inch higher. Then, calling up retired reserves of strength, I rise another inch. Within seconds, I'm high enough to reach a leg over the car the way Will did and drop into the seat across from him.

He falls back into his seat, breathless, hair windblown, and face bright with effort. "Drama queen," he teases.

"Says the adult who's afraid of the dark."

"Good thing we're taking care of each other now."

My cheeks flush, and the skeleton of what the abandoned amusement park once was floats into view. A place that brought so much happiness is just visible beneath the overgrown greenery and broken-down rides. Wind whistles between us, tasting impossibly of cotton candy.

"What do you think?" he asks.

"It's sad," I say. "Everyone forgot about this place. Like it never meant anything to anyone."

"Sad? No. It's—you're looking at the wrong part." The Ferris wheel whines, and we descend. "Close your eyes."

"What? No."

"Just trust me. Hurry."

The eagerness in his expression convinces me. Will's hands come to my shoulders, the touch light, but firm. He adjusts me to face to the right of where I was looking.

"Wait for it," he says, his voice a breath against my neck. My heart drums a new beat against my rib cage.

"This is . . . bizarre, you know."

I can feel his grin inches from my ear. The sensation of rising again makes my stomach feel like it's floating. "I know. Open your eyes."

Sunshine explodes in the space where darkness was just moments before, and a surprisingly well preserved ten-foot ice cream cone rises up from the overgrown greenery.

"Wow. We walked past that. It looked like a decrepit ice cream stand."

Will's eyes light up. "I know. Did you see what's written on it?"

I look closer at the faded letters visible just above the wild brush and weeds.

ADVENTURE STARTS WITH HOPE AND ENDS WITH ICE CREAM.

"Kind of perfect, right?" Will asks.

"Kind of," I say, because the lump in my throat is preventing me from telling him that this is the nicest thing anyone has done for me in a long time. I'm in a forgotten place with an unlikely friend, and for the first time in a long time, feel like I'm where I'm supposed to be. "It's strange, too, right?"

"Strange?" A current of wind pushes back Will's hair as we descend, highlighting the planes of his face and the defined lines of his jaw.

"Yeah. I mean how Maeve gave me a tea for courage, and now here I am, doing one of the bravest things I've done in a long time."

20
WILL

Listening to Hope tell the story of the Ferris wheel at Adventure Land feels like being there again, only this time the colors are brighter and the air is crisper. Her eye for detail makes the story come alive in a way that feels at once real and surreal.

I wonder if anyone has ever told her how rare that ability is. Or how when she gets animated, the yellow in her eyes turns golden.

"Did I miss anything?" Hope directs the question to me, but her attention is focused wholly on Maeve, whose face remained expressionless as she twisted my mother's ring around her finger and listened. Sure, she smiled when Hope gestured excitedly and looked thoughtful when Hope relayed the part about the failed locket, but there was—and is—an intensity in Maeve's attention that feels almost predatory. The urge to hide Hope away becomes a physical need.

"That's all of it," I say. Hope skipped the part where I crossed three lanes of traffic and nearly gave her a heart attack. I doubt she forgot.

"It sounds like you two had quite the adventure," Maeve says.

Her choice of word sends a lightning bolt down my spine. Hope locks eyes with me, as if we're both in on the same private joke.

"No regrets," I say, and Hope flashes me a private smile.

"That's good to hear. You do know what they say about regret, don't you?" Maeve asks. "It's a poison."

"I hate that expression, actually," I say, feeling the words tumble out of my mouth too fast. "Regret isn't really a poison. Poison kills you. Maybe makes you suffer a few hours, but eventually, it runs its course. It kills you. Or it doesn't. Regret is something worse. Regret won't kill or run its course. It'll just corrode you from the inside out forever."

Regret creeps into your system when your fight-or-flight response is going haywire, when the words coming out of your mouth are not words you would ever say.

Poison is a death sentence. Regret is a life sentence.

I glance toward Hope, whose expression shutters, a curtain clamping down on light.

"Hmm, that's one way to look at it." Maeve purses her lips. Shadows shade the hollows of her cheeks, giving her face a predatory harshness.

Maeve stands to stir one of the pots simmering on the stove. Bubbles on the surface of the liquid pop, and a floral aroma winds through the cottage. "Hope, will you give me a hand?"

"That smells like apple," Hope says, taking the spoon from Maeve's hand.

"You're right. Apple and a hint of cranberry. For love and healing."

Something low tugs in my belly. Too many lines blurred the moment I arrived at Maeve's and found Hope already here. Hope looked at me funny, the way she had the first time we ran into each other here, and then smiled and invited me in.

"It's for our little patient," Maeve says.

"He looks fatter and bluer than yesterday." The cloudiness in Hope's expression disappears.

"Isn't turning bluer usually a bad sign in a patient?"

Hope laughs. My heart adds a patter to its rhythm.

"For a human patient, yes. Not for the bluebird Maeve has been nursing back to help," she says. "I named him Icarus . . . though I expect a happier ending for this little guy."

"Don't give me all the credit," Maeve chimes in. "You've been instrumental in caring for the bird—and the garden. Honestly, without Hope here, I don't know what I'd do. She's really something special."

Maeve's pale eyes hold mine, and an entirely new rhythm takes over my heart. The slow way she speaks, the smoothness of her movements, all of it makes me uneasy. It's like she's always planning her next move, which means I can't let my guard down around her.

Color flushes Hope's cheeks. "Speaking of, I only have a few hours until I start my shift. I didn't come to chat, and Will didn't come to hang out with me. I'll get started on the eastern half of the garden."

Maeve delivers instructions on which flowers need water, which need a special plant food she prepared, and which need to be pruned back. All the flowers have exotic-sounding names that I almost believe are made up.

Hope leaves with a shy wave in my direction, as if we haven't accidentally spent nearly every day together since we met. Or maybe because we've accidentally spent nearly every day together.

Maeve puts a lid on the simmering brew and comes to sit beside me. "What can I do for you, Will?"

"I heard, um . . . Hope told me, and I saw Bailey . . ." I clear my throat, not quite sure why I'm suddenly tongue tied.

Maybe because I'm not sure what I'm doing here anymore. At first, I just wanted to meet the woman who was responsible for my mother's uncharacteristic behavior. I didn't like what I saw, but so what? Exposing Maeve as a fraud—if that's even my goal—isn't going to make the Inn run better and probably won't convince my mom to come back.

"My brother is suffering from addiction. It's ruining his life. I was wondering if you had any remedy for that."

"Oh," Maeve says, her forehead creasing as she sits back heavily in her chair. "That must be heartbreaking for you. It's always difficult to witness the ones we love hurt themselves."

"Yeah." My throat tightens.

"Is that truly why you came to me?" Maeve narrows her eyes, revealing a sliver of color like a cat's. Or a snake's.

Over Maeve's shoulder, a pale-blue butterfly flutters above a rosebud. Its wings pause, as if it's listening. The image is eerily similar to the butterfly inked onto Maeve's bicep.

The lump in my throat makes my "yes" come out as a croak.

Maeve's shoulders sag. "In that case, I'm sorry, Will. Some addictions are beyond my scope."

"Why?" The intensity of the question heats the space between us. Maeve sits up straighter, her eyebrows drawing together. "I mean, he needs help. I'm willing to pay anything."

Maeve twists my mother's ring on her finger. She cocks her head to the side to study me. "Why did your jaw clench just there? When you mentioned payment?"

"It didn't."

"You have a problem with me accepting payment for the services I provide?"

"No, I—"

"Do you have a problem when Annette charges for coffee?"

"She doesn't claim—"

"Doctors charge for medicine. Sometimes the cures work, sometimes they don't. Sometimes they harm. My teas are no different."

Maeve's cavalier attitude to the idea of her teas doing harm makes my entire body clench. "You're not a doctor."

"The truth," she says, continuing, either oblivious to or unbothered by my reaction, "is that I'd prefer to do what I do for free, but that's simply not realistic. I need money to eat and care for my plants. Our society is structured in a way that I'm forced to buy into the capitalist system, even if I don't want to. And don't get me started on how undervalued women are, especially women who provide the kind of services I provide. We're more likely to be burned at the stake than offered union benefits.

"Let me show you something." Maeve stands abruptly and heads out the door. She grabs a box of gummy bears on her way out.

She leads me to her infamous tree near the front of her property. Thick roots grip the soil and disappear beneath the ground. Its wide branches extend out from the trunk, almost as if the tree were cupping something at the heart. Hundreds of names mark the tree—some carved so long ago, they've blackened. Hope's name is there, freshly carved, as are Bailey's and Ashley's. And my mother's.

"Each of the names on this tree belongs to someone who came to me with a wound. A heartbreak, a loss, a devastation, and they needed help, the same way they would for a broken arm. I gave them that help. That's worth something, and every person with a name on that tree knows it."

Ashley said Maeve had carried this tree from Tucson. I knew then it was impossible. Now, I'm sure.

"I didn't mean to offend you."

"You didn't. I won't force you to trust me, Will. But if you change your mind, I'll be here waiting."

From the corner of my eye, I catch sight of Hope working in the garden with a set of pruning shears. Following instructions. Completely in Maeve's thrall.

"I have something for you, while you decide," Maeve says. Her extended hand tears my attention away from Hope.

"What's this?" I say, taking the small flowerpot and smooth, blue rock—identical to the one I gave Hope at Adventure Land—that Maeve seemed to produce from thin air.

"The rock is a token from me for your father. For the next time you go to Adventure Land. The flower is a blanchefleur. You might know it as the hundred-leaved rose," she says. "It'll help you find the place you're supposed to be."

"How?" The single word is soaked in disbelief, and Maeve's resulting smile is a thing of feline glee.

"It only starts growing once you've found home. As long as you care for it, that is."

21

HOPE

It was stupid to get my hopes up. Of course, the locket wasn't waiting for me at the local jewelry store. Of course, the owners—who've known me my whole life—would have called me years ago to tell me they had something of Brandon's for pickup. Of course, they'd be offended I'd think otherwise.

I had known all of that. Why had I suddenly convinced myself otherwise? Why had I let myself start to hope?

The glares of the jewelry-store owner and his wife heat the back of my neck long after I turn the corner into the heart of downtown Kingsette, where the bars that dominate the street have set up outdoor tables and music pours out of open windows. It's not quite as charming as Newport, but a close second, according to the pamphlets in Kingsette's visitor center.

A few women sitting at a table across the street yell out my name, and I force a smile. Another table full of off-duty nurses calls out too. I wave and pretend not to hear the invitation to join them.

In another life I might have gone over. In another life, I would have had a drink and gossiped and compared notes about marriage and mortgages while killing time before meeting Tessa to hear a potential band for Noah's party. That other life was easy, stable. It made sense.

There were no midnight blooms or Ferris wheels that spin against all odds in that life.

The awareness that it's an either-or life lodges in the space beneath my ribs. The weight of it stays there, an uncomfortable invader, as my thoughts shift to Will.

He hasn't said much about why he went to Maeve after Adventure Land, but I hope she was able to help him. He needs . . . something.

Despite the confident air Will puts forward, he always seems a little lost.

My phone vibrates with a text from him—as if just thinking about him made him reach out.

I just finished another useless manager interview. This is beginning to feel hopeless. Made me think of you. HOPEless— get it?

I roll my eyes and respond. I'm supposed to believe you were a writer for a popular TV show with that kind of joke?

His response is instant. Well it did get canceled. Thanks for that reminder.

I thought the first two seasons were phenomenal. You've got one fan dying to know what you had planned for season three.

This time, his response takes four long minutes. You watched?

Binged. You're really talented.

It was a team effort. Another text arrives with lightning speed. What are you up to now?

I hesitate. Will would have come with me today. Thanks to that cultivated LA charm, he probably would have asked about the locket without insulting anyone too. But Will has his own problems at the Inn. Which he'll solve, eventually, before returning to LA.

The queasy feeling that unfolds in the pit of my stomach when I think about that is the reason I didn't ask him to come. That and Kingsette's rumor mill. The last thing I need is to show up downtown with Will and add fuel to whatever rumors ignited the night of Logan and Tanya's wedding.

I type: I'm downtown. Meeting Tessa in a while to see a potential band for the party. I'm in trouble, though. Totally forgot to make an appointment with some fancy baker.

A low-grade anxiety vibrates beneath my skin as I think about the baker who is too booked to even take a meeting with me now. I should have made the appointment weeks ago.

My phone rings seconds after I press send.

"What baker?" Will asks.

"Hello to you too."

"We can skip the pleasantries. We were in the middle of talking." His impatience makes me smile.

"We were texting," I correct.

"Semantics. What fancy baker?"

"Sunshine Bakers in Newport. He only accepts meetings with new clients one day of the month." I admit to Will how I lied. "I'm screwed, right?"

A creaking sound comes through the phone, as if Will is sitting back in his office chair contemplating the question. "Not necessarily. Let me call you back in a few."

He hangs up with a suddenness that makes me wonder whether LA did away with hellos and goodbyes.

A flurry of pink streamers and pink balloons at the restaurant on the corner catches my attention. A foam board, the words *Welcome to Selena's Baby Shower* printed in elegant script, stands guard at the door.

My heart drops into my toes and anchors me in place as Brandon's cousin appears on the restaurant patio, in a body-hugging dress and hoop earrings that mimic the curve of her belly. Her gaze catches mine, and her eyes widen in a reflection of the look on my face.

"Hope, hi," she says, seeming to recover faster than I do. She steps down to my level, and we're eye to eye. A telltale flush of pink rises up her neck. At least we're both uncomfortable.

"Hi, Selena. This is . . . beautiful." The crash of my heart against my rib cage makes it impossible to tell how I sound. If I had money, I'd put it on *unhinged.* "Congratulations," I add.

"Thank you. I just—" She clears her throat, glances behind herself at the event I wasn't invited to. "I—my mother wanted to keep this event small. Just family."

"Just family." The words razor through my heart, through memories of extended family dinners where Brandon's large family gathered around our table and gave toasts and laughed and welcomed me as one of their own. A stark contrast to the quiet dinners at my house—where my mom did her best to be two parents while Tessa and I did our best to let her know she was doing a good job.

"Oh, God." She closes her eyes. "That's not what I meant. Of course, you're still family. I just—" Her eyes snap to mine. "We all know how hard the wedding was for you. I'd be in an absolute shame spiral if I embarrassed myself like that. We just thought . . . a baby shower? So much harder, right? I mean, we know how much Brandon wanted to be a dad."

She continues rambling, and her words *Brandon, dad, family* begin to lose meaning. Brandon wanted to be a father.

The reason he wasn't—me.

"Hope, you're so strong. We all think so. But this—honestly, I'm trying to protect you from another . . . you know." She sucks in a breath through her teeth, as if the memory of that night physically stings.

The fight-or-flight instinct that has always bent toward flight freezes, shifts. Will's words echo through my thoughts: *I just wanted her to find her voice.*

"You used my wedding song!" I blurt out. "I pushed my grief aside for your wedding because we're . . . we were . . . family, and then that song begins to play. Do you know what that was like? You had a thousand songs to choose from, and you chose ours."

Too easily my mind summons the way my throat tightened as the first notes of our wedding song began to play through the room.

"Oh please. It's a song. It's not sacred just because you and Brandon danced to it. News flash, Hope, not everything you and Brandon touched is off limits now. You two weren't some, like, perfect couple that turned everything to gold. Everyone else might think so, Kingsette's own star-crossed lovers. But I know the truth. Brandon told me everything."

Inside my chest, my heart goes silent as the meaning of her words registers. "I don't know what you're talking about."

Selena takes a step toward me. Her nostrils flare. "I think you do."

"Selena." Brandon's aunt emerges from the restaurant and startles when she catches sight of me. "Where did you—Hope, you're here. What a surprise." She looks between her daughter and me with a deer-in-the-headlights expression.

"I was just leaving."

I speed walk as fast as my legs will allow. Tears burn behind my eyes, blurring the sidewalk. My heart has resumed its rhythm with renewed ferocity, and my lungs strain to keep up.

I need air.

I need space.

I need—a friend who will listen without making me feel worse.

Before I can talk myself out of it, I dial Will. At his half-swallowed "hello," a broken sound escapes my throat.

"Hope, what's wrong?"

"I found my voice."

22
WILL

"Come on. I have a good feeling about this place," Hope says as she drags me into a bar with a view of Newport's fishing pier.

I pull a face but follow her, for the second time, into a bar with bad lighting and questionable cleaning protocols.

How exactly we went from Hope's phone call to a bar in Newport is a mystery. There was a phone call from a friend who co-owns Sunshine Bakers, followed by a whirlwind of a meeting, during which Hope agreed to a ridiculously expensive birthday cake for her brother-in-law, and then—two tequila shots at the first bar we walked into.

Throughout it all, Hope just seemed to need to keep moving. The instinct to flee was familiar.

The kindest thing I could think to do was to give her space to run, and make sure she didn't fall.

The way once, a decade ago, Darren let me.

Memories of that hazy afternoon play in the back of my mind as Hope waves down the bartender sporting a shock of blue hair.

Darren was at the gas station with a few buddies, guys who'd graduated years before Darren, who were well known for all the wrong reasons. He saw my car, nearly exploding with all my worldly possessions, and knew.

"This will kill Mom," he said, lighting a cigarette pinched between his lips. "I'll be all she has left here."

"I know," I said, shooting a nervous glance in the direction of the forty-ounce beer bottle in his other hand. "Are you going to be okay?"

"Is your engine light still on?" He whistled, and one of the guys loitering by an idling Ford Mustang swaggered over. Darren told him about my engine, and the guy popped the hood.

Forty-five minutes later, I was gone. He was my only goodbye, and only because a twist of fate had put him in my path.

"Don't look at me like that," Hope says, bringing me back to the present and misreading the expression on my face. "You said you couldn't find people to work. I'm getting you people to work."

"Other people would just help me post on social media. Maybe offer to read a few résumés. They wouldn't go bar to bar poaching talent."

"Other people have no vision." The alcohol has turned her cheeks as pink as mine feel, and her eyes have a shine, like some of the heaviness from earlier has lifted.

My teeth worry over my bottom lip. "Is this even legal?"

"It's definitely not not legal. Ethically and morally questionable, probably. But ethics and morals went out the window hours ago." Hope leans so far over the bar her legs lift from the ground.

"That doesn't make me feel better," I say and fight the tequila-fueled urge to check out her ass. No more drinks for me. Women sabbatical.

"It's called networking, getting the word out that the Inn is hiring. You might even be doing these guys a favor. They might hate working here and be thrilled to learn there's a well-paying job owned by a famous TV writer just outside of Newport waiting for them."

"Famous TV writer is a stretch." I sweep my gaze around the bar. A band with a familiar *S* logo sets up on stage, and a few people mill about the empty high-top tables. Possibility crackles in the air. Soon enough, this place will be buzzing with college kids spilling drinks.

"How about this? I'll do all the talking so your conscience can remain clear."

"You'll bear the weight of moral bankruptcy for me?" I mean for the words to sound cute and cheeky, but my voice catches in a way that makes them sound vulnerable and true.

"For you, anything." She resumes trying to get the blue-haired bartender's attention, and maybe Hope's had one too many drinks too. Because though I'm out of practice, I would bet money that she was just flirting.

And that I was flirting back.

Hope's not by the bar when I return from the bathroom. In her place is a cluster of early twentysomethings who make me feel like I should apply for my AARP card. A moment later, I spot her across the bar, chatting up the second bartender.

She gives new meaning to the word *determined*.

I'm halfway back to Hope when a woman steps in my path. Her drink sloshes over the side of her glass and spills between us. Her gaze stays fixed on mine as her eyes narrow. "Look who's back."

My thoughts play catch-up as I try to reconcile the angry brunette in front of me with the desperate-to-fit-in blonde girl from my memories. "Natalie?"

"Hi, Will. I heard you were home."

"I'm not—"

Natalie raises an eyebrow, and my brain stutters over all the words I owe her. "I mean, I'm home, but just for a few weeks. Helping my mom."

"Right, your mom. I heard all about that too."

The way she says *that*, as if my mother is little more than a piece of gossip, makes my pulse tick up. "I wouldn't believe everything you hear."

Heads swivel in our direction.

"Oh right. It's only true if it's in print." She air quotes *true* for reasons only she knows. "You can't be bothered with small-town things like gossip and goodbyes."

The hurt in her voice is a sucker punch. I steel myself to say the thing I should have said a long time ago. "I'm sorry, Natalie. I should have been more mature about how I handled things."

"Which things do you mean exactly? Not having the courtesy to break up with me in person before you left town or letting rumors about me fly?"

"I didn't—what rumors?"

She scoffs. "That I was clingy. That I was desperate. That the extent of my life goals were to get married to whatever sucker asked first."

Discomfort tugs low in my stomach. I was halfway across the country by the time those rumors reached me, and when I heard them, I said nothing. I told myself I didn't have to say anything—I was out of Kingsette in every way. But the truth was, I was relieved that they'd moved on from talking about my mistakes and failures. "Natalie, I—"

"You have no idea what you're talking about."

I swivel around to see Hope standing beside me, her hands clenched by her sides. Her expression is fierce, that temper I first caught sight of on the roof-deck on full display.

"Will would have stopped the rumors, if he'd heard them." There's not an ounce of doubt in her eyes.

The look undoes me. No one has stood up for me, or been on my side, no questions asked, like that, in a long time.

"That's what I believed too." Natalie blows out a breath. Her gaze sweeps the bar, and her eyes widen as she registers the circle of voyeurs around us. She returns an unflinching gaze to me. "I didn't come here to make a scene. I just wanted to tell you you're an asshole."

She turns to Hope. "I'd be careful if I were you. He has a way of promising one thing and then doing the exact opposite."

Natalie disappears into the crowd. For a single, fragile moment, Hope and I just stare at each other. An entirely new set of words prickles along my tongue. I take a deep breath, inhaling it deep into my lungs.

"Sooo . . . ," Hope says breaking the awkward silence, "that was a blast from the past."

I breathe a laugh. "Understatement of the century."

"You okay?"

I nod. "So . . . do you moonlight as a bodyguard . . . or?" I force lightness into my voice. "You were like a ferocious little pit bull back there."

She laughs. "I hope you mean that as a compliment. Pit bulls are misunderstood animals. My neighbor had one when Tessa and I were growing up. He was the sweetest, smartest dog. He used to sit outside, watching us play, and he'd growl at anyone who came too close. Our own personal guard dog."

"What happened to him?"

"Older kids trying to provoke the dog to prove that he was vicious. My neighbor moved before anything really happened."

"I remember that scandal. The dog was Fido or Fifo or . . ."

Her next laugh fills the space between my ribs with something warm. "It was Coco, but close. How do you remember that scandal? As far as scandals go, it was minor."

"I had a front-row seat to Kingsette scandals." I brace myself for the next part of my confession. "My mom was close with Annette Martina. They grew up together."

"Oh," she says, the word a blend of understanding and sympathy. "So, you knew everything happening in town?"

"Well, my mother did. But the walls were thin."

"Aah." She taps her full lower lip with her pointer finger. Her top lip puckers. "So you knew all about my mother?"

I hang my head. "I remember when your dad left. It couldn't have been easy."

Snatches of old gossip find purchase in my thoughts. My mom, Annette, and Delilah in the kitchen, discussing Hope's mom's alleged affair with Peter Wilkens, a man ten years her junior. Judging her, as if she were the one who'd cheated and blown up a marriage. No one talked about Hope's dad, how he'd left his family high and dry two years earlier to take up scuba diving with his secretary. "It was awful how people treated her. Like she was a pariah."

"When my family broke down, I think it made them realize their families could break down too. It was easier to blame my mom rather than face the ugly truth about their own lives." She shrugs.

"I get that. It wasn't too different for my mom. No one blamed her, but they started to treat her like she had a disease, like she was . . ." My eyes widen, and now would be a good time for the earth to swallow me whole.

Hope's laugh feels like an absolution. "Don't worry. You didn't tell me anything I didn't already experience. But I didn't know your mom had it tough like that. Too bad we didn't figure that out years ago. Our moms could have been friends."

"It's not too late."

"Oh, it is. My mom moved out of town years ago. She has very strong opinions about small-town life. If Noah and Brandon didn't love this town so much, she would have found a way to force us to move."

"Now I know where you get that fierceness from."

She beams up at me, her eyes bright, her long lashes dusting her cheeks as she blinks. My chest fills with warmth.

Her attention snags on the band members preparing their instruments. "Oh my God, that's Ian Summers's band. Noah would love to have them perform at his party. They're impossible to get."

"So I've heard."

The tuning sounds of Ian's band wrap around us. The scent of something sweet filters in.

Ian strums a note on his guitar, and the crowd energizes. I'm pushed closer to Hope as she loses her balance. I reach out and catch her, steady her. She sucks in a gasp. My fingers linger on the curve of her hip.

The crowd pulses around us. The energy shifts. What had been light and friendly arcs toward something dense and electric. A current vibrates beneath my skin.

"Maybe we should leave the dance floor to the coeds," I say.

"Yeah." She sounds as breathless as I feel.

I lead her off the dance floor, my hand firmly around her waist. She shuffles forward, staying close, as if she feels the invisible magnet between us too.

Once we're far enough away from the dance floor, I look down at Hope. Baby hairs curl around her forehead. The flush in her cheeks brings out the flecks of gold in her eyes. Her mouth falls slightly open on a breath. My heart loses track of its rhythm.

"Probably time for the old folks to get out of here?"

"I don't know. More than a few of these girls will be disappointed when you leave with me." She bites her lip.

My gaze dips to her mouth. A current surges between us, thumping to the energy of the crowd, the beat of the music. My heart finds a new rhythm, and it's a timeless one—one I've known and forgotten.

"I haven't noticed." I take a step closer, and with that step, the crowd melts away. It's just us.

"Will," she says, and her hand finds the constant, steady beat of my heart against my chest.

A moment passes, and then a lifetime. She doesn't pull away. I don't release her.

She tilts her face toward mine. Between us, there's a whisper of space. For the first time in a long time, I feel like I'm where I'm supposed to be.

I feel like Hope is where I'm supposed to be.

I inhale. And then that space is gone.

Her lips are warm and soft and gentle. My hand slides around her waist, and the warmth of her exposed skin feels like a branding.

A small sound escapes from the back of her throat, and God help me—maybe it's the tequila—but my mouth presses more firmly on hers. She takes a step in, pressing flush against me. I spread my hand flat along her lower back, wanting to feel more of her.

She deepens the kiss, and there is nothing except this moment— Hope's lips and Hope's hand and this kiss—and Hope.

I pull back and rest my forehead on hers. We both need to catch our breath. More than that, we need to talk.

"Oh my God, Hope Gold out and about in a bar."

She nearly jumps out of her skin putting space between us. With the little room around us, that's next to impossible.

Black spots cloud my vision, and I see only the outline of a man's shoulders.

My vision clears, and my stomach inverts. Logan. Brandon's brother. He looks between us, looks down at the nonexistent space between us. His brows draw together, carving out a distressed groove in his forehead. For too long, he just takes us both in. Hope's shoulders round forward, as if she's trying to make herself smaller.

I take a microstep forward.

"Will, right? I'm Tanya." The woman with Logan extends a hand toward me, her gaze only briefly sliding past Hope's before returning to Logan's.

"I remember. You had a beautiful wedding," I say, trying to sound gracious. With the music and the crowd, it's hard to tell if I succeed.

Logan's nostrils flare, no doubt as he connects my face with my name . . . and reputation.

"Thank you." Tanya interlaces her fingers with Logan's.

He glances at their clasped hands, confusion smoothing out the lines in his forehead. "What are you doing here?" he asks, directing the question to Hope.

"I—Will's helping me look for Brandon's locket, so I'm helping him with . . . poaching . . . staffing." She shakes her head. "With stuff at the Inn."

Logan's expression hardens.

"You mean the locket Brandon gave you?" The urge to protect Hope from the sharpness in his voice makes my shoulders tense.

Tanya tugs Logan back, shows him her phone. "We should get going. We just stopped in before dinner with my parents to see Ian

Summers's band. But, looks like we have to go. Hope, we'll see you back at home?"

She nods, but the gesture is little more than a head bob, as if all the strength has vanished from her body.

As soon as they disappear, I turn to Hope. "Talk to me."

"I should go," she says and shoves her drink into my hand, pushes through the crowd.

More than a few glares and angry words chase me as I follow after Hope. She's halfway down the sidewalk, nearly swallowed by the pitch-black night.

"Hope, stop." Night air blows across the back of my neck, cooling the heat that collected there. "Please. What can I do?"

She turns to face me, and the relief I feel is blotted out by the way her broken expression guts me.

Hope is off limits. She's not the kind of woman you can have a casual fling with. Despite that sparking temper and the fact that she would hate being called fragile, there's something vulnerable about her, something I can't help wanting to protect. Even from myself.

"Hope, I'm sorry. I shouldn't have kissed you."

"Don't say 'I'm sorry.'"

Something nameless ignites inside me. "Why? Why can't I say 'I'm sorry'? You owe me that explanation."

"I owe it to you?" She scoffs, but the sound is layered with a swallowed sob.

"Yes, Hope. You do."

She stares at me, unblinking. People heading into the bar stare and give us a wide berth. Music and laughter flow into the space between us—that last friend who doesn't realize the party's over.

"Tell me," I say, my voice softening.

Seconds pass. A minute. Our gazes remain locked on each other's.

She sighs. "Because I don't deserve anyone's 'sorry' until I can say 'sorry' to Brandon."

"To Brandon? What would you need to say 'I'm sorry' to him for?" Brandon died in a car accident. A drunk driver ran through a red light, and Brandon died at the scene. Hope was in the passenger seat. She spent three weeks in the ICU and defied a thousand odds to walk away. At least that's the story I've heard a few times since I've been in Kingsette.

"Brandon and I were fighting in the car that day." Hope's gaze drops to the sidewalk. "We'd been fighting since the night before."

"What were you fighting about?" It's a struggle to keep my voice gentle and keep true to the space she put between us.

"Everything. We were . . . not on the same page anymore. Brandon was ready to start trying for a baby, and I wasn't." Her eyes are heavy with guilt as she lifts them to me and shakes her head. "He and I had gotten so stuck here. We'd had so many more plans, and I just wasn't ready. I didn't understand why Brandon was being so pushy. He didn't understand why I wouldn't just consider it."

Her chest rises as if she's carrying the weight of the world on her shoulders.

"People get mad at each other. Even people who love each other. It doesn't matter that you were fighting."

"It's more than that. Brandon was angry and already not paying attention to the road. Then I said to him—" Her voice cracks. Tears stream down her cheeks. "I said maybe we should take a break from each other. Maybe we want different things."

The force of Hope's guilt and heartbreak slams into my chest, and even I can't breathe.

"But I didn't mean it. I didn't want a break. I wanted forever."

"People say things when they're angry." The words fall too short to be comforting.

"He looked at me. He turned away from the road and looked at me, horrified that I'd say that. I didn't even mean it, but I was so angry. So stupid." Hope's tears stream down her cheeks. "The other driver hit us then. Ran through the red light. And Brandon—he died. He died, and

145

that's the last thing I said to him. If he'd been watching the road instead of reacting to me, the stupid thing I said, he'd be alive."

"Oh, God. Hope." Words rise and fall in my throat. "I'm sorry."

She doesn't flash a warning look at the apology. Her shoulders shake with the force of her sobs. "That's why I need Maeve's magic to be real, it's why I need to connect to Brandon. I keep telling myself that if I can just tell him I didn't mean it, tell him that I love him with my whole heart and always will, it will . . . I don't know what it will do. But it will make this hurt less. It has to."

Her hands shake, and I have to swallow hard against the rising wave of emotion.

"It's not your fault."

She steps back, into the gathering shadows. "I don't know why I lied to everyone about the fact that we were arguing. I just . . . I didn't want people to blame me. I blamed myself too much already."

"It's not your fault," I say, and Hope shakes her head. She looks up at the sky, where the moon and stars have gone invisible.

As if they don't know how to fix Hope's truth either.

23

HOPE

Tears slide down my cheeks as I head to Tessa's house the next morning. They do nothing to wash away that final image of Will's expression after I admitted what had happened in the car between Brandon and me.

If Will was that horrified by what I'd admitted, I can't even imagine how horrified he'd be if he knew all of it. Or if Tessa knew. Or Logan.

Yesterday was the closest I've ever come to telling the truth. And it only confirmed that I cannot tell. Ever.

Tessa's doorbell is broken, and my knock is answered by a little voice that dries up my tears.

"Mommy, Aunt Hope is here."

I swipe underneath my eyes and don a happy-aunt smile.

A commotion sounds on the other side of the door, like the girls are fighting over who turns the lock. Eventually, the door swings open and Tessa stands in front of me, a white bathrobe wrapped around her body. Everything about the way she's glaring at me and holding herself is hard and cold, and maybe I miscalculated how early parents of young kids actually wake up on a weekend.

"Hey, did I wake you?" I ask, in my softest kids-have-been-up-since-sunrise voice.

Emma and Macy rush toward me, squealing my name. I bend and wrap both girls in my arms. They smell like Cinnamon Toast Crunch and gummy bears. "I've missed you two." I lean backward to take in their full height. "You both have grown like a foot since the soccer game. How is that possible in two weeks?"

"Mommy says I have big feet and that means I'll be tall," Macy says, lifting a foot to show me. She's a mini Tessa, down to the Lululemon headband holding back her curls.

I crane my neck to see Tessa, who hasn't softened. I need Tessa to be Tessa right now. I need my big sister.

"Mommy's very smart," I say.

"Girls, why don't you go inside and finish your cereal. Maybe Daddy will put on a show. I need to talk to Aunt Hope alone."

Emma turns to me with a serious expression. "I've been working on my magic tricks. I'll show you later, okay?"

"Definitely," I say, remembering the magic set I bought her from one of the first mediums I visited. Tessa wasn't pleased.

Both girls disappear, giggling down the hall, and I face my sister.

She glances down at her white robe and white slippers. "You're wearing all black."

"Is everything okay?" I ask.

"No, not really, Hope." Her eyes are puffy—and it's not just from regular exhaustion. She's been crying.

My stomach bottoms out.

"What's wrong? Is Mom—?"

"What happened to you yesterday?"

"Yesterday?" The failed locket attempt, downtown, Selena's baby shower, a call to Will, a kiss . . .

Tessa waiting for me at a bar to watch a band. *Shit.*

Excuses crackle and wither on my tongue like the Pop Rocks candy we used to fight over as kids.

She stares me down, an unfamiliar glint in her eyes. "I waited for you for an hour at the bar. You didn't answer my texts."

"Will and I went to Newport, and my phone died."

The hardness in her expression develops a layer of ice.

"God, Tess, I messed up. It's not like you never went out for a fun night and let your phone die. You've even dropped your share of phones into the toilet, if my memory is correct." More ice and silence. "You do remember fun, don't you?"

She exhales a sharp laugh. "Glad you think lying to me is fun."

"I'm not lying to you."

"It's hard to believe that since every time I turn around you've got a new lie for me. You even lied about seeing Maeve." Tessa's face undergoes a series of microexpressions I know are meant to keep her from crying because I cycle through those same expressions.

"Maeve. How did you—who told you?"

She breathes a jaded laugh and pinches the bridge of her nose with her hands. "That's your answer. Who told me? You know, the worst part is that I could almost forgive you for ditching me for Will, but it never even occurred to me that you'd lie to me for Maeve. I thought you learned your lesson."

"Learned my lesson? As if I'm one of your kids who you can just send to their room?" Tessa's elegant foyer, the chandelier, and the spray of white orchids turn red as heat pulses beneath my skin. The intensity of the heat melts away the barricade I put up. "Must be nice—to live here, in your beautiful house with your perfect children, and pass judgment on everyone else. Well, guess what? You went to Maeve too. You never mentioned that. What did you go for, huh?"

Tessa's jaw goes slack; then she grinds her teeth together. "I went as a joke. To see what it was all about. You know what I saw—a sad woman, with a sad story, who needs to take advantage of other people to make herself feel better. I saw your future, if you're not careful."

I step back. My heels hang off the back edge of her cement steps. "That was cruel, Tessa. Maeve is my only chance to connect with Brandon."

"Why, Hope? Brandon's gone. He's been gone, and you're the only one who refuses to see that. Why are you so desperate to connect with Brandon." The cruel emphasis she puts on *connect* makes the word sound nonsensical. "Explain it to me. Because you know what? I don't understand."

It's my turn to pinch the bridge of my nose to stop the tears burning the backs of my eyes. "I just want to know I'm not alone."

"You're not alone. I'm here." Hurt darts across her face. Brandon's horrified expression smolders against the backs of my eyes.

My mouth goes dry. The words I need don't come, like they haven't come time and time again. "It's—never mind. It doesn't matter."

Tessa shakes her head. "You're right. It doesn't matter. The only thing that matters is I've been there for you every day, trying to help you get your life together, and you don't care. You lied to me. Lied to my kids. I can't keep saving you. I just . . . it's exhausting. If you're determined to self-destruct, I can't stop you anymore. I don't want to."

My throat is thick, and I can't respond. Tessa and I are separated by a few inches, but the chasm that has opened between us feels too wide to ever even begin to cross. She's my sister, my first friend and first soulmate, but right now, she feels like a stranger.

The last time I felt a chasm like this with someone I loved was that last morning with Brandon. I said things I can never take back, that led to his death. Tears fill my eyes. I can't do this again. Can't be at fault. Can't lose someone else because of something I said.

I pivot and walk down the steps. She makes a noise from the back of her throat, half sob, half laugh. "Yeah, that's a good plan. Run away. Go hide. You've gotten good at that these past few years."

Her words strike the vulnerable place just beneath my ribs. And I let them.

24

WILL

In the morning, I text Hope to ask how she's doing. Her response comes back within seconds: thumbs-up emoji.

The equivalent of *I'm trying to be kind, but leave me alone.*

I don't blame her.

Hope deserved better last night. She deserved someone who looked her in the eye and told her in no uncertain terms that you can't blame yourself for things that aren't in your control.

The logical part of my brain tried to say that. The emotional part got tongue tied. Because I can't give that advice unless I'm ready to hear it myself.

My first stop is the bank to speak to Seth Richards—or S. R. Chard, as he's known in the Inn's guest book—about a personal loan. He rejected my business-loan application—Annette's influence, no doubt. Up until last night, when Hope stood up for my character, I'd planned to use that nugget of information to encourage him to change his mind.

Since I couldn't sleep anyway, I spent the night scouring the internet for a plan B. A personal loan means tethering myself to the Inn and Kingsette more than I'd like, but it buys me time to figure things out. Right now, time is more valuable than money.

More importantly, when it comes to personal loans, the bank requires that loan officers assert the reason for their denial. In writing.

I strongly doubt anyone at the bank is willing to put in writing that they're letting Annette dictate bank business.

Two hours later, I'm stepping back into the day's oppressive heat. Seth has not only granted me a loan, but he's agreed to a more-than-reasonable rate.

The next stop is to the Friendly Bean. Annette flashes her signature closed-lip smile when she spots me, and I steel myself for the conversation ahead.

As long as Annette thinks she can do whatever she wants with no consequences, she's going to keep doing it.

My phone pings as soon as I walk into the Friendly Bean, which is as busy as it was the last time I was here with Delilah.

It's not Hope.

This is the first time my agent's texted me in five months.

He answers on the fifth ring. "Will Reynard. Just the man I was thinking of."

I roll my eyes but do my best not to sound jaded. "Hey, Jimmy. Sorry I haven't checked in. Family stuff."

"Yeah, yeah, I get that. Family stuff. Listen, though. Get that family stuff taken care of. The original producer of *The Burning* wants you back. He's got a new show, and you're top of the list. He wants to talk."

"What?"

He's speaking too fast and sounds distracted. I imagine him at a restaurant, craning his neck to see whether there's anyone in view he should be watching or navigating to get attention from.

"A job, kid," Jimmy says, and his voice becomes clearer as if he's leaned forward and curled his other hand over the phone.

His words suddenly start to make sense. A job in LA. "They want me back?"

"When can you get yourself back here?" Jimmy asks.

I breathe through the tension in my shoulders and clutch my phone. There's a strange kind of déjà vu occurring in my brain, only twisted, as if I'm gazing into the past through a kaleidoscope. As if it's being superimposed onto the present in all its distorted glory.

Another chance to leave.

Once upon a time I took it, and it was the easiest decision to make. Things were stable then. My mother was running the Inn. Darren was . . . Darren, but a better version. LA was an exotic place where anything was possible.

Could I do the same now? Leave the Inn to fend for itself. Leave Darren to be Darren without any family nearby. Leave Hope to—

Friends.

She said *friends.* Could she have been any clearer?

"I'll be back in LA as soon as I can, but—" He hangs up before I can finish my sentence.

"You're leaving."

I whip around to face the stern male voice.

Logan is wearing the exact same loathing expression he wore last night. It gives me the same square-peg-in-a-round-hole feeling.

"Probably a bad time to make a you're-following-me joke, huh?" My voice falters. The three-inch height advantage I have shrinks to nothing.

His lips purse. "Does Hope know you're leaving?"

"I'm not leaving."

"That's not what I heard."

"Maybe that's because you heard one side of a private conversation." My voice rises, and heads whip in our direction. A table of young mothers lean in to whisper toward each other. "If you have something to say, I'm happy to discuss it. But not here."

Logan scans the restaurant. My gaze catches on Mrs. Lemmings, who's watching me through narrowed eyes.

"I'm just looking out for Hope. I have nothing to hide." Logan crosses his arms over his chest. A muscle flutters in his jaw.

"Have you ever considered that she might be able to look out for herself?"

"I know she can. I saw her walk out of that hospital when no one thought she would. But in some things, she's just—she's too trusting. She wants to believe the best in people, and that gives her a huge blind spot."

"Maybe that's what gives her strength."

Hope believes in people no one else believes in. That's rare.

"You have no idea what she's been through."

"She told me about the medium in New York." My voice rises in challenge. "Have you never made a bad judgment call? Or is it only Hope who gets one shot at figuring things out before she's branded for life?"\

"I'm trying to help her. She's my sister." Logan blows out a breath. "The medium in New York was my fault. I knew something was fishy, and I should have stopped her from going. She was just having such a hard time with grief and guilt. She kept blaming herself because of that stupid fight they had."

"You know about that fight?" My heart rate spikes. I thought no one knew.

Logan bites his lip and slips his gaze left and right. "Hope doesn't know that I know. When she was in the hospital and out of it, she told me all about the argument she and Brandon had in the car. She never mentioned it again, and I didn't have the heart to bring it up to her."

Lies by omission are lies. Hope said so. But who am I to pass judgment?

"And now she's spending time with Maeve, and a guy with a reputation for stirring the pot and then running away from people who need him the most. So you can guess why I'm concerned. I won't make the same mistake twice."

"I won't do that to Hope. And Maeve . . . I won't let her hurt Hope either. I promise." My lungs swell with the gravity of the promise. It's the first time in a long time that I've made a promise I don't want to run away from. "You'll be the first person I call if she does."

"How do I know I can trust you?"

The truth rises up and shoots across my consciousness, a shooting star lighting up the darkest parts of the night.

"Because I'm falling for her."

25

HOPE

Flickering light from Maeve's window is the first sign that she's awake. The second is more obvious—the sight of Maeve's door being thrown open.

Maeve steps out onto her porch wearing a pair of old jeans and a vintage New Kids on the Block concert tee.

"I didn't expect you until later," she says.

"I—" My voice cracks, and Maeve's gaze softens.

"Why don't we go inside to talk? The gardening can wait."

I drop onto the wood chair by the kitchen table while Maeve opens cupboards and removes dishes. She moves with the grace and speed of a dove, and after a few minutes, she pulls out the only other chair and sits across from me. She slides a mug across the table.

"What's this?" I've gotten pretty good at identifying Maeve's herbs. I can make some of her teas and tonics by heart now. But this one is unfamiliar.

"This is a more advanced brew. It's for truth."

I wrinkle my nose. "A truth serum?"

She smiles, and the smooth skin around her eyes crinkles with wisdom. "No, nothing like that. You won't be bound to tell only the truth. But you will be able to access the truth in your own heart, and maybe you'll feel comfortable enough to share it with me."

"I know the truth in my heart."

"Are you sure?"

I sigh. "I don't even know where to start. Everything just got so messed up so fast."

"Start from the beginning, and I'll listen as long as you want."

The gentleness in Maeve's offer is enough to lessen the weight of the brick sitting at the base of my throat. I sip her tea, and tears begin to pour down my face as I tell her everything.

Somehow, Maeve is the only person I have left. In less than twenty-four hours, I've alienated Will and broken my relationship with Tessa. Both have left giant aching holes in my chest. Not as big as the hole Brandon's death left, but—how many holes can one person live with?

"You did nothing wrong. You're allowed to be happy, Hope," Maeve says when I run out of words.

The truth pulses in my chest—a sharp, jagged rejection of her words. "You sound like my sister. I know I'm allowed to be happy. I know Brandon would want me to be happy. I know all of that."

"Will makes you happy."

"He's just lonely. He needs a friend."

"Yes, there seems to be a lot of that going around." Her gentle gaze should not make every muscle in my body tense. But it does.

"He's probably only staying here for another few weeks. I don't think he's all that happy in Kingsette."

"Are you?"

"Tessa is here, and my nieces. My job."

"That's not an answer."

"It's my home," I say.

"That's not an answer either." In the gray morning light, Maeve's pale eyes look colorless. There's a wistfulness in her expression I haven't seen before.

"What about you? Are you happy in Kingsette?" I glance out the window at the garden. At least a hundred flowers have set down deep roots.

Maeve flashes me a knowing smile. "I'm not quite welcome to call Kingsette home, am I?"

"You know what they're saying?"

"They're not exactly discreet, are they?"

"No. They just—they're not used to different." It's not an excuse, but hopefully it's an explanation. "They don't mean harm."

At least most of them don't.

Maeve's brow rises in wry amusement. "Well, no one believes they're the villain in their own story. Cronus ate his own children and still believed he was the hero in his story."

"Maeve . . ."

"No, don't worry about it. Honestly. One day I will settle down and find a place that is mine forever, but for now, the universe has a different calling for me. To travel and help people connect with those they've lost."

"How did you know what that calling was?" Once I thought I knew what my calling was—a straight line. Brandon, Kingsette, the hospital. I gave up so much of what I thought I wanted to follow that line. Point A was supposed to bring me to point B. But point B wasn't where I thought it would be.

Now point A is a memory and point B is nonexistent, and I'm on an unlabeled, unknown spot. An infinite number of new lines with invisible end points spans out in every possible direction. How am I supposed to know which line to choose? What if I choose wrong again? What will the cost be this time?

It feels easier to just stand still. To go through the motions of living without actually living. Like on the Ferris wheel with Will.

"Sometimes you just know," Maeve says. She gazes out the window, where a trio of butterflies has landed on the sill.

"What happened?" My voice is barely a whisper, but anything louder might shatter the intensity of the moment.

Seconds tick by.

"Please. I want to listen."

She turns back to me, her eyes a shade of stormy gray. "A long time ago, I ignored my calling. I didn't want to be like my mother—eccentric, outcast . . . other. I married someone who was the exact opposite—from a white picket fence family—and we bought a white picket fence house. I got pregnant." A ghost of a smile traces her lips, and my heart breaks for her. I know the bittersweet taste of that ghost smile.

"I went away for a girl's weekend. I smelled smoke and could not get that smell out of my nose. Some part of me knew it was a warning. I ignored my intuition. I didn't tell anyone. I didn't tell my husband to check the smoke alarms. He—Nathan—died that night.

"I had a miscarriage two days later. Stress, they say."

"Oh, Maeve."

"I feel Nathan's energy in butterflies. My baby . . . she's in the sunrise."

We both look to the window, to the sun coming up over the lake. The cottage has a perfect view. "It's not your fault."

"I don't blame myself anymore. But I never want to ignore my intuition again. Especially when it can help save someone."

Maeve reaches for a bag of gummy bears. Red, yellow, green. She chews, and there's a rawness in her expression I haven't seen before. A vulnerability. A humanness. It's the first time Maeve feels more like a friend I'm walking beside, rather than someone I'm following.

It must be lonely to always be the one forging the path for others. "Maeve . . ."

"If you've finished with your tea, I'd like to show you something in the garden."

In one graceful motion she's up and out the door.

Maeve leads us to her rosebushes. Icarus tweets as we pass, and Maeve scoops him up and nuzzles him to her neck. The bird sighs into her affection. There's so much more I want to say to Maeve, so much more she needs to hear, but the words I wanted to say vanish. What she needs from me isn't language, but presence. What she needs is the thing I wish others had done for me—let her take the lead and respect the boundary around her grief.

Maeve points to the rosebushes, which have grown so much in the last day they need to be pruned back. She beams. "Look at these roses. They were withering until you came. You made these grow when I couldn't. Because you believed you could. You did what your heart told you to do, and it worked."

"It's easy with flowers. They're just plants."

Maeve frowns. Lightness returns to her eyes. "Shh, they'll hear you. Flowers have feelings too." She takes a breath. "Choices are never easy. There's always a push and pull between our hearts and our minds, our fears and desires, our shoulds and our what-ifs. I'll never know what might have happened if I'd listened to my intuition. Maybe the story would have ended the same way. The point is that choosing to stand still is still a choice."

A cloud skids past the sun, and the tree casts a shadow over us. Without the sunlight blurring Maeve's edges, her white-blonde hair looks a shade of brittle gray. Lines on paper-thin skin I hadn't noticed before gather around her eyes, her mouth. Age spots darken the hands holding the bird.

I blink, and sunlight streams through the tree's branches again. Maeve is Maeve. "So, Hope, your turn. What's your choice? What do you want?"

It's an echo of a question I've asked so many times since I survived the accident and Brandon didn't.

My gaze sweeps around the garden. The colors blend. "I don't know."

"Hmm . . . ," Maeve says. "I think maybe you do know. You're just afraid to admit it."

Maeve turns at the same moment I do at the sound of a twig snapping. Three men stand on the hill watching us. Wearing various shades of green fishing vests with poles attached to their khaki backpacks, they look like they just walked off the pages of *Field & Stream* magazine. They smell like they walked out of a brewery.

The tallest of the three assesses both of us, and his attention focuses on Maeve. It remains there as a hardness sets into his features. My pulse kicks up.

"I thought you'd be taller," he says.

"Can I help you boys?" Maeve asks, stepping toward them, seeming to grow taller under their glares.

"We were fishing over there." He gestures vaguely to the lake. "Got turned around. Found you. Lucky coincidence."

"Looks like you didn't catch much."

"No." He glares at Maeve. The space between them feels fragile. "Seem to be having some bad luck holding on to things lately."

Maeve sucks her teeth. "Some things aren't ours to hold."

"Some things aren't any of your business."

The other two cross their arms over their broad chests, their shirts straining against the flexed muscles.

Maeve tilts her head. "I'm not quite sure what you're talking about. If you'd like to come in, I can get you some water. It's a steep hike, and the day is pretty warm."

As if hearing their cue, the last puffs of cloud stretching across the sun slide away, and sunshine floods the space. My temperature spikes.

"We don't accept water from witches." He sneers and turns to me. "Or their friends."

Even with the heat and light now beating down onto us, my teeth start to chatter.

Maeve sighs audibly. "Honestly, is this how you want to spend the rest of your morning? Harassing a single woman working in her garden?" Her hands go to her hips, and she studies the three intruders. "Let me guess. You're born and raised in Kingsette. Your father is a science teacher at the high school, and your mother runs a day care from her home. Your older brother moved out a few years ago and is waiting tables in Manhattan. You feel abandoned by him. It makes you feel unworthy."

A red flush laces up his throat. His fists clench by his sides. "What, did you stalk my social media?"

"How could I have known you were coming?" Maeve touches a finger to her lips. "Hmm, you said yourself, I was a witch."

The boy stalks toward Maeve, and his two friends follow on his heels.

She stands straighter and lifts her chin, meeting him glare for glare. He's three inches taller and at least seventy-five pounds heavier. Still, Maeve somehow overshadows him.

"You're a scam artist. You're manipulating people, making them act in all kinds of crazy ways."

"Am I a scam artist or a witch? It would be best if you made up your mind."

The boy makes a sound like a growl, and recognition sears through me. "You're Rory Lefner. You're engaged to Bailey."

He swivels his head toward me. "Was engaged to Bailey. Until Bailey started coming here and got her head all messed up. And how do you know that?"

The boy flanking Rory's left startles when our eyes meet. I realize I recognize him too. All of them are familiar.

Maeve sighs. "Have you said what you needed to say? It's getting quite warm out here, and if you boys won't come in, then I think we're done here."

"What'd you do with the engagement ring? She told me she doesn't have it anymore, so that must mean you have it." A muscle flutters in his jaw. "Is that the scam? Is that how you keep this pretty little garden alive? Not on my dime."

He pivots and stalks into the garden, heavy boots trampling delicate blooms. As he moves, he snatches flowers up from their plots and discards them as if they are nothing. As if they are worthless.

His hand reaches for my rosebush. The moment he tightens his grip, a yelp escapes him, and he wrenches his hand back. A rivulet of blood leaks down his hand. He smears it on his pants and reaches instead for a plant with dull-purple bell-shaped flowers. He yanks as his foot stomps at the roots. I gasp. A shadow crosses Maeve's features, darkening her eyes, the hollows of her cheeks. Making her look other. In that moment, I believe every menacing rumor whispered in town.

Rory drops his first victimized flower to the ground and crushes another in his fist. The crunch of stem and crinkle of delicate petal grate along my panic. The flowers are blameless, yet they are bearing the brunt of Rory's cruelty.

"Rory!" We both startle at the sharp bark of his name from my lips. My heart crashes against my rib cage as I carefully step over the plants to put myself between Rory and any more damage.

"My sister plays bridge with your mother every Thursday night. They belong to the same garden club, and my sister hosts the annual Memorial Day barbecue for the club. If I tell her I saw you here and describe how you were acting—" I click my tongue the way Tessa does when she's disappointed. He takes a step back. I close the space again. He doesn't get to slink away.

"My mother . . . she'd . . . she'd support me."

"Would she?" I hold up my cell phone, useless with no service. "We can call and find out."

"No," he says and then yelps. He releases the plant. An angry red rash blooms across the pale skin, spreading to his wrist.

Rory's friends gasp. Rory's gaze darts to Maeve, who hasn't moved, hasn't spoken. Her mouth is a straight line—her expression neutral.

"You did this," he accuses, cradling his injured palm.

His two friends shrink back as if Rory's hand were contagious.

"I haven't done a thing." Maeve's voice is light but not gentle. "That flower you crushed is belladonna. It's harmless unless you have an open wound. Like from a rosebush thorn. Which you did to yourself."

Rory cradles his hand and glares at Maeve. "This isn't over."

Maeve and I stay silent until the sounds of their feet crunching through the forest floor are long gone.

"Thank you for standing by my side."

"You don't have to thank me. It's what friends do." My gaze sweeps over the carnage of Rory's attack. "Why aren't you more furious?"

"Because he got his due punishment. And holding on to anger is as helpful as living with regret." She laughs a bit as she scowls at her ruined flower beds. "At least he didn't make it to the midnight blooms."

"Will you be able to save them?"

She shrugs. "Most things that look irreversibly broken can often be repaired with a bit of effort. As I always say, where there's a will, there's a way."

She raises her eyebrows suggestively. "If you know what I mean."

I roll my eyes. "I think even the birds know what you mean."

26
WILL

If weddings are for former frat boys taking shots to relive college, then retirement parties are for executives drinking vodka martinis to chase away their regrets.

Pete, the man of the hour, orders three vodka martinis with a different kind of vodka in each glass. A taste test, he tells me, with a wink, as if trying to serve 150 guests while short-staffed were a time for taste tests.

I glance toward the door and try to decide if I'm punishing myself by even holding out any hope. She's not coming to help tonight. Not after the way I messed everything up.

I make Pete's drinks and start on a round of gin and tonics for a group of women who've ordered every drink with a frown. Annette's influence, too, if I had to guess. At least she couldn't work fast enough to encourage Pete's company to cancel this party. The Inn needs the revenue more than ever.

The women take their drinks without a thank-you, and I start on the next order shouted at me.

It's going to be a long night.

The email that arrived minutes before the party slams into my thoughts, a reminder that *long night* is an understatement.

The private investigator had decided to look into Maeve—had called it professional curiosity. And charged me for it. What he found is . . . worth knowing, especially considering all the issues with the Inn's finances, but that doesn't mean I have any idea what to do with it.

Shoplifting, disturbing the peace, destruction of personal property. A few unproven allegations of identity fraud.

An arm brushes against mine, and I whirl around, ready to reprimand Pete for climbing behind the bar again.

It's not Pete.

Hope's tying an apron around her waist, her long hair pulled up in a ponytail, her expression set. "Sorry I'm late."

"What are you doing?" I blink to be sure the stress isn't making me hallucinate.

"I promised to help, didn't I?" Hope turns to take a drink order, and I'm flooded with relief and a dangerous desire to kiss her again.

For the next two and a half hours, we work. The only break from the endless crush of people comes during the speeches, when Pete's coworkers share some questionable stories about him.

Hope nudges me. "You think Pete's retiring or being kindly pushed out."

There are so many things I want to talk about other than Pete, but now's not the time. "I've personally served him three drinks tonight, so I'm going to go with not-so-kindly being pushed out."

She grimaces as the guests begin to clap. The man of the hour stands, his wife's hand clutched in his, and says a few words about how much he'll miss everyone. Clapping begins again, but Pete isn't done. His voice is thick with emotion—and slurred—as he launches into very detailed apologies to his secretary, to the new hires, to everyone who he hurt.

Around the room, nervous giggles erupt, no one knowing whether to let Pete go on or stop him. Clearly Hope and I aren't the only ones wondering where the idea for retirement sprang from. Pete finishes his speech and sits. For a moment, everyone sits in silence. Then the band begins to play. Around Pete's table, people reach across to shake his hand. Others, not at Pete's table, sit stone faced or exchanging furious whispers.

The lesson is clear enough, though. An apology isn't always enough to repair the damage.

Every muscle in my body aches. I feel as if I just completed an Ironman competition rather than tended bar for four hours for a bunch of middle-aged accountants. Beside me, Hope massages her right shoulder, stretching her neck to the left and exposing the smooth line of her collarbone. Around us, busboys collect dishes and stack chairs in the corner of the room.

"Thank you for your help. I don't think I would have been able to get that done without you." I head toward one of the tables that has already been cleared of everything except a tablecloth stained with sauce and coffee. "I owe you."

She trails me and falls into the seat at the opposite end of the table. No one has turned on the bright overhead lights, so the room is still lit only by the soft light leaking from the antique brass chandelier. "Let's call it even."

She glances at the table. The space in front of her is stained deep red. "Think we'd have been less busy if people didn't spill all their drinks?"

"Yeah. Every time I saw Pete tip his glass, I cringed."

She breathes a laugh and then rakes her teeth over her bottom lip. The silence between us stretches into uncomfortable territory.

"How was Maeve today?"

She narrows her eyes. "How'd you know I visited Maeve?"

"You have a leaf tangled in your hair."

Her eyes widen, and she reaches up to her hair, finding the shredded parts of a leaf. "Why didn't you tell me earlier?"

"It didn't seem important. Besides, it gave you a little character."

She shoots me an unreadable look. The tension between us snaps taut, and I've never been comfortable with the uncomfortable.

"So . . . are we going to talk about it or just pretend it never happened?"

"Talk about what?" There's something in her voice that makes my heart shudder.

"The other night." My pulse ticks up; the memory sends my body temperature soaring. "That kiss."

"What about it?" A flattering pink flushes up her cheek, as if her temperature is rising too. I'm more excited about the idea than I have any right to be.

"I feel awful about how I handled what you told me. And that Logan saw us . . . I'm just . . . God, with your 'I'm sorry' ban, you're a really hard person to apologize to."

Her mouth twitches up. I lean closer, drawn toward that small break in her hostility. A moth to a flame.

"You don't have to apologize. You did nothing wrong."

"You ran off. I've never seen anyone call an Uber so quickly. I was worried about you."

"I'm fine," she says, her voice rising. "I just—emotions were high. I've never told anyone about that fight. And then . . . the kiss. We both know the kiss meant nothing, right?" Her voice drops to a whisper. "Because we're friends?"

We're more than that, but it's not fair to admit that when it's not what she wants. When there's so much else between us. "Totally. I got caught up in the moment. It was a mistake, that's all."

"Right. A mistake."

Butterflies—not the good kind—take flight in my stomach. For long moments, we don't speak. The ballroom clears out, and we're alone.

"So, we're good?" I ask and realize I'm holding my breath waiting for an answer.

"Two wrongs cancel each other out, right?" She smiles. It's a fraction of a smile, but it's enough.

"Something like that is true." I take my first deep breath since Hope walked away the other night.

"Did you hear from the Newport bartender?" Hope asks with the kind of forced casualness usually reserved for strangers asking about the weather in an elevator.

"Not yet."

Not yet? That's the best I came up with? I wrote for a semipopular television show, which once earned critical acclaim for its witty dialogue, and *not yet* is the best I can come up with to keep the conversation smooth.

"You will," she says.

More silence. My mind is full of stories I want to share with Hope—about Annette and my agent's news—but somehow Hope is the only person I can't tell. More lies by omission. She chews on her lower lip, as if there's something she's struggling to keep inside.

I lean forward, unable to help myself. "Something's bothering you."

"Is it that obvious?"

"Well, I wouldn't join a poker tournament if I were you."

She flashes a soft smile. "Brandon used to say the same."

I want to reach my hand across the table, but I hold back.

"Rory Lefner paid Maeve a visit. It didn't go exactly as he'd planned, though."

My mind zigzags to put the name together with the gossip I heard. "Bailey's ex-fiancé? What did he want with Maeve?"

"To intimidate her, I guess." She tells me about his threat and the way a coincidence with the order of his plant rampage saved them.

My fists clench, and it's a struggle to keep my voice even. "Were you there? Are you okay?"

Hope nods. "I'm fine. He ran away screaming like a colicky baby."

I breathe deeply through my nose and force the smile I know Hope wants. "Is Maeve . . ."

Hope throws up her hands, exasperated. "She's not even flustered. Wouldn't even consider letting me get her a room at the Inn."

"She's . . . something else," I say and stop myself from telling Hope she needs to keep her distance from Maeve. Hope said we're good, but I don't need to test how good by telling her what to do. "I should have been with you."

Her eyes snap to mine, and yes, I said she was a terrible poker player, but I cannot read that look. Because I would bet money that it's full of heat from the memory of that kiss, but I know it's not. *Mistake.* Could she have been any clearer?

"Hope, I have to tell you something. It's about Maeve. I . . . I haven't been exactly honest with you. Or her." My stomach knots at the way she stiffens. "That first night I showed up at Maeve's, I wasn't there to connect with anyone or because I believed in Maeve. I went because I knew my mom had been going to see her, and then my mom left so abruptly . . . I heard the rumors, and I didn't trust Maeve. I hired a private investigator to find my mom, and he ended up learning a lot about Maeve instead."

I slide my phone toward her and watch as she reads the summary document from the investigator.

She looks up with an unreadable expression. "Have you shown this to anyone else?"

"Just you."

She nods. She reaches for a napkin and wrings it in her hands. "If we're being honest, I should tell you that I heard the rumors about Maeve and your mom. I guess I thought I was protecting you by not telling you."

Hope wanted to protect me. The thought makes my heart swell. "Do four wrongs make two rights?"

She laughs, but the sound disappears too fast. "If you go public with this, they'll come with pitchforks for Maeve."

"I know."

"Please don't. I know I have no right to ask you that, but I know Maeve. You don't know her full story, and you shouldn't judge someone by her worst decisions. She's . . ." Hope turns the full intensity of her green eyes on me, and it's terrifying how desperately I want to give her everything she asks for. "If you can't trust Maeve, I understand, but please trust me. Trust me when I say she deserves the benefit of the doubt and she's a good person who would never hurt anyone."

A charged moment passes between us. "I trust you, Hope. I'll keep this to myself."

"Hey, Will?" A young waiter appears in the doorway leading to the kitchen. He has the shifty, nervous look of the kid who drew the short straw. "There's a ton of food left over. Some of the guys want to know if they can take leftovers?"

"Of course. Everyone should help themselves."

The waiter bobs his head in a grateful nod and disappears.

Hope's shaking her head, a smirk playing on her lips. "Your boss really is a pushover."

"Hey, I'm not the one who let a patient's husband sneak a dog into the ICU." I click my tongue in mock reprimand.

Her jaw drops. "You promised you wouldn't tell!"

I make an *X* with my finger across my chest. "And I won't. Doesn't mean I can't bring it up whenever you question my judgment."

She crosses her arms over her chest, feigning offense. With her back ramrod straight, her hair still pulled back from her face, and that light flush in her cheeks, she's never been more stunning.

"How about we call a truce and you help me with one more thing?" I stand and reach a hand toward her.

She raises an eyebrow but puts a hand in mine. I grasp it and lift her up. We each take two bottles of wine from behind the bar and make our way to the kitchen. The waitstaff freezes as we enter, forks in midair, wine bottles lifted to lips.

Hope giggles at the dozen deer-in-the-headlights looks darted our way. I lift both bottles in my hand over my head. "Tonight, we eat and drink. I owe you guys for being here."

Whoops and cheers follow my words. Hope's smile is as wide as I've ever seen it as she uncorks a bottle and begins filling the empty glasses raised her way. For the next hour, we drink and eat and chat with the waitstaff. They regale Hope with stories about my leadership skills as I found my footing doing this inn-manager gig, and she laughs, fully and wholly from her core. The sound warms every place inside my chest. More than once, I catch her eye across the room, and I can't help but think what it would have been like if Hope had been in my life before I left for LA.

Would I have gone? Would I have wanted to leave Kingsette? If I hadn't left, would Darren be on his way to rehab and my mother MIA?

The answer doesn't matter because we can't go back in time.

Even if we could, Hope would have been with Brandon. She was his.

Around two, after we've cleaned up the kitchen, Hope and I are the only ones left.

"I'm starving," she says, surveying the sparkling kitchen.

"Seriously?"

As if to prove her point, her stomach growls. A laugh roars out of me, and she turns toward the industrial-size freezer behind her. "What have you got that's sweet?"

She opens the freezer door and peers in.

Heaven help me, I cannot resist coming to stand beside her, brushing my arm against hers. The freezer is embarrassingly empty.

"I'm a little behind on ordering things."

She rummages around past the frozen meats and produces a carton of mint–chocolate chip ice cream. The colors are faded, and it's crusted in ice crystals.

"Where in the world did you find that?" I take it from her hand, flipping it over to check the expiration date. "You're in luck. Exactly six weeks until this baby expires."

I feel the smile slide down my face as I take in her expression, the intensity of her focus on the carton of ice cream. "What's wrong?"

She blinks a few times, as if when she looks again, the carton in my hand might be something else. "That's mint chocolate chip."

"Is that a problem?"

"No, it's just—that was Brandon's favorite flavor. We always kept it in the freezer, and when we were in college, he'd eat an entire carton after exams ended to celebrate." Her attention is fixed on the carton in my hands, as if it were a bomb. As if it might explode and destroy everything.

"You know, I remember Brandon from high school. Not well, or anything. But I remember he always hung out by the basketball courts. He and his friends tried to steal our ball. They'd knock over our water bottles, stupid pranks. Now that I think of it"—I feel my face pucker as the memories float in—"he was kind of a punk."

Hope makes a sound that's half laugh, half cry. "He kind of was in high school. He grew out of it."

"He had to, if you married him."

"Yeah," she says, her eyes darkening with whatever memory my ill-considered monologue ignited.

"I wish I had gotten to know him better," I say and mean it. I'd like to meet anyone who made Hope smile the way I saw her smile in those old photos with Brandon.

"He would have liked you. I bet you guys would have been friends." Her attention returns to the carton melting in my hands. "Thanks for sharing that with me—about Brandon being a punk. Everyone talks about him like he was perfect, and it's nice to talk about him like he was a real person again."

"Anytime." I spin around and notice that the kitchen was reorganized again. "If I can find a trash can, I'll get rid of this."

"Wait. Don't." She steps toward me hesitantly, as if the carton might take flight from my hands. "I think . . . I think I'd really love to eat late-night mint–chocolate chip ice cream again."

27
HOPE

We need to talk. Please.

I expected this text.

If I'm being honest, I've been expecting this text for a long time. Though that doesn't make it any easier to respond.

I read Logan's message for the dozenth time and am no closer to deciphering his tone. He seemed so angry and has been avoiding me at home. But the *please* . . . that doesn't sound angry. It sounds . . . like a text message, and I need to stop treating text messages like real communication.

His next text arrives in my inbox while I'm still working out a response. I have something that belongs to you. I'm at my mom's house.

I delete what I was going to write and type a new response: I'll be there in twenty minutes.

Driving up to Logan's parents' house, which is the house he and Brandon grew up in, feels like driving up to a memory. Even though Brandon's mom painted the formerly yellow house a modern blue gray, it still feels like an echo of a life long gone. The trellis that I used to climb to reach Brandon's room is still there. The pond behind the house where Brandon and I hunted for frogs is still there. My house—or the house that was mine before my dad left and we moved—is still next door.

It's all still there. Just smaller than I remember.

Logan's waiting at the door when I arrive. He's wearing Brandon's we-need-to-talk expression beneath Brandon's faded Yankees cap. "Thanks for coming."

"Thanks for asking me." My throat feels thick, and it's an effort not to turn and run. I force myself to make eye contact. "What are you doing at your old house?"

He glances over his shoulder at the old Victorian. "Tanya and I are thinking of buying this place from my parents. Since Brandon died, they never come up from Florida, so it's just sitting here empty, and it's bigger than our house now. More yard space for family one day."

"Oh." A rainbow of emotions overwhelms my nervous system. According to the support groups and social media memes, widows are supposed to be good at navigating two opposing emotions at once—grief and joy, love and loss. I haven't gotten the hang of it yet. "Congratulations," I say and hope I sound genuine.

He toes a loose paving stone with his shoe. "Nothing's definite, obviously."

"No—don't—you don't have to do that. You don't have to act like this isn't an amazing thing for you because you think it'll hurt me."

"You're my sister, Hope. That was true even before you married my brother, and the last thing I want to do is hurt you." An expression darts across Logan's face. It's there and gone so fast that if I didn't know Logan, I might have missed it. Or misread it.

"Logan, I need to explain—"

"I have your locket." Logan holds out a hand. My eyes take a moment to adjust to the thing dangling in the space between us. Even once it comes into focus, I still blink to make sure I'm seeing correctly.

The diamond in the heart's center sparkles. Breath whooshes out of me. "That's my . . ." My words catch on a sob.

It is. There's no mistaking the interlocking *H* and *B* on the heart-shaped medallion. The delicate diamond stud. My locket.

"How?"

"I'm sorry I didn't give it to you sooner. I just—I thought—" He shakes his head. "The police gave it to me while you were in the hospital, and you never asked for it. Somehow I thought returning it would be too hard on you. Like it would remind you that he was gone." He breathes a laugh. "As if you'd ever forget."

He puts the locket in my hand. It's weightless and heavy, real and surreal. I close my hand around it and then instantly open it, worried it disappeared. "I was afraid of what you'd think of me if you knew I lost it."

"I want you to be happy, Hope."

I tear my gaze away from it to look at Logan. His eyes, which are so like Brandon's, shine.

"I thought you were angry when you saw me with Will. I thought that's why you wanted to talk."

His expression hardens, and the fluttering in my stomach makes it feel as though the ground were shaking.

"Are you with him?"

"I don't know," I admit. He called the kiss a mistake. But last night scraping mint–chocolate chip ice cream from the bottom of the carton felt like coming back to something that I thought I'd lost for good. Not Brandon. Obviously. But something else. Something different than what I had with Brandon, which is maybe why I didn't recognize it at first.

"We're . . . more than friends, I think."

It takes all my strength to admit that. To Logan. And to myself. Because admitting that means admitting Brandon is gone. Intellectually, I've known that for two years. But grief is so rarely intellectual.

"I know that's hard to hear," I say, wanting to bridge the gap widening between us.

"No, Hope. It's not." He reaches for my hand. "I know you love my brother, and always will, but he's not here. You can't choose him right now. At least not without giving up yourself. It's just . . . Will. I don't trust him."

My throat tightens. "I know what people say about him. But he's not that guy. At least not anymore."

"I don't want you to get hurt," Logans says.

"Will won't hurt me."

My phone vibrates, and I know who's texted me even before I turn the screen to face me. It's a photo of a cat wearing a party hat and the words DRINKS LATER? stamped on the bottom.

I look up from the text and find Logan watching me with a gentleness that should not make every single muscle in my body tense as if I were caught red handed doing something immoral. But it does.

"You're allowed to be happy, Hope."

Tears spring to my eyes. If he knew the whole truth, he might feel different. "I hope you're right."

Logan wraps his arms around me, squeezing me with all the love I don't deserve from him. "Just be careful. And know that if he hurts you, even a little bit, I will chase him down and tear him to shreds."

28

WILL

The plan should have been to forget Maeve and focus on the Inn. But since Hope told me that Rory had threatened Maeve, had threatened her, it's taking all my willpower not to march over to his place and warn him against ever speaking to Hope again. I can't help myself—even though some part of me knows that Sheriff Wilson's presence on these nights means Hope is safe.

I'm the last to arrive to watch the midnight flowers bloom. Bailey acknowledges me first.

She tells me she's moving next week—earlier than planned.

She seems calmer. Lighter. Like she found the peace that's been eluding her.

That makes one of us.

I spy Hope chatting with a man I don't recognize on the far side of the bonfire. As I approach, she turns, grinning at me with none of the nerves I expected. She's holding a mug of Maeve's tea in her hand.

"Will. You made it," she says breezily, casually, as if she hasn't been consumed by thoughts of last night.

Our shared night has replayed in my mind no fewer than a thousand times a day. The taste of mint chocolate chip is still on my tongue.

"Wouldn't miss it." I gesture toward her hands. "More tea for courage?"

"I needed to be more than brave today." She holds the mug toward me. The smell of sweet cinnamon and something spicy is heady. "This one's for hope."

"Are we talking in the third person now?" I raise an eyebrow, eliciting a laugh.

"No, it's for hope—that vague, indefinable concept. Maeve said this tea will help me be open to hope, to make space for the thing that comes next, and trust that it'll be okay, even if it's not what I expected."

The hair on the back of my neck rises. "That's . . . powerful stuff."

Hope's gaze turns up toward me. Her eyes reveal a vulnerability I'm not used to seeing in her. "I needed something stronger than courage tonight."

"Why?"

Maeve calls for the group's attention. The man Hope was speaking with glances between us. A primal part of my brain makes me square off my stance, pull back my shoulders to take up more space.

Hope seems oblivious to the admittedly embarrassing staring contest going on around her. Something is different about her. More than usual her focus is fixed on Maeve, whose silver hair is glowing with shades of orange and red, making it seem as if she is on fire too.

Maeve leads us into the garden. Once again, Hope and I are the last to follow.

"I'm going to get a message from Brandon tonight. I can feel it." Hope turns to me. Even in the darkness, the wild, heartbreaking hope in her eyes shines through. She needs Maeve's flowers and teas to be true so desperately that a small part of me wants it to be true for her.

And maybe for me too.

My grief has always felt like a tiny iron ball in the pit of my stomach, something I wrangled and rationalized and shoved away. Hope's grief is different. She lets her grief rise to the surface. She lets it swirl with that boundless hope she was named for, in a way that makes grief look like love, not just sorrow.

Grief is never light, but maybe it doesn't need to be so dense.

Maeve glances back. Her gaze slides to Hope. An expression passes over Maeve's face, and my blood runs cold. Her gaze ticks away, and panic shivers along my spine.

"Hope—"

A defiant caw ripples across the night sky, slicing my warning in half. Hope gives my hand a squeeze and disappears into the garden. Leaving me in the dark.

The smell of pine and lavender and something musky curls around us as we make our way to Maeve's midnight blooms. We stand for long minutes, watching the flowers unfurl in the moonlight.

Maeve begins her affirmations. Beside me, Hope's holding herself taut, nearly trembling.

Maeve turns her ear up to the moon, as if listening for something. Hope isn't breathing.

"Please." Hope whispers the plea echoing in my thoughts.

"Long before I arrived in Kingsette, I felt the call of Ahava Cottage and this group. I knew there would be something special here in this place where light and shadow meet, where impossible feels possible, where strangers become friends and guardian angels. What I hadn't realized is that some liminal spaces can be more than what they seem. They can come to feel like home." Emotion chokes Maeve's voice. "There's so much energy tonight. Do you all feel it?"

Maeve's question is met with murmurs of agreement.

"There are many who seek connection tonight, but there's one vibration coming through louder than the others. It's . . . Vincent, it's your sister."

Air puffs out of Hope on a broken breath. The new guy who Hope was speaking to steps forward.

"She's been sending you ladybugs. Have you seen them?"

"That's her?" His voice quivers.

She asks Vincent more questions. He answers, his back straightening as Hope's rounds.

"He could still come," she whispers and sips the tea. "Right?"

"Yeah, Hope. He could."

Maeve and Vincent speak for something like an eternity. Hope finishes her tea and shifts forward onto her toes, a boxer ready to jump into the ring.

The first flower curls into itself. Hope makes a small sound that echoes loudly in my chest.

Vincent returns to his place in the circle, his forehead slick with sweat, eyes bright. Maeve's gaze skims over Hope. Roaring fills my ears.

Hope takes an incremental step forward. "Maeve? Is there . . ." She glances up at the star-flecked night, at stars that are fifteen hundred light-years away. So close, and yet forever unreachable.

A small headshake.

"But you said—he . . . ask again."

Another midnight bloom folds closed. Hope's attention snaps to it. "Oh, God."

My fingernails dig into my palms. This is Maeve's doing.

Maeve repeats the affirmations that signal the end of the night. The others join, their voices uncertain rather than exhilarated.

"I need to get out of here," Hope says, her voice rising above the roaring. She rushes out of the garden and into the woods.

I'm right behind her.

"Are you okay?" I ask once she's slowed to a walk. "Maeve shouldn't have told you to expect—"

"I found the locket Brandon gave me," she says, her breath jagged. "He still didn't come."

"You—when? You didn't tell me."

She turns tearstained eyes up to me, and somehow I know where the locket came from—who had it all along.

"I'm so glad you brought it," Maeve says, appearing from the shadows. "And I'm sorry Brandon didn't come tonight, but I never said he'd come if you found the locket."

"You—" A breath puffs out of her. "You said if I brought the locket, I'd find the thing I was most looking for. Brandon is that thing. He was supposed to come."

Her words echo through the hollow darkness, and a part of my brain goes cold. It takes less than a heartbeat to shake the jealousy away. If Hope lets me into her heart, I'm sure she'll have more than enough space for both of us.

"I said you'd find the thing you've been looking for. But Hope, didn't you find it?"

"No." The words release the emotion Hope's been holding back. She covers a single broken sob with the back of her hand. The sound carves out a hole in my heart. "I needed to tell Brandon 'I'm sorry.' I can't do that if he doesn't—"

"That's bullshit." I only realize the outburst belongs to me when Hope's head swivels in my direction. Accusations scorch up my throat, coming to a screeching halt at the tip of my tongue. "You and your cryptic shit. Of course, Hope believed Brandon was coming. Why else did she spend all that time looking for a locket to bring to you."

I'm on the verge of giving away too much, saying the wrong thing that will reveal what I really feel about Maeve. Only the heartache etched in Hope's face makes me stop. Everything else fades away.

"It's okay, Will," Hope says, her voice small as her arms wrap around her. As if she needs to physically hold herself tight to keep from falling apart.

My arms ache with the need to scoop her up, to take her away from here.

"It's not Maeve's fault," Hope says. She looks up at the sky, the universe, before settling her attention back on me. "It's mine."

"How is it yours?" I take a step toward Hope. For long moments, no one speaks. The air is thick with the thing Hope hates the most—pity.

Hope's gaze falls on Maeve, who's watching her with a tenderness that almost—almost—makes me want to trust Maeve too. You can't look at someone with that much affection if you're actively trying to hurt them, can you?

"You'll have another chance." Maeve sets a gentle hand on Hope's arm. She shoots me a meaningful look and announces she's going to meditate by the water. Hope and I are alone again.

When I reach for Hope, she steps into my embrace like it's the most natural thing in the world. My arms wrap around her waist as her hands slide around my neck. "Are you okay?" I breathe into her hair, which smells like fire smoke, and think of our first night here.

We promised to take care of each other. What started as a joke has taken on gravity.

The words I should have said outside that bar in Newport churn somewhere in the pit of my stomach. It's an effort to drag them past the sharp edges of my bad choices.

"I understand why you won't say 'I'm sorry.' But, Hope, Brandon knows you didn't mean what you said, even if you can't tell him. The fact that you stayed is all the proof anyone needs."

The bonfire crackles. Hope startles. She looks toward the flames, half her face bathed in light, the other half concealed.

She shakes her head. "That's the thing. I did mean it." Her voice is hollow, sending chills shivering down my spine. "I lied."

"What?"

"I lied to you. I told you I didn't mean what I said to Brandon—but I did. I did want a break. Maybe even more. Everyone thought Brandon and I were destined for forever, and so that's what I thought I wanted. But I always felt like I was living someone else's life, and I just—I loved Brandon, with my whole heart. But I wasn't in love with him anymore. That night was the first time I'd said it out loud to him. And it was the last thing he heard."

My heart squeezes. "Hope, you're allowed to want something different. You're allowed to choose something else."

"I don't want to be absolved of my guilt." Her gaze lifts to mine, full of disbelief.

"What can I do?" I would give anything to fix this for her.

"Please just let me go. I need to be alone." She steps back again. Disappears into the darkness.

And this is what it feels like to be the one left behind.

29
HOPE

That fleeting hour before night gives way completely to day used to be our favorite time of day. It was when I used to crawl into bed after a long night shift and Brandon would curl his body around mine before he'd have to get up and go to work. Brandon and I spent that entire hour talking about everything and nothing as gray light filtered into our bedroom. Sometimes we listened to birds chirping, sometimes to the sigh of the garbage truck rumbling down the street. Sometimes we just listened to each other breathe, matching our breaths by instinct rather than choice.

It was our hour, our time to be just Hope and Brandon—not sister, son, nurse, lawyer, all the things that made it hard to remember who we were.

All the things that broke us. That had been breaking us for months.

"I want a break." I wanted more than a break. I wanted a new life.

Be careful what you wish for, I guess.

The few early risers walking the streets flash me strange looks—maybe because I'm wearing last night's clothes and makeup, or maybe because the truth I've been trying to hide is now at the surface.

Brandon and I weren't soulmates. Our story wasn't special. We were just two people who fell in love as kids and got caught up in the story everyone else wrote for us.

The air around me thins as I get closer to Birch. Blood roars in my ears, and each step is an effort. My aimless drifting has not been aimless. I'm done walking . . . and running.

Goose bumps prickle along my skin as I spot the bench in the corner. My breath saws in and out of me as images and moments come—the same ones that haunt my dreams and the hours that I haven't been able to fill with work.

On the street, cars follow a familiar traffic pattern. The traffic light—*the* traffic light—flashes from red to green. A blue van honks at the driver of the white sedan that's first in line to go. The driver, a teenage boy, pops his head up from his phone and presses down hard on the gas, overcompensating for not paying attention.

The wheels screech as they work to find purchase on the gravel. It's not brakes squealing, but the sound sends my stomach to my toes. The world feels as if it's narrowed to just the intersection.

My legs threaten to give, and I drop onto Brandon's bench. A plaque with his name and birthday gleams to the right of where I've sat. The town erected this as a tribute to the loss of one of their own. I should have come to see it earlier.

I sit back and stare at the spot of the accident, letting the memories come, letting myself remember all of it.

Brandon was wearing a blue-and-yellow-striped button-down shirt that set off the golden hues in his brown eyes. It was his favorite shirt, the one he'd been wearing when he proposed, and he'd started calling it his lucky shirt.

His lucky shirt, which was stained with his blood after the accident.

An invisible fist reaches into my chest and squeezes my heart. A familiar urge to clamp down on the memories grips me. But I don't. I can't. The lock keeping the memories buried broke at Maeve's.

I let myself remember my anger. How hurt I was that Brandon had stopped seeing me. How terrified I was that I had stopped seeing Brandon. How heartbreaking it was to admit this life that we both believed was our destiny actually wasn't.

I let myself remember how I told him I wanted a break, and the way he turned to me, looking at me as if I'd slapped him. And then that split second that changed everything.

It happened fast, but in my memory, it's slow motion. I see the truck barreling toward us. Some part of me knew the truck wasn't slowing down and I needed to warn Brandon. To save him. And I did. I shouted his name. It was too little, too late.

My voice was drowned out by the squeal of brakes, and then metal crunching against metal. He didn't hear me. He didn't know I wanted to save him. Then I woke up in the hospital.

And the world was still spinning.

It was the cruelest discovery: that life could continue to go on. That the world had not stopped, though my world had.

My world never restarted. All the ways I thought I've been living since Brandon died have been a lie. I have built nothing, not a home, not even a shadow of a real life. Instead, I've been running. Not the way Will did when he picked up and took off. But from the truth and the accident and my grief and my guilt.

I don't know how long I'm sitting there with the contents of my dark box strewn around my consciousness before I realize I'm not alone.

"I never expected to find you here," Tessa says.

My throat tightens. "I didn't expect to find you here either."

Neither of us says anything for a long moment. Tessa's anger has softened, but it's still there, still billowing off her in a way that makes her feel too far. Beyond reach, even.

"I'm sorry that I ditched you at the bar. I ran into Selena at her baby shower, but that's not an excuse." I slide a glance toward her. "I'm sorry about Maeve too."

A muscle tenses in Tessa's jaw, but she relaxes her shoulders, releasing a huge sigh. "I get why you did. I cannot even imagine what it must be like to go through every day without Brandon. I just—" She turns to me, eyes lined with shimmery tears. "I just miss you, Hope. I miss my sister, and I've been missing her for more than two years."

Tessa's words swirl around me as I try to make sense of them, but they remain blurry and out of reach. "What do you mean? I'm right here. I've always been right here."

That's been the problem. I'm right here, and Brandon is not. I survived, and he did not.

"No, you're not. I didn't just lose a brother-in-law the day Brandon died, Hope. I lost my sister too. You haven't been the same. You've been a shell. You and I—we used to . . . we'd go to Newport together and check out the latest hot restaurant, and we'd run 5Ks, and we'd . . . we'd have fun." Her words catch. "We don't anymore. Because *you* didn't die at this corner, but the thing that makes you, you did. It's like a light went out. That's why I'm here. This is where I go when I miss my sister, to this corner—the place I lost her."

"Brandon died. My husband, my first love, died. I will never be the same. I will always be changed and different."

The traffic light shifts to red, and a car comes to a screeching halt. The sound of brakes squealing lingers in the air long after the car has stopped, and I brace myself against the terror that comes.

Tessa touches a hand to mine. Emotion crashes over me but doesn't drag me away. I can still breathe.

"I don't expect you to be who you were before the accident. I know you won't be. But you haven't tried to *be* anything. You've just let yourself fade, done the bare minimum to survive." There's no bitterness in her voice, just a sadness that molds perfectly to the edges of my grief. "If you want to get your master's degree in nursing, apply to the program. Or don't. If you want to go to Greece to study Greek literature. Go. Do it. Just stop not doing. Stop going through the motions, and start living."

Tessa has said these words to me so many times, in so many ways. So has Maeve. So has Will.

Living with Logan and working endless double shifts all felt like movement. I don't know what else to do, if not that.

I'm in the exact same spot I was in the days after Brandon died—a bit less weepy, but just as unmoored.

"I miss my sister who used to leave brochures from exotic places she wanted to visit, who quoted obscure Greek poetry, who'd show up at my house without warning for a spontaneous beach day. God, I even miss the way you made every party a theme party when you hosted."

"I don't know how to do any of that anymore. I don't . . . it's not fair that I get to live and Brandon doesn't." My voice comes out small. "That's why I went to Maeve. I need Brandon to forgive me. Tell me it's okay. And he didn't." The admission is a dagger through the center of my heart. "Maeve told me to find my locket. She told me if I did, I'd find what I needed. Brandon didn't come, though."

The moment when Maeve said someone else's name felt like losing Brandon all over again. It felt like some part of me was dying all over again.

"Maybe it did work." Tessa's voice pulls me back from the edge I crawled toward.

"What if the locket did bring you what you need and what you need isn't Brandon. What if what you need is to face that Brandon's gone? Or to forgive yourself for being the one to survive."

Hearing Maeve's words in Tessa's voice is a firecracker exploding beneath my rib cage.

She turns to me, her expression fierce. "Something has changed in you these last few weeks. You're going out, you're working less. I haven't seen you so bright and happy in a long time. But we both know it wasn't Maeve who made that happen. It was you. And whatever you've been doing, that's what you need to do. Every day. Even if it's hard. I'll be there every step of the way."

I swallow against the barbs in my throat. My eyes fill with tears again. "I have been happier."

My heart twists. "Even admitting that feels like a betrayal. How can I feel joy or happiness or love when Brandon can't?"

"It's not a betrayal. It's moving forward. No one is telling you that you have to forget Brandon. I loved him, too, and I never want to forget him. But you didn't die, Hope. You lived, and it's okay to live. Not because you owe it to Brandon. You don't. You don't owe it to Brandon. You don't owe it to me, to Mom, to anyone. You owe it to yourself."

The truth of her words cracks open something I didn't even know was tightly nailed shut inside my heart.

"I don't know how."

Tessa exhales a teary laugh. "Oh, I have some ideas. Starting with that closet you call a bedroom and ending with Will."

My teeth scrape my lower lip. A feeling that's become all too familiar rises up inside me. "Will's not an ending, though, Tessa. He's just a fling."

"Is that what you want?"

A lump climbs up my throat, and I nod. "He's not here forever."

"You're allowed to believe in a happy ending," she says, as if reading my mind.

"I'm working on that."

We have so long still to go to heal our relationship, but it's a start. A step forward.

Tessa nudges me with her shoulder. "I owe you for planning Noah's party, by the way. You and Will made a good impression on the baker. He's throwing in a few dozen red velvet cupcakes."

My chest fills with a laugh and a sob. "That was all Will. He worked some magic on that snooty baker. He might want to be a writer, but he was born to be in the hospitality industry."

Tessa smiles warmly. "You sound like you when you talk about him. Brandon would want that."

For the first time, her words don't grate on me.

Tessa and I sit for a while longer in silence before she checks the time. Her nail polish matches mine. "I should go. Emma has soccer in a few hours, and I'm sure neither she nor Noah have any idea where her cleats are." She rolls her eyes, but the expression is marked by love. Tessa wouldn't give up any of it for the world.

With all my heart, I hope she never has to. I hope the randomness and cruelty of the universe pass over her.

Of course, there's no way to ensure that. Bad things happen. The more people you let in, the more you can lose.

30
WILL

"I see you've made a friend," Maeve says, appearing from behind the veil of mist twining through her garden. Above her, a purple-black sky slowly dissolves into pinks and oranges. "Icarus likes you."

"He's a needy little thing," I tell her, looking down at the bluebird that has been perched on my armrest since before sunrise, keeping vigil right alongside me.

For nothing, as it turns out. Hope never returned to Maeve's.

"Here. You must be exhausted." She climbs the steps up her porch and extends a black mug with white lettering that reads LIVING MY BEST LIFE!

"What is it?"

Maeve sits in the rocking chair across from me eating gummy bears. "Coffee. No additives."

A sniff confirms it's coffee. I bring it to my lips and hesitate.

Maeve breathes a laugh. "You don't trust me, do you?"

"Of course I do." Exhaustion drills through my bones and my lies. The bluebird pecks at my free hand. I take a small sip. It tastes buttery and spicy and, most importantly, strong.

"I have an ear for lies. I suspect you do too." Maeve leans forward, fixes her pale eyes on me. "Only one of us has lied to the other, and I still trust you."

"I haven't—"

"A mutual friend of ours would argue that a lie by omission is still a lie."

A breeze ruffles Icarus's feathers. Early-morning sunlight stabs into the space separating Maeve and me. The angle of the light makes her skin appear translucent, as if she's been carved from glass.

"When did you figure it out?"

"From the moment you crested the hill that first night. Your mother is truly an excellent photographer and artist. She captured your likeness expertly."

"You didn't say anything."

"I assumed you had your reasons, and I wanted to respect that."

I sit back heavily. The porch creaks under the added weight of new awareness. "I thought you stole money from my mother. Maybe even brainwashed her to leave for some nefarious reason I haven't figured out yet."

It's a relief to give voice to the accusation. For the first time since that conversation with Bailey, the maelstrom in my head quiets.

"Aah, so you were investigating me." Maeve crooks a finger, and the bluebird lifts and glides toward her. "What's your conclusion? Do you think I did it?"

"You have my mother's ring."

"I didn't take her money." Maeve holds my gaze, and against my better judgment, I believe her. As if eyes that colorless couldn't hide lies. "Your mother sent me something a few days ago. Now that we're being honest with each other, would you like to see it?"

Maeve rises. The bluebird soars into the thinning mist.

"I guess he's healed," I say, following Maeve into the cottage on legs that feel weak with exhaustion.

"Mm," Maeve says.

"You don't think so?"

She raises an eyebrow at the challenge in my voice, which surprises me too. "I think appearances can be deceiving."

Maeve leads me into the kitchen and opens a drawer. Inside, there's a purchase agreement for a building near the edge of town and a blueprint for something that looks like a café.

Maeve ignores my questioning look and pulls out a thin stack of postcards. Each comes from a different city. Each is signed only with the initials H. G. Except the last postcard, which is postmarked two weeks ago.

This made me think of you. H. G.

"My mother sent you this?"

Maeve nods. "She's staying at an energy-healing resort in Arizona run by a friend of mine. Very off the grid. Even the best PIs in LA couldn't find them."

An apology sticks in my throat, but Maeve waves it away. "Look at the card, Will. I think she was hoping this one would make its way to you."

"She could have called me. Or returned my calls." Or turned on her phone.

I flip over the card, and Maeve's tree—no, a crab apple tree with carved names similar to the one here—is pictured on the front. The only legible word on the postcard tree is *Hope*.

"Not exactly a subtle message." I raise an eyebrow, and Maeve arranges her face in a picture of innocence.

"I didn't tell her a word. I guess it was a mother's instinct."

For the thousandth time, I check my phone. A no-service signal glares back at me from the top right.

Maeve glances out the window. The sun has lifted above the horizon, burned away the last of the mist. "Hope isn't coming back. I thought she might too."

"Do you know where she could be?"

Maeve shakes her head.

"Why didn't you summon . . . whatever you call it . . . Brandon for Hope? You broke her heart."

Maeve dims. "It doesn't work like that. I can't summon someone. They have to want to come."

"Couldn't you—"

"Lie? Fake it?" Icarus taps against the kitchen window, and Maeve opens it. "No, Will, that's not what I do."

The bluebird swoops around the kitchen, weaving through a pair of butterflies. I duck out of his way—and God, I hate birds.

"I—you're right. I shouldn't have said that. But . . . she was heart-broken." The heartbreak streaked across her expression is branded into my memory.

"She was. She is." Maeve reaches into the drawer and hands me Hope's locket. "When you find Hope, can you give this back to her? It didn't do what she'd hoped it would do, but that doesn't mean it's useless."

I take the locket from Maeve. Up close in the light, the diamond is colorless and clear and worth far more than my mother's ring. "You're not keeping it?"

"For what?" Maeve shakes her head. Her fingers are conspicuously ringless. "The necklace belongs to Hope. She gave it to me because she thought it might call forth Brandon's energy. Now that I'm sure it won't, I don't need it."

"You have Ashley's ring. And my mother's."

"Ashley asked me to find someone to give the ring to, someone who could use it for luck. I'll do that for her. And your mother—well, you'll have to ask her. Now go. Get coffee you won't pretend to drink—Hope probably needs one too. And tell your brother I said hello. I've been worried about him."

"My brother?"

Maeve cocks her head. "He didn't tell you he'd been staying with me?"

Fatigue has only made me hallucinate once before—I'd been driving eighteen hours straight and started seeing winged specters on the side of the road. I'd blink, and they'd clear, only to return moments later at the next mile marker.

Three blinks later, this hallucination hasn't cleared. She's perfectly crafted—a hallucination in high-def.

I blink again, and the woman barreling toward the Friendly Bean's front door, phone pressed to her ear, looks up just in time to avoid a collision with me.

"Will," she says, coming to a stop. "I was just calling you."

I hold up the two coffees in my hand. "I couldn't answer."

"I see that." Hope licks her lips, and it's the absolute wrong time to notice the rosebud set of her mouth. "I was calling because . . . I need to talk to you about last night. I'm sorry I walked away from you like that. I—"

"I get it. I'm sorry I didn't come after you. I should have—wait, are we saying 'I'm sorry' now?"

"I think we are. I think we—" She takes a step toward me and goes still. Her gaze lifts and snags on something behind me. I follow the direction of her gaze and see a few dozen sets of eyes trained on us.

On us in our clothes from last night. Hope has a leaf trapped in her ponytail—again. The reflection in the Friendly Bean's storefront window reveals a smudge of ash on my cheek. My clothes have the telltale creases of a night spent on a porch swing.

I reach up and take the leaf from her hair. "I guess you've been up all night too?"

She nods. "Clearing my head."

"Why don't we take a walk? Here, this is yours." I hand her the coffee Maeve suggested I order for her. "Extra milk and two packets of that gross yellow sweetener, right?"

She shakes her head and accepts the coffee. "You didn't have to do that."

"To be honest, it was Maeve's idea."

Hope laughs a little. "It's weird how she does that."

"Very." More weird is how Darren ended up staying with her. That's a question I've filed away for later, when I have the emotional bandwidth to deal with the guilt associated with the fact that Darren ended up staying with her, not me.

She drops her chin to her chest. "Will . . ." She blows out a breath.

"You don't have to say anything, I understand."

"No, you don't understand." She exhales sharply and breathes a laugh. "Oh, this sounded better in my head."

I turn to face her and am struck again by the perfect lines of her face.

"Last night—"

My phone rings, the noise cuts across my thoughts like a blade across metal. "Shit. It's my brother. He never calls . . . he . . ."

"Answer," she says, her mouth pressing into a worried line. "It's family."

The voice on the other end is loud and stern.

"Sir, this is Officer Thompson. Your brother's been taken to Kingsette Memorial. He was found passed out on the side of the street. You were listed as his emergency contact in his phone."

"Is he okay?" My voice cracks.

Hope steps closer. Her nearness is a balm to the jagged edges of the officer's words.

"I'll be right there."

"You don't have to come with me. I can drop you off on my way." My voice sounds sufficiently earnest, even though the last thing I want to do is walk into that hospital by myself.

"No, I'm going with you. I may be able to get you better answers than you would get on your own." Her chin lifts, and she sets her gaze on the road ahead.

Her support makes whatever words I should say in gratitude stick in my throat.

Hope stays quiet, looking determinedly ahead. The silence between us teems with her resolve. It's a backstop against my spiraling nerves. I drive as fast as I can. Kingsette and all its trivial problems blur into the background.

She directs me to the visitor's lot. Signs point the way, too, but they don't register half as well as her voice. Her steady presence.

Later, I'll need to examine why I need her steady presence so badly, why I feel so unsteady in the first place. Darren and I aren't that close. And based on how disheveled and wild he was when I last saw him, I could have guessed that a police officer might one day call to tell me he'd been passed out at a bus stop. Yet it feels as if everything around me has turned inside out and upside down. Everything except Hope.

She waves to the security guard, who does a double take. "Are you working on your day off again?"

She flashes a thousand-watt smile. "I am not, as a matter of fact. Just helping my . . . Will. His brother got brought in earlier today."

Bill's expression changes, similar to the way Hope's did when the officer called. Like she was ready to rush in to save the day, do what needed to be done. My instinct has always been to turn the other way.

It's an effort not to give into that instinct as Hope leads me to the ICU.

Anxiety, raw and sharp, throbs through me. I keep my attention fixed on Hope's back—the set of her shoulders and her confident stride—to keep myself grounded. I hate hospitals. This hospital, specifically. The way the air moves through the vents like a constant funeral song. The way it smells—like sweat and antiseptic. The way it keeps standing, even though the rest of the world has crumbled.

Hope stops in front of a room near the corner and turns to me. "You go in, and I'll find a nurse to talk to."

I nod, though I want to grab her hand and pull her inside with me. No, I want to grab her hand and race out of here, go back to poaching bartenders and impressing her with my limited Kingsette social savvy, and . . . none of that is really an option either. If we weren't here, we wouldn't be there either.

She walked away from me. She asked me to let her go.

Hope slides open the door, and I enter, instantly missing her.

Beeps and shrieks from the machines monitoring my brother greet me. A machine for his heart. One for his blood pressure. Another for—I don't even know. I swivel around, but Hope is gone.

Darren lies in the bed. The blanket pulled over him hugs his torso, revealing narrow shoulders and bone-thin arms. Shrunken even from the man who I saw just weeks ago. A deep-purple bruise circles his right eye. A bandage across his left cheek completes the tableau.

The only other time I saw Darren with a black eye was when he'd fought some older kid who'd been bullying me. Our mother didn't punish Darren. Instead, she told him violence wasn't the answer, but that sometimes rules had to be broken. We went out for ice cream afterward.

The thought of her makes my jaw clench.

My mother should be here. She should be here for her son. She should be here to take care of things at her Inn. She should be here to pay back her loan, deal with her staff that's abandoning ship faster than I can keep track, and fix everything that's broken.

Hope and a doctor find me pacing the room.

The doctor explains how Darren was found, the condition he was in, and the medications they administered. Her words go in one ear and out the other. Overdose. Stomach pump. Permanent damage. I catch just enough to understand. He's stable now and will be monitored overnight.

"He may be discharged as early as tomorrow afternoon, but I suggest he not go straight home," the doctor says, handing me two sheets of paper. "He needs a treatment facility, or he'll end up right back here."

I thank her, and Hope walks with her to the doorway. They exchange a whispered conversation, and then Hope returns, dimming the lights on her way toward me. She pulls over the second chair and sits beside me, as if she has nowhere else to be.

Like in the car, her silent company feels like a grounding. Or maybe like the calm in the eye of the storm.

Cool air hums through the vents. Hope shivers and then smooths Darren's blanket. His fingers flutter at her tender touch.

Memories rush up like floodwater. The rattle in my father's lungs as he struggled for breath. The small light my mother kept on in the evening as she sat vigil by his bedside night after night. The hole Darren punched through the wall. The hollow hiss of a last breath.

"My dad died in the hospital," I say, because giving voice to the words that are drowning me feels like reaching for a lifeboat. "He was diagnosed with lung cancer when I was twelve, went to the hospital— this hospital, actually—and never came out."

Darren's heart rate monitor shrieks, the numbers climbing as if he's remembering the same moment.

"Darren was never the same. I mean, none of us were. But Darren . . . it was too much for him. He started stealing liquor, and I started covering for him. I think I knew it was bad, but he seemed so fine most of the time, and I thought . . . I thought I'd know when he hit the tipping point. Or someone else would know and they'd pull him back, but it doesn't work like that."

"You and Darren had to grow up fast."

"It's not an excuse. You and Tessa had to—"

"I'm not feeding you an excuse. I'm not saying you can't or shouldn't feel guilty. I am saying you did the best you could with what you knew as a kid. Now you know different, and you have the choice to do different. If you want to show up for Darren, show up. See him for who he is, though, not who you think he can be or used to be."

I frown. "You sound like Maeve when you lecture me."

She grins, flashing all her teeth. "Young widowhood made me wise, what can I say?"

My heartbeat finds a new rhythm, the inverse of the one it has played my entire life.

Hope turns serious. "What do you need right now?"

I press my elbows into my knees and cradle my head in my hands. "I don't know, but I imagine asking for a strong drink wouldn't be appropriate at this moment."

Hope breathes a surprised laugh, and I want to hold on to the lightness of the sound in this dense room.

"Sorry, that joke was probably in poor taste."

She waves off my apology. "Wisdom and morbid humor are my widow superpowers. The darker the better. You should see some of the memes my online widow group shares."

She begins to describe some of the memes and jokes she's heard from her online widow tribe, as she calls them. Her stories fill in the space between beeps so that my thoughts can't take over. It's the kindest thing anyone has done for me in a long time.

Around midnight, she's exhausted her stories. She curls her legs up underneath herself, somehow fitting her entire body onto the small square of the chair. I don't know how one person can make herself that small and still fill a room.

Darren stirs. His eyes flutter open, and he groans. I lean forward, "Darren? Can you hear me?"

He mumbles something incoherent, and one of the machines monitoring his vitals hits a high note. I shoot a glance at Hope.

"It's okay," she says, though her attention never shifts from the screen.

"You're at the hospital. They had to—" The words get caught in my throat. "They had to pump your stomach, and you've got some nasty cuts and bruises, but the doctors said you'll be fine. Probably hurting for a few days, but okay."

"You came." Darren's voice is like nails against sandpaper, and weak. Still, that note of surprise breaks through and shatters me. Even in this state, his instinct was to assume I wouldn't come. That I would run in the opposite direction.

His eyes drift closed.

"Darren?"

His head lolls to the side; a quiet snore slips from his mouth.

Something in my chest deflates. I feel heavier than I did a moment ago.

"He knows you're here," Hope says, as if she knows exactly what I need to hear. The concern in her voice shatters me further.

I'm not sure I deserve that concern.

"It never should have come to this. My mother gone, the Inn barely holding on, my brother—"

A machine beeps. The rail-thin body barely visible underneath the white sheet doesn't stir.

"Will, this isn't your fault."

It is, though. I was too little, too late.

I need space. I need air. The walls of the room press in closer, and too much energy pulses in my bones. I can't sit here. Doing nothing for Darren, failing him. The same way I've failed so many other people in my life. My father. My mother. Even my agent, when I ran out of town the moment things stopped going the way I'd planned.

I'm up and running, my legs moving toward the exit as if propelled by muscle memory.

I turn left and right, hardly seeing where I'm going. An exit sign glows in the distance, but it doesn't seem to be getting closer.

Her voice reaches me before she does. A featherlight touch grazes my arm. My body comes to a stop.

Green eyes the color of stormy seas lock onto mine. "You didn't let me run alone. I won't let you either."

She's forgetting that I did let her go. I didn't keep going after her. But her arms wrap around me, and I can't bring myself to remind her. She holds me to herself, anchors me to the place I need to be.

My arms wrap around her as if they have done so a thousand times before. She fits perfectly against my chest. When my heart rate slows, I find the words I should have found so many times before. "Thank you for being here. I couldn't do this alone."

"You're not alone," she says, the vibration of her words rippling across my chest. "I'm right here."

She looks up at me. Her lashes dust her cheeks when she blinks. I want desperately to read the expression on her face. Reading people has always been my talent, but Hope is the exception.

"There's nothing more for you to do tonight," she says. "We should go."

The events of the night puncture the bubble we created in these stolen moments.

"Oh. Yeah. I'll . . . drive you home." It's the last thing I want to do.

"No, not home," she says and takes my hand. "My turn. Will you trust me this time?"

31

HOPE

A full moon brightens the night, casting a luminescent white glow over half of Kingsette, leaving the other half drenched in darkness. Luckily for us, we have the light. The same way we did that first night one month ago.

"Tell me again why we're on the roof-deck?" Will arranges us on cushions against the wall of the Inn's roof-deck and smooths a blanket over our laps before opening up the bottle of wine he grabbed on our way up.

"You took me to the Ferris wheel when I needed a place to escape. I'm taking you to the roof-deck. Best place in Kingsette to stargaze, and you seemed like you needed space to breathe."

"Back to where this all began," he says, pouring a glass of wine into a red plastic cup he also picked up on the way to the roof.

"At least we've upgraded and aren't drinking straight out of the bottle," I say.

He chuckles, and we clink Solo cups.

"And you're not using cheesy pickup lines about generous pours. What was it you said?" I slide my gaze in his direction, my lips already twitching up with the start of a laugh. "'Beautiful women never have to thank me for generous pours.'"

"Hey! Low blow!" He nudges me with his elbow. "That's definitely not what I sounded like."

"Oh, there's a good chance you did. I got whiplash from how fast you went from directing me to the gazebo to hitting on me."

He laughs, a full, deep sound that vibrates down my entire body. "I was just trying to keep up. One minute you're sweet and sad—the next you're all temper and sass."

Heat floods my cheeks. Of course he hadn't forgotten. "Fair. Not my finest moment."

"I might disagree with that." The look he attaches to that claim makes my toes curl.

A measured silence crawls between us, heavy with all that's happened. For long minutes, we drink and it's just easy, like slipping into another life I've always belonged to. The lake and hospital and all that happened and didn't happen tonight feel impossibly far away.

"Are you ready to talk about the other night?" Will asks with heartbreaking tenderness after we've both finished our first glass.

"Are you ready to talk about what happened tonight?" I ask, arching a brow.

"Touché."

"Can we just pretend for a little while that none of it happened?" The wine he brought is light and sweet and exactly what I need to calm the storm of my thoughts. I'll have to face it all soon enough. But not yet.

Will nods and lifts a finger to the sky. He points out obscure constellations and stars, and I'm so grateful for his chatter, for this moment when we're safe from it all.

"Tell me about the astronomer in Dublin who taught you about stars."

"You remember that line, huh?"

"I remember a lot of what you say."

He blows out a breath. "It was my dad on a trip to visit family in Dublin. He was into space and stars. I think the biggest disappointment of his life was when neither Darren nor I were that excited about a space camp he'd found. He thought it was the greatest thing in the world, and we didn't."

"You miss him a lot, huh?"

He turns to me, a crease forming between his brows as if he hasn't considered this before. "I guess I do. I don't talk about him much. Except with you."

"I can't tell if that's a good thing or a bad thing. I don't mean to dredge up old memories."

"No, I like that you do. I've been running from the memories and the feelings too long. Maybe I need to finally confront them head on." He studies my face like it's a puzzle he's trying to solve. "I got scared when my dad died. It made everything feel unsafe. I thought leaving Kingsette would make that feeling go away."

"That sounds familiar," I say, my pulse ticking up at the vulnerability laid bare on his handsome face. "Do you want to tell me about him?"

For a while, he tells me stories. About his dad and nights that they camped under the stars, how sometimes his mom came with them and how she hated the mud and the cold, but inevitably would be the one making the s'mores to keep them awake just a little longer.

Every inch of me melts into his stories, the pictures that he paints with his words. Will might be the best storyteller I've ever met, and I can't imagine a time that I'd be sick of hearing him talk.

"There was this one time that my dad convinced my mom to drive cross-country. He'd always wanted to see the country, but my mom worried about the Inn. He used every trick in the book to get my mom to agree. He recruited Darren and me to draw pictures—we'd leave maps for her with cool sights circled . . . whatever he could think of.

"My mom finally agreed. We packed for days. The car was stuffed to within an inch of its weight limit. I mean, the back bumper skimmed the road. My dad couldn't see a thing out the back window. When we drove up a hill, Darren and I would lean forward to take some pressure off the back."

I laugh, able to visualize a young Will and Darren leaning forward, believing they're helping. As he talks, I graze his fingers with mine.

"About a day into the drive," he continues, "the car breaks down."

"Oh no," I say.

"Oh yes. By this point, we're in the middle of nowheresville, there's not a car in sight, Darren's feeling carsick, my mom is terrified, my dad is angry—we're all arguing. Full dysfunctional family meltdown. Then my dad just stops and points to the sky, to the clouds that look like blankets of fire across the horizon and the deep blue leaching into the bright orange. He said, 'Even if this is as far as we get, this is all I need to see with you.'"

Warmth filters through my chest, trickles down to my toes. "He was a great guy."

"He was." Will's mouth splits into a mischievous grin. "Although he did ruin the moment about thirty seconds after that when he ran away screaming because a spider had crawled up his arm."

Even as I laugh, my heart breaks for all Will has lost, how much death has taken from him. From me. Would Will have felt compelled to run away if his father hadn't died? Would he feel responsible for his family's breakdown?

Would I be living a life so small I've left myself no room to breathe?

I don't realize that he's gone silent until the silence is filled with the sound of crickets.

"You're shivering," he says, pulling me from my reverie. "We can go inside if you're cold. I doubt hypothermia was in your plan."

"No, I'm okay." Inside is the last place I want to be. Inside I can't see the stars and sky and be reminded that there's so much world outside this moment. When Brandon first died, looking up at the sky made me feel insignificant, made me feel as if I was too small to take on the world by myself. But right now, the vastness of the sky feels like potential. And hope. And all the things that it felt like before Brandon died. It feels like if I go inside, I'll lose that again.

I turn to find his warm brown eyes fixed on me in a way that makes every nerve ending down my spine spark to attention. The moonlight accentuates the perfect angles of his face. My hand trembles slightly as I brush a lock of hair off his forehead.

He leans into my touch, and my breath catches. My body is humming as this man who runs, but has only ever run toward me, catches my hand. Logan's warning flickers in the back of my mind and then vanishes. I know Will. I know where his heart is going, and I'm okay with it.

"Hope, if we're being honest with each other tonight, I have one more confession."

I can't bring myself to blink, to do anything that might stop the flow of energy vibrating between us. Long moments pass. Maybe more than moments. My heart races so fast, it feels like it's made up of a thousand butterfly wings.

"Yes," I say, and oh God, my voice is huskier than it should be.

His focus dips to my mouth. Heat pools in my core, and it's not the cold making me shiver.

"I lied to you." His voice drops an octave, and all that heat rushes right back. If I tried to stand right now, I don't think I could. "When I called that kiss a mistake."

"Lied again? This is becoming a terrible pattern, I think." As I speak, I'm drawn closer, as if we're two stars who've finally come into each other's orbit.

"*Terrible* is a harsh word," he says. His breath skitters along my skin.

"You're the writer. What word would you suggest?" I breathe, and his answering breath mingles with mine.

"It depends on what you want. *Predictable*, as in 'predictable pattern,' if you're looking for alliteration. *Vicious*, if you're looking for exaggeration." His finger wraps around a lock of my hair. "What do you want, Hope?"

The question again.

I still don't know, but the answer feels closer. Like it's on the tip of my tongue.

I lean forward, and my lips brush his. He hesitates for only a fraction of a second before he kisses me back. Light, at first, and then deeper. I taste the wine on his lips, smell the night breeze on his skin.

Something that was building inside me erupts, pushing away everything except Will and his lips against mine. And then . . . the feel of his tongue as my mouth opens for him.

He pulls me closer, his fingers spreading along my lower back. I melt into his touch. We're a perfect tangle of lips and tongues and teeth. It's exhilarating and new and every sensation in between.

A sound escapes from the back of my throat, and his mouth presses harder against mine. His energy takes on an urgency that mirrors a growing flame in my chest.

He tastes of wine and late nights that should never end. In that moment, I know I don't want this night to end. I want to reach for the edges of the sky and wrap them around us, cocoon us in a blanket of stars and moonlight for as long as Will stays in it with me.

He pulls away, lips swollen and eyes glazed. "Hope."

My name is a breath on his lips. I know what he's asking, the choice he's leaving up to me.

Sensation explodes across my body as his hand slides up and down my spine and this—

This is what I've been missing for two years. The feel of hands on my body and breath mixing with breath. The feel of doing something for the now and not thinking about what it will mean later.

I pull him flush against me. "Will, I want this. I know you're leaving. I know this isn't—"

He captures my mouth with his, and his urgency is met with an equal amount of softness.

We kiss, and every time my thoughts knock against my consciousness, his hand and his lips find a new way to pull me back. To keep me just in my body. Just in this moment. His hand reaches under my shirt, and each fingertip is a lightning bolt on my bare skin.

He drags his mouth away from mine and alternates soft kisses along my jawline and down my neck with gentle nipping and scraping with his teeth. Every nerve ending ignites, shoots sparks of light and heat into places that I forgot.

A whimper escapes, and I feel his smile against my neck. "You're not worried about my boss wondering where I went this time?"

"Nah. He's a pushover, right?" I trace the line of Will's shoulder, feeling the corded muscle underneath.

Will laughs, a low, quiet sound, and floats a kiss to the hollow of my throat. "Exactly. Lets me get away with whatever I want."

"And what is it that you want, Will?"

His lips find mine again, and his hands reach for the hem of my shirt. We separate for only a moment. I answer the question in his eyes by lifting my arms. He grins and pulls my T-shirt off.

The heat of his attention on my skin burns away any thought besides those about him.

He swallows, eyes on mine, staring with open fascination. "God, Hope. Holy hell."

The reverence in his words makes my blood heat. My hands tremble as I unbutton his shirt. He puts a hand on mine, and I feel the question in his touch, the concern. I touch my lips to his in answer.

His hands fall to his sides, letting me take charge, go at the pace I need to go. After the last button, I slip the shirt off his shoulders, letting my hands move across his skin, across his sculpted shoulders. He shivers, with cold or restraint.

I slide a trembling hand down his chest, along his stomach. His skin is smooth and stomach taut. He hisses as my hand comes to a stop above the button of his jeans. We lock eyes, and his nostrils flare at whatever expression he sees on my face.

His fingers trace the curve of my hip. A current of electricity surges beneath the surface of my skin. I haven't felt this wholly in my body in years, and the sensation is like waking up from a deep sleep. Even my toes tingle.

I draw back slightly, needing to catch my breath as much as I need to make this moment last. "All those rumors about you leaving—and not one about what a good kisser you are," I tease. "I'm going to have to tell Annette. People need to know."

He strokes a lazy line up the side of my body. "You wouldn't."

"I don't know . . . I feel inspired to tell—"

He pulls me back toward him, and his mouth captures mine as his arms wrap around me, holding me close, holding me like he never wants to let go. Holding me like nothing in the world could ever make him let go. I forget whatever I was going to say.

He sweeps me up without breaking our kiss and lays me down on the blanket. I'm peering up at the endless sky, seeing stars. Our bodies are touching in a thousand different spots, and still it's not enough.

"Oh, God." The words come out in a rush as my hips reach up toward his.

"Hope. We—"

I lift my mouth to meet his, swallowing his *we*. His hand slides open the button of my jeans and pulls them down. My thoughts vanish, and again, it's just a thousand familiar and new sensations rippling through me. It's just this. Him and me and the way our bodies just fit.

His mouth lowers down my body, licking and sucking as he goes. He finds the birthmark on my hip and traces a line with his tongue to my belly button and back up to my breasts. My back arches, needing more. Needing him.

He moans, and the vibration roars through me. My body temperature rises, pressure building in my core. It's all I can do not to beg him for more.

More of this. More of Will. More of the pure delight of just feeling and not thinking.

I reach down for his pants, and this time, he doesn't wait for me to do it on my own. This time, his patience is hanging by a thread. But he's hanging on to it. For me. He lifts up just long enough to kick his pants all the way off and resettles himself onto me.

"Hope." It's a plea and a promise and a question.

"Will." It's the only answer I have, but it's the one he needs.

He lowers his mouth to mine, and then nothing else in the world matters. Not his questions. Not my answers. Not our names. Nothing. My eyes close, and the stars behind my eyes burn a thousand times brighter than the ones in the sky.

32
WILL

I haven't been able to stop thinking about Hope since she left early this morning with a promise to return.

I shouldn't have slept with her. It was too soon, too impulsive. I don't know what I was thinking. I wasn't thinking, obviously. It was stupid. Stupid and selfish and . . . life changing. Which is crazy. Everyone knows sex isn't life changing. Sex is just sex, regardless of what the actors, writers, producers, and directors make it seem like on the big screen.

But holy hell. Sex with Hope. I've replayed it in my mind a thousand times, and the memory doesn't seem to fade. Each time, it glows brighter.

Which is probably why my first interview for a new manager was a bust and why preparing for my second is next to impossible. The candidate isn't half-bad. Young, educated, and experienced—but something about her impressive résumé is lacking. I scan the education, experience, and languages spoken again, and it's only then that I see where the problem is.

She's a stranger.

She didn't grow up avoiding the second step on the back staircase because it creaked or playing hide-and-seek in the formal dining room, which was supposed to be off limits to Darren and me.

This is a family inn, and saving this Inn, restoring it to its glory, is a job for someone who sees the echo of their childhood inside these walls.

I think back over these last few weeks, from the wild bluebird debacle to the understaffed retirement party. Running the Inn is exhausting. There's always a new emergency that needs my attention, always a new disaster that we're barely skirting.

But some of the guys are starting to look at me like I know what I'm talking about when I speak. In town, people started saying "good morning" when I stop for coffee. And that night sky . . . I could live forever in a place where so many stars glow every night.

My phone vibrates, and my heart does a little dance, already imagining Hope's name on the screen. Some part of me starts picturing what it'll feel like to tell her I'm going to stay, that she can take all the time she needs, but that I'm here, with her.

The saner part of me is telling the other part to tone it down a notch. We had one night together. I can't assume Hope wants anything more than that.

Her text is nothing but a waving-hand emoji. My mouth splits into a smile picturing her sending that text, the adorable V her forehead would make as she decided what to send.

I send back a string of waving-hand emojis. We've come so far since that first kissy-face emoji.

See you tonight? I promised I'd go to Emma's soccer game this afternoon.

I type back: Definitely. I have a surprise for you.

Three dots appear. Then disappear. Then appear. Then disappear. Finally, her response comes. Can't wait.

Could I give up LA, my dream, for Kingsette?

No. I can't.

But staying in Kingsette with Hope doesn't feel like giving up a dream. It feels like making space for a new one, because maybe, the truth is, we're allowed more than one.

Three hours later, the receptionist at the hospital is looking at me with the head tilt Hope told me about. She's speaking in that measured, apologetic tone Hope complained about too.

All because Darren said no. He doesn't want to see me.

"I brought him clothes," I say, holding up the bag of clothes I packed from my mother's apartment.

The receptionist sets down her tea tumbler to reach for the bag. The infuser is stuffed with petals and broken twigs. "I'll see that he gets them."

"Will you tell him I came by? And that I'll be back again in a few days?"

She nods, as if resigned, as if she already knows the truth I know—a few days won't make a difference to Darren. "I'm sorry."

Hope was right. "I'm sorry" is boring.

"What's your tea for?"

The receptionist's face flushes. She slides the cup behind the computer screen. "I don't know what you're talking about."

Outside, I debate where to go. There's always work to get done at the Inn, but I haven't had a day off in forever. Maybe I can surprise Hope at Emma's game—see her in best-aunt-ever mode.

My attention snags on a woman being wheeled out by an attendant. She looks more annoyed than ill.

"My friend should be here any minute. She obviously should have left earlier. She knows there's traffic on Main at this time of day." The patient cranes her neck to see farther down the empty street.

Her hair is a tangle of limp knots hanging down her back. Her lips are pale without the ever-present shock of red they're always painted with. She's almost unrecognizable. Though I'd know that voice anywhere.

"Annette?"

Her gaze darts toward me, and within seconds, her face is buried in her hands and she's crying.

I never saw Annette cry before. Some part of me assumed she was incapable.

"Is everything okay?"

"Oh, Will. It's not." She lifts her face from her hands. Her makeup is smudged where her fingers held her face. "That awful woman poisoned me. Or she tried to. Luckily, I made it to the hospital in time."

"What?" My gaze lifts to the attendant. His expression gives nothing away.

"I know it was the tea Maeve gave me." The hardness in her tone doesn't fit with the tears.

I must have heard wrong. "You went to see Maeve? Why? I thought . . ."

She sniffs. "I just wanted to help. The whole town's changed since Maeve arrived. Even the sheriff's drinking her tea now. He hasn't been in for coffee in over a week. I thought it was time she and I had a face-to-face conversation. Woman to woman."

"I don't understand." The words she's saying are all familiar, but they aren't fitting together in a way that makes sense. "You actually went to—"

Annette begins to wail. "She tried to . . . she wanted to harm me."

No. Maeve wouldn't. Annette must be—

Rory's hand. Maeve's own admission that sometimes her teas do harm.

The warning bell from that long-ago conversation with Maeve begins to ring with insistence.

"It was so frightening. I drank it, and then suddenly felt so dizzy, like I might faint. And nauseous. And . . . Will, she's dangerous. More dangerous than I first thought." Annette's gaze finds mine, and her eyes widen. "Has Hope been drinking the teas? They've been spending so much time together, and she's so trusting. Who knows what terrible things Maeve's been slipping to Hope."

Hope. The warning bell becomes a war drum.

From the beginning, my instinct about Maeve was right. She was dangerous.

"Will, did you hear what I said? We have to work together to get her out of town. She's—"

"Dangerous. I know. I've seen her criminal—"

Annette's hand snaps to my wrist. "Criminal what? William, tell me what you know."

The promise I made Hope sits on the tip of my tongue. Terror fills my mouth. It's not that I don't trust Hope; she's just too close to see the truth. She's too good to see the bad in Maeve.

But I see it.

And Hope's not going to be the next sad story.

Not if I can help it.

For the first time, I'm not running away from a problem. I'm running headfirst to fix it.

33

HOPE

The bicentennial organized behind the high school is exactly as I imagined it. Balloons and streamers in Kingsette High's green and gold decorate the trees on the perimeter of the field. People mill about, red Solo cups in hand, while their children run wild, shrieking with laughter, throwing loose popcorn to the birds swooping down to eat. A raging, ill-advised bonfire crackles and snaps against the sky, carving rivers of heat across the field. Combined with the drought and the brooding sense of discontent in Kingsette, the air feels stifling.

The town has always felt like a tinderbox, one errant flame away from disaster.

Tonight, for reasons I can't pin down, it feels as though the flame's been lit.

For the hundredth time, I check my phone. Will hasn't texted since he told me he has a surprise for me. I don't know whether it's the idea of a surprise or his sudden silence that's making me feel restless.

"Hope! You're here." Annette Martina saunters up to me. Her teased blonde hair is styled to just barely hide everything her low-cut shirt is revealing.

"Hi, Annette. Great job on the bicentennial. Everyone is having a great time."

Elaine Roth

"Oh, I don't put in all this time and hard work for the thank-you. I just like to know my community is taken care of." She glances at Sheriff Wilson, who is standing at the perimeter of the field, speaking into a two-way radio, and frowns. "I don't turn my back on community."

"Of course. So gracious of you." I flash her a closed-lip smile. After what she's done to Will and the Inn, it's an effort just to share space with her. "I should find Tessa and the girls."

"Speaking of the community, have you heard the news about Maeve?"

"No, but I'd rather not—"

"Apparently she's got a criminal record—no surprise there—and a trail of other suspicious activity. There was awful business with a politician's wife, and I heard—" Annette pauses, her eyes gleaming with something resembling malice. "Will didn't tell you any of this? He's the one who hired the private investigator to look into Maeve."

"Will?"

Annette's eyebrows perk up. If she didn't know that Will and I slept together, then she does now. "Who knew he'd be this story's hero, right?"

"He wouldn't—he told you?"

Annette places a hand on my shoulder. "He must have wanted to protect you, but fret not. I'm already taking care of it. The first meeting of the Keep Kingsette Safe committee is tonight, in fact. Our first order of business will be to get that cottage condemned."

The rising tide of hurt pauses just long enough for the rest of Annette's words. "Maeve's cottage?"

"Yes. Once it's condemned, we expect she'll leave. I can't imagine anyone in town will rent to her."

No one will rent to her because Annette won't let them. Like she tried to stop people from working at the Inn.

"You can't do that."

Two little girls run past us. A pair of crows flutters behind them, scavenging the popcorn they leave in their wake.

"Oh, dear, Hope. I see that I've upset you. I know this must be hard for you. You're such a trusting thing." She pats my forearm. "Oh, speak of the devil."

"Annette," Will says, looking between us as if I'm the one who's been accused of spreading rumors. "You're looking much better than the last time I saw you."

"Hi, Will. I'm glad you could make it. Yes, I'm feeling much better, thank you for asking. And I was just telling Hope what your private investigator discovered about Maeve. Awful business. Really awful."

Behind us, the crows caw at a man shooing them away.

"You told her?"

He turns to me. "Hope, let me explain."

"You promised. You . . ." The words to describe the shattering happening inside my body don't exist.

"I had to break my promise. I—Annette was in the hospital, and she told me . . ." He drops his chin to his chest. "I wasn't thinking. I just panicked. I saw a problem and didn't want to run away. For you. I wanted to protect you."

"Protect me?" The sting of those words penetrates my chest. "Because I can't make my own decisions? Because I'm vulnerable?"

He lifts his gaze to mine. Will's expression is confirmation, and something in my heart collapses. "No, of course not. I just—"

His attention snaps to Annette, whose gaze is ping-ponging between us. "Can we talk about this somewhere else?"

Words don't come. Even if they did, I'm not sure I'd want to say them.

A flame snaps and stretches to the sky. For one bright moment, everything is clear—the field, the faces of the people watching us intently, the truth I should have known.

He pulls me to the side and puts his back to Annette.

"Hope." His voice feels like an arrow in my chest. "Please."

"I've told you from the beginning that I don't need you or anyone else to protect me." I taste the bitterness of my own words in the air. His mouth snaps closed, and I know that he does too.

"I care about you. You and I—"

"No, Will." Somehow my voice sounds steady, though distant. "There is no you and I. I thought we could be something for the little while you were here, but we're not even friends." The admission that I made to Tessa less than two days ago about my budding feelings for Will flashes through my mind. I drive it down, into that dark pit of memories that recently reopened because of Will. It fits easily in the newly vacated space. "Natalie was right about you."

"Hope."

It's a plea that I ignore without trouble because swirling around the ashes of that extinguished ember is another feeling. One I haven't let myself fully feel: anger.

Anger at Will. At Brandon. At the truck driver and Kingsette and the universe. The universe most of all.

The anger unfurls inside me, turns every breath ragged.

I turn on my heel and storm away before I say the words boiling through me. My breath comes in jagged rasps that will open into sobs later.

Behind me, crunching grass tracks Will as he comes after me. I don't look back. I move faster, pushed forward by muscle memory and the heat of the bonfire on my back.

It's not supposed to be this hard. We can't both keep running anymore.

I let Will catch up, because this needs to end.

Will reaches me. His eyes, full of desperation, hold mine. "Please listen to me," he says, breathless.

"I think I've listened enough." The venom in my voice makes Will stumble back a step. He winces, as if he's been wounded.

"What's that supposed to mean?" Will's nostrils flare.

He knows exactly what I mean, and he's going to make me say the words anyway.

"Last night shouldn't have happened." The words rise up from some vicious, angry place inside my chest. "You made me think . . . made me believe . . . after we—I—"

"After we what, Hope? Say what we did." His anger rises to meet mine, and it's an absurd relief to feel it pushing against mine, driving my anger hotter and higher.

"We did nothing, Will. It was just sex." My tongue feels coated with the sharp tang of bitter things and lies.

"That's all it was." His eyes have gone hard, cold. "It takes two, you know."

"Yeah, it takes two, unless one of them is lying and using the other." I step toward Will, fueled by the righteousness of my next words. "You were so worried about Maeve taking advantage of a vulnerable young widow—well, congratulations. You got to me before she did."

I pick my way across the field, past trees that are nothing but shadowy silhouettes, until I reach my car. I listen for Will.

He hasn't followed me.

He's not going to follow me. Because he told me himself—he's the guy who runs.

I was so wrong about him.

34

WILL

For the next week, I try to contact Hope a few thousand times. Her phone goes straight to voice mail. My text messages go unanswered. She's shutting me out. With good reason.

I can't get the expression on her face out of my mind. Stripped down to the most vulnerable layer. Pale and wild and brimming with the effort of holding herself together.

I did that to her.

I should have told her my concerns about Maeve the moment things between us changed. But—when was that exactly? When I kissed her in that bar? When I held her hand and told her she could trust me?

The moment I met her.

She won't forgive me. I felt her walls soar up around her, locking me out. By now, they've probably only been reinforced.

I don't blame her. I should have told her the truth.

Even the flower Maeve gave me is withering, failing because of my tendency to be too little, too late. It was thriving for a short while. I'm not sure what changed.

I pour water into the planter and then drop onto the couch in my mom's apartment, where I've stayed these last few days.

This was my surprise: that I was staying.

For Hope, but also because Kingsette has started to feel like home.

My phone beeps, signaling a voice mail. I didn't hear it ring, and as I reach for it, I have to tamp down the hope that it's Hope who called. Of course she didn't.

It's Darren's rehab facility, where he was transferred once he was stable.

I listen to the message, the financial coordinator returning my call confirming the bill's been prepaid for three months by a woman named Maeve. Which is strange to start with, and made stranger because the amount that's been paid is the exact amount that went missing from my mother's closed retirement account. It's too convenient to be merely a coincidence.

The financial coordinator ends the call by asking me to pass along a thank-you to the woman who's been leaving donuts and other treats at the nurses' station at each visit.

A click in the lock distracts me from the rest of the voice mail.

I bolt upright as my mother strides into her apartment, looking tan and rested and pulling in her suitcase. A man with salt-and-pepper hair trails in behind her, chuckling.

My jaw drops at the sight of her, this woman who I've been searching for, who just strolled in as if returning from a planned vacation.

They both freeze when they notice me.

My mother recovers from her surprise faster than I do. "Good morning, Will."

"Good morning?" I blink at the absurdity of the greeting. "That's it? Months of nothing and all you have to say is 'good morning'? Where the hell have you been?"

The man she entered with takes a protective step forward, and I round on him. "And who the hell are you?"

"Will, it's nice to see you too," she says and looks me up and down, assessing my bare chest and faded basketball shorts. She surveys the apartment next. My clothes are scattered throughout the living room. A pizza box with two congealed slices hangs open on the counter. Dishes sit unwashed in the sink.

I grab the T-shirt I discarded on the coffee table two nights prior and pull it over my head. It smells like tacos. Old tacos.

"I see you're still as messy as you were in high school."

"I've been busting my butt trying to keep this place afloat. The Inn is in debt because of you. Everyone quit." I reach for my phone and show her the missed call from the rehab place. "And Darren's in rehab."

Her hand goes to her heart, as if the news about Darren physically hurt. Some of the stress I'm so used to seeing in her face returns in the crinkles around her eyes. Guilt nibbles at the edge of my anger.

"Is he . . . how is he?"

Some vindictive part of me that wants all this to be her fault is ready to tell her that of course Darren's not okay. But another part of me, that part that understands needing to escape, that remembers how she tucked us into bed every night, even when she'd barely had a moment to herself all day. "He's in rehab. He . . . he needs a lot of help."

My mother's shoulders slump. "I'm glad he's getting it."

The man behind her steps up and puts a supportive hand on the small of her back.

"Who are you?" My words come out almost as a growl.

"My name is Mike. Your mother and I met in a photography class at the retreat." He holds out a hand.

"Photography?"

"Yes, Will. For once, I wanted to follow my heart, follow my passion. The way all those years ago I encouraged you to follow your own."

"Only after I had no choice."

Her hands come to her hips, and the look on her face is a mixture of disappointment and heartbreak. Maybe it's because her old photographs are hanging on the walls, but it takes only a moment to place where I've seen that look before—the day she quit her photography class, even though she loved it, because our dad had just died. She stepped up. For us.

Another memory presses forward. The same look of disappointment and heartbreak when I told my mom I'd been rejected from my top-choice local school and maybe I would push off college for a few years to stay and help her. After that, my mother started leaving film-school applications on the kitchen table. She started conveniently collecting boxes in the garage, which I used to pack up my stuff. She encouraged me in every way to go—I had just been too wrapped up in myself to hear. It's so clear now, it seems impossible that I was so oblivious.

Mike's unshaken hand drops in slow motion to his side.

I shake my head to release some of the pressure building behind my eyes. "It would have been nice if you'd told someone."

"I tried." My mother's voice doesn't rise to meet mine, which makes my hysteria feel out of place and uncalled for.

"You tried. When?"

"Every time I called you. You hung up on me so quickly I never had a chance to tell you how unhappy I was, how I needed a change."

"You just left, though. You didn't even check in." I hear the double standard in my words, and the quirk up of her eyebrows tells me she does too.

"I didn't just leave. I set everything up, and Terry was here to oversee things."

"Well, he quit and the Inn is falling apart. We're so far in debt . . ." I gesture vaguely to the suitcase behind her. "If you'd answered my calls, I would have told you that."

My mother turns to her companion, who looks at her with unfiltered compassion, with a promise in his eyes. She's not alone. He won't run, no matter what she admits.

"If I'd answered your calls, I would have come back. I would have dimmed my light, shrunk my dreams, again, to fit into a life that has become too small for me. But, Will, if I did that—again—I would have suffocated the last bit of light I had left inside me, and once that light's out, it's impossible to get it back. I just—I saw my future if I stayed here. It was lightless, and we need light. We're not meant to live our lives in dark, cramped spaces. Going off the grid is radical, but it felt like the only way to save my light, save my life."

The sunlight shifts, and my mother's face sharpens more fully into view. For the first time, I see her.

She sighs and looks me over. "You're an adult. The Inn was struggling, sure, but Terry was handling the accounts, and he assured me we'd be fine. And Darren—he was in a good place when I left. He even seemed happy. I thought there might even be someone special in his life."

"But you came back?" I ask.

My mother tilts her head and considers me, as if sizing up whether I can handle the truth.

"A little birdie told me I should. But mainly, it was time. I missed the Inn and Kingsette. I was worried about Darren. And mostly I realized that happiness is mine to claim wherever I am. I love running the Inn, but it doesn't have to be the beginning and end of my life. Leaving showed me what I was missing here. But also that I want both. A full life." She brings a hand to rest on Mike's wrist.

A thousand questions press on my consciousness, but there's one question that rises above the others. "Why does Maeve have your sapphire ring? Did you give it to her?"

My mother brightens, her eyes shining with amusement. "Do you think she stole it?"

My cheeks redden. "I don't know what to think."

"Yes, I saw the hoopla about keeping Kingsette safe around town as I drove through. I hope you haven't succumbed to that kind of groupthink. Your father and I raised you better than that."

Because I can't bring myself to admit the truth or make eye contact, I stare out the window.

"I see." She makes her way to the window and pulls the curtains the rest of the way open, flooding the room with light, before pushing open a window. Fresh air pours in. "That's better. It was smelling like a frat house in here."

"The ring?" I prod. I need to know. I need to know how wrong I was about all of it.

My mother whirls on me. "I gave Maeve that ring because I couldn't bring it with me, and I truly worried Darren might take it. It breaks my heart to admit that, but it's true. Even though he seemed better, I just . . ."

"You trust Maeve that much?"

She quirks an eyebrow. "You think you're a better judge of character? You think that despite all I've been through, the way I've led this family for decades on my own, that I'm incapable of seeing through a lie. You think she talked me into giving her tens of thousands of dollars and then encouraged me to disappear? Do you know me at all, William?"

Hearing the accusation that's been brewing in my mind, I see better the flaw in my reasoning. I've failed to give my mother any kind of agency, any responsibility for her choices. I've failed to take into account that my mother raised two boys by herself, kept one of Kingsette's most historic inns running by herself. I've failed to remember that my mother has never needed someone to save her. She's always saved herself.

They are nearly the exact same assumptions I made about Hope. The ones she has shown me time and time again aren't true. That her loss made her incapable of deciphering what was right for her. That I knew better. Knew what she needed. All because I thought I had done grief right by locking it up, instead of letting it take up space. As if that were strength, and not the other way around.

I didn't think I could feel lower than I had minutes earlier, but somehow I do.

"Maeve is like family to me now. For a long time this past year, she's been the only one who has been like family to me."

Her voice quiets as she lands this blow, which crashes into the soft space beneath my rib cage with stunning sharpness. The meaning is clear—Darren and I abandoned her, and Maeve hasn't.

"Maeve helped me realize that I'm allowed to live my life on my terms, like she does. She helped me contact your grandmother and your father, who both confirmed they wanted me to be happy, in whatever way that meant." A softness filters into my mother's expression. "I think for a long time I was afraid that living on my own terms would be a betrayal of your father. Once Maeve helped me get in touch with him, I realized I didn't need his permission to live. I just needed to give myself permission."

I think of all the days and nights my mother spent at the Inn. I took it for granted that she wanted to be there. All along, she just felt trapped. Like me. Like Darren. I should have asked.

"I'm sorry I wasn't there for you."

My mother approaches me and puts a soft hand on my cheek. "I'm sorry you've had so much on your shoulders because of me. But I'm so proud of how well you've kept it all standing." She takes a step back, nudging an empty Oreo package with her foot. "Mostly well, I should say. We probably should cover the basics of housekeeping."

She pauses and looks at Maeve's withering flowers on her windowsill. "And plant care. Assuming, that is, you're planning to stick around."

35

HOPE

A week passes. Then another. I can't bring myself to go to Maeve's. Luckily—or unluckily—the hospital's been unusually busy, so Lydia hasn't complained about my extra shifts.

Brandon didn't come.

Will betrayed me.

And Maeve—I'm not sure I know who she is anymore. I don't know what to make of the rumors that are supported by police reports.

All those truths hurt in ways that are wildly different and at the same time suspiciously similar.

A crystal Maeve gifted me scatters rainbows across the room, illuminating the piles of laundry, discarded water bottles, and books I started and never finished. Something about the contrast of glittering colors and dirty laundry makes me immeasurably sad, makes me want to run. This place—this room—isn't my home.

Tanya's soft knock on my door startles me from my thoughts. "Hope, are you okay? I'm worried about you."

"I'm fine. Just fighting off a cold." For two weeks.

"Okay," Tanya says, sounding unconvinced. "Well, umm . . . Will sent another flower arrangement. Purple hyacinths, I think."

"You can toss them."

"It's none of my business, but—he meant well, Hope. Anyone can see that."

Anyone can. But I expected better from him.

Maybe because I'd gotten my hopes up too high believing he expected more from me.

"It's complicated," I say, my voice hoarse.

"I know. Just . . . think about it, okay?" She sets something heavy by the door. "We're going to go. Text me if you need anything."

I squeeze my eyes shut. The *we* crashes through me, a storm cloud cracked open. "Have fun."

The shadow of Tanya's feet beneath my door remains still. "There's one more thing. Annette got the town council to say Maeve's cottage is condemned. They're going to make her leave."

"That's ridiculous—"

"Totally," Tanya says quickly, confirming she's solidly in the I-haven't-given-in-to-hysteria camp. "I just thought you should know."

Tanya's feet disappear. A moment later, murmuring filters in and then the sound of the front door opening and closing.

In the silence, Maeve's cottage locks into my thoughts. Maeve, who wasn't afraid when Rory confronted her, but cannot stand up against an entire town. She needs help. I reach for my phone to call Will and drop it.

Will cannot be my first call. He cannot be my first anything anymore.

The loss is like a hollowing, and I try not to think about how familiar it feels as I throw on clothes and stuff my feet into sneakers.

Maeve is seated on the porch swing drinking a cup of tea when I arrive. Gummy bears are scattered across the table, and she's plucking colors at random. Today she's wearing cutoff jeans and hot-pink Reeboks that somehow survived the eighties. Her gray-white hair is pulled through the back of a baseball cap. She looks young and . . . normal.

"I don't think I've ever seen you sit still," I say as I climb the steps and try to keep any assumption from my voice. Maeve has always been a whirl of energy when I've arrived—pruning flowers or blending herbs. To see her sit is . . . startling. Worrying.

"I'm just taking in the view. It really is beautiful here." She slides over to make room for me.

"It is." I sit beside her. The swing creaks with my extra weight. "You're drinking tea?"

"Jasmine, rose, and a touch of chamomile to help me find and give grace." She breathes a laugh. "Although I suppose I should have added something stronger."

"You heard about that committee, I guess?"

She nods. "I should be flattered that so many people believe I have so much power."

"I'm sorry. It's—I hate them for what they're doing. I wish there was a way to stop them."

A cloud drifts across the sun. A shadow falls across the woods, the trail leading away from the cottage.

"We talked once about how sometimes I find myself needing to move on from places. I thought Kingsette would be different, but—I smell the smoke in the air, and I don't ignore the warnings anymore. Besides, I'm not sure I'm helping anyone anymore," Maeve says, her tone indecipherable.

"I'm sorry I haven't been by . . ."

"I understand," Maeve says. "You don't owe me an explanation. I wouldn't be surprised if you questioned me after all of this—after hearing Will's accusations, after Brandon didn't come."

"No, that's not—"

Maeve flashes me a knowing look, and I relent. "Fine, I did question you for a bit, but then I thought about how people here overreacted to rumors about you, and how easily one side of a story becomes fact. I thought about you and everything you taught me and everything I've seen you do, and I know the truth. I know you aren't a scam artist or a fraud or any of the awful things they're saying about you. You have something they don't, a power they can't understand. I hate that they are being so awful to you. I'm sorry."

Maeve waves away the apology. "I'm not the only one with a power. You have a gift of your own, Hope. There's a reason you turned to nursing, healing, and a reason the universe brought you and me together."

"I think you're giving me too much credit." The master's degree application with the blank lines is proof.

"No one's ever accused me of that before," Maeve says with a smirk, and I laugh.

"Where will you go?"

"To wherever the universe takes me next. To the next town where I'm needed." She shrugs, as if setting off with no plan in a universe with no safety net is something anyone can do. Unlike when I first met her, though, I see the loneliness in that small shrug. I see the fear and the hope too. I see Maeve as she is—a woman seeking her own answers the best way she can.

"I wish I'd had more time with you," I say.

Maeve stands and braces herself against the railing. She tips her face up to the sky and exhales. After a beat, she spins around. "What about you?"

"What about me?"

"When I leave, what will you do?"

"I . . . don't know." A crystal clear image of what tomorrow will look like forms in my mind. It's followed by a series of identical images. Hospital. Home. Rinse, repeat. A life of moving, but never getting anywhere. "Maybe I'll finally finish my school application. Get a place of my own."

"That's one choice. There are others too. Other doors you haven't opened." Maeve's expression is free of judgment, free of that pity tilt. "Greece?"

Greece would mean breaking out of the box. No longer being defined by loss.

It would also be Greece. On the other side of the world.

Noah's surprise party is coming up, Macy has a dance recital next week. Emma's soccer team is probably going to make it into the championship tournament. Tessa roped me into training for the 5K in the fall. Will—

His name trails behind the others so inconspicuously I don't realize he's entered my thoughts until his image is fully formed in my mind.

For about a dozen reasons, he should not be a motive for me to stay or go. He never should have been part of the equation.

"Is that a yes?" Maeve steps toward me. Her eyes have gone a shade darker, which should make her appear more normal, but instead makes her seem more other.

I shake my head. "No, I think . . . I think leaving now would be running away. It would be another form of hiding. I owe myself more than that."

For so long I didn't believe that.

Maeve puts a cool hand on my arm. "I know you don't trust the universe anymore, Hope. But trust your instincts. Trust yourself."

"Trust me," Will said, and I did.

That didn't work out.

But trusting myself—that idea shouldn't sound so radical. My instincts were right about Maeve. They've been right countless times for my patients. Maybe even if I'd trusted my instincts and told Brandon how I'd been feeling, he'd still be alive.

Or not.

I have to stop blaming myself for things I can't control.

Maybe all I can do is begin trusting myself. Maybe the only apology I need to give is the one to myself—for not trusting my own heart.

"I wish there was some way to fix this. So you didn't have to leave."

"Some things can't be fixed. They can only be weathered."

Like loss. And grief. And heartbreak.

"Have you spoken to Will?" Maeve asks, reading my thoughts as always.

"No." My voice is hard, foreign. "It's his fault all of this is happening."

"We would have found ourselves here whether or not Will got involved."

"You're defending him?"

"He made a mistake, Hope. He's on a journey just like all of us, and he stumbled."

I shake my head. "He didn't just stumble. He used me. He made me believe in him."

Worse, he made me believe he believed in me.

"You're entitled to your anger, but I can't help but wonder whether there's something else driving that rage."

"Like what?"

She shrugs, her shoulder lifting and lowering like tucked wings beneath her shirt. "I don't know, Hope. Only you know if there's some reason you're choosing to run away."

"I'm not running anywhere," I say.

"You can't stay still anymore."

"I know." It's long past time to go.

Maeve brightens. "Oh, I almost forgot. I have something for you."

She retrieves a postcard with a recipe written in her neat block handwriting. "Brew this tea when you're ready."

"What's it for?" I flip the card over. The back is blank.

Maeve's eyebrows raise, and mischief glimmers in her eyes. "You'll find out."

36
WILL

If I were a better person, I'd let my mom take over planning Noah's surprise party. She'd take this meeting to confirm outstanding details. But if the last few weeks have proven anything, it's that I'm not that guy. The one who does the right thing.

The clock strikes 2:15. Hope was supposed to be here at two. I glance at my phone and debate texting her, but if she hasn't answered any of my other messages, I doubt she'll respond to one accusing her of being late.

My knee jiggles under the desk. The picture frames vibrate. I stand and pace the office. This is how a caged elephant must feel before it's about to perform.

I check the time again. 2:17.

I'm going to lose my mind.

2:18.

A knock on the door has me jumping out of my skin. "Come in," I say in an uncontrollable high-pitched voice.

The bartender from Newport with the blue streak of hair opens the door just far enough to poke her head in. "Sorry, Will. I didn't mean to bother you. Have you seen your mom around? She wanted to talk about references for a few of my friends who need jobs."

It takes all my strength to keep my voice neutral. It's not her fault she's not Hope. "I think she's in the pantry doing inventory."

"Great, thanks."

"You're welcome," I say, mostly to myself because she's already disappeared, having left the door ajar.

I sit again and look through the stack of résumés my mom handed me this morning. She's got a gift for finding college kids who need jobs. Or a better grasp of using social media to recruit. At the very least, she's found a way to recruit without going bar to bar. I look through the stack of candidates and select the best of the bunch to call for interviews.

Only half my brain manages to function. The other half is listening for the sound of someone walking down the hallway.

"Hey, Will. Sorry I'm late."

I snap my head up, ready to crack a joke to make Hope smile, but feel whatever hope I was holding on to extinguish.

"You don't look that happy to see me," Tessa says, coming into the office and taking the seat across from me. She has Hope's eyes and Hope's smile. Without Hope's bright energy to light it up, it's just a beautiful face.

"I'm just surprised. I thought Hope was the point person on this— to keep the surprise."

Tessa shrugs. "No one's talking about much besides Maeve right now, so I felt pretty safe to just go about my business. It's a shame it takes a witch hunt to get some privacy in this place. When Maeve leaves, it'll be ten times worse, I bet."

"Maeve is leaving?"

Tessa nods. "Hope says she's leaving tonight."

"Hope says?" Something desperate has crept into my voice, but I don't care.

"I just spoke to her. She's with Maeve. You know Hope, loyal to the end."

"Yeah. To the end." Pain I have no right to strikes the back of my throat.

Tessa's cool gaze runs over me, and in that moment, I'm sure she's the inspiration for the phrase "if looks could kill." "You're an idiot, you know that."

"I know. I didn't mean to hurt her. She—"

Tessa makes a noise from the back of her throat and holds up a finger. "I don't care what you meant to do. I only care about what you did and how you're going to make it better."

"She's not going to forgive me." Thinking about the extent of my screwup makes bile churn in my stomach again.

Tessa leans forward, her forearms on my desk, and looks at me without pretense. Directness must be genetic. "She's hurt, but she'll forgive you. She's . . ." Tessa scrunches up her nose. "She doesn't quit on people she cares about."

Her gaze slips behind me to the two suitcases I have stacked behind the desk. The ones waiting to go to LA, where I accepted the job for the new show. "The only thing she won't forgive you for is leaving without saying goodbye."

37

HOPE

A bouquet of lavender roses, my favorite color of rose, sits on my work-station when I return from dealing with a patient. My heart beats a little faster, which feels like a betrayal—until I read the card. Then I wish all my heart felt was betrayal.

Congratulations on your move. You're going to do amazing things.

On the back—*PS: We'll miss you.*

P.P.S.: We heard Lydia's friend loved your essay. You better come back to celebrate with us when you get your acceptance letter.

I tuck the card into my pocket. Now that I officially have a plan to leave Kingsette, the struggles of living in a small town feel less import-ant than the joys. A boss who will push you to be your best self. A coffee place that knows exactly how many sugars you take—even if you have to take them with a side of gossip. A safety net, because you'll always have a place to land.

The final patient's room I enter is a familiar one, and even without checking the chart, I know it's Mrs. Matthews. The wife and mother with a brain tumor.

Unlike the first time I entered this patient's room, which swirled with silence and sickness, I'm met with bright overhead lights and a man and woman sitting up in bed. IVs trail out of her arm. Her skin is pale and lacking luster. But her eyes are bright, and she's alert and happy to see me.

"Mrs. Matthews," I say. "You look great."

A hand self-consciously reaches up to touch the bandage on her shaved head. "All things considered, I feel great too. We're going home."

"As soon as the doctors give you one more examination," I say, confirming the order in the chart. "I just need to take your vitals one more time too."

Mr. Matthews makes space for me, and I work, checking her blood pressure and temperature and reassuring her that everything is normal.

"The doctor should be in shortly. Can I get you anything before I go?"

They both shake their heads, and I turn toward the door, wishing there were something I could get them that would ensure their happy ending.

"Hope." I pivot, and Mr. Matthews bounds up from his seat. "I just wanted to say thank you."

"You don't have to thank me. It's my job. And my pleasure."

His mouth tilts up in a warm smile. "That's actually not what I wanted to say thank you for. I mean it is, but also for what you said that day."

My mind tries to flip back to the afternoon, but so much has happened in the interim that the only clear memory I have of him is of a small dog poking its snout out of its hiding place.

Seeming to realize that, he prompts, "I asked you how I'd do any of this without her, and you told me 'you just do. You live. One day and then the next.' Everyone else told me to 'be positive' or promised it would all work out."

"Oh." Guilt washes in along with the memory of that long-ago conversation. "I'm sorry. I should have been more encouraging."

"No, no," he says quickly. "You shouldn't have been. I can't tell you how much your honesty meant to me. I didn't need positivity. I needed to face what I was afraid of. And I did—with your words. They helped more than Maeve's teas." He winks, and I shouldn't be surprised that he found himself at Maeve's too.

"You're welcome," I say, feeling pressure build behind my eyes. "The doctor will be in soon, but let me know if you need anything in the meantime."

He nods. "Oh, I almost forgot. When I went back to see Maeve, she gave me a message for you." He glances back at his wife, who smiles encouragingly. "She said to remind you that doling out advice is the easy part, but where there's a will, there's a way."

My eyes fill, and a laugh escapes my throat. "Thank you for telling me that."

"You understand?"

"Yeah. It's a bit of unfortunate wordplay, that's all."

"I can't believe you're really leaving." Logan stands at the entrance to our kitchen with an award-winning pout on his face. "I already have a new queen-size bed in your room in the new house."

I blow out a breath. "I can't keep living with you and Tanya, going through the motions. It's time to leap or drown."

He quirks up an eyebrow. "I think you mixed your metaphors there. Sink or swim?"

I laugh. "Yeah, one of those."

"You're just mad that you'll have to referee your own decorating fights now," I tease as I wrap my favorite mug in bubble wrap and place it into a box containing the few kitchen things that were mine. The dishes from the house I shared with Brandon are already sitting in a box waiting to be unpacked in the new place—a sun-drenched apartment about an hour outside Kingsette, with a view of the water and not far from campus.

It's somehow both a new beginning and an ending. A rebuilding.

He starts to walk away, and something on the hall table catches his attention. "What's this?"

"A tea recipe from Maeve."

"For what?"

"She didn't say, actually."

"That's . . . completely in character." He laughs. "Are you going to make the tea?"

I bite my lip. "I haven't decided yet."

He raises an eyebrow. "That's not in character."

"I know. I guess a piece of me wants to hold on to her magic a little longer. Once I brew this, there will be none left."

"I think you're selling yourself short."

"What are you talking about?"

An impish smile lifts his lips. "Just a rumor. A little birdie told me you had a knack for gardening and a heart for helping people."

38
WILL

No more holes.

Well—one. The gaping hole I left in Hope's heart. I tried at least. Some holes just can't be mended.

But no more beyond that if I can help it.

The private investigator I hired to find my mom was happy to work on a new project for me—and I was even happier when he got me an address within the hour.

Terry's house is just a few miles outside Newport and within walking distance of a boat club. When I pull into the gravel driveway, I'm met with a manicured lawn and a man I haven't seen in nearly ten years, pruning overgrown hydrangeas. He's wearing a Hawaiian shirt and shorts, a far cry from the buttoned-up khaki wearer he'd been.

He peers into the car window. When I step out, the pleasant, neighborly expression gives way to something else. The shears fall from his hand as recognition registers on his face.

"Hey, Terry," I say. "Nice place you got here."

"What are you doing here, Will?" His voice is hard.

I raise my hands. "Sorry to drop in on you. I came to ask for your help. With the Inn. I know it's a big ask, and you deserve your time, but you know the Inn better than anyone."

The screen door pushes open, and a woman with strawberry-blonde hair emerges. She startles, her hand dropping protectively onto her round belly. "Dad, is someone here? Is that—"

"Lacey, can you go inside, please?" The question slips from between Terry's gritted teeth.

Lacey glances at me, and then does as she's told.

"I really don't mean to intrude. I know you're dealing with family things."

"I am. It's not a great time . . ." Terry gestures toward the hydrangeas, as if that's what's keeping him busy and not the very pregnant daughter.

"I'm sure. I mean . . . congratulations. You're going to be a grandfather." I take a step toward Terry, hand outstretched.

He stiffens and doesn't take it.

I let my hand drop, dusting it along the side of my jeans. "I'll keep this short then. My mom is back, and she needs a hand around the Inn. It's too much for her, and I'm going back to LA. I don't want to leave her alone again."

"Sorry, Will. I don't think I can go back right now." Terry bends to grab the shears. His posture is too stiff, his words too stilted.

"I understand," I say, glancing at the house, at the curtains, which are fluttering, hiding Lacey's eavesdropping. "I'm sure my mother would work with you if you needed a different schedule. It's not—"

"I said no."

The hair on the back of my neck stands on end.

"Listen, Terry, you've been like family to us for as long as I can remember. If there's anything I can do for you, you know I will. My mother too."

He nods, and it's a dismissal. Another hole that can't be mended.

He steps back and knocks over a basket full of flowers.

I drop to my knees. "Let me help."

"What about 'no' do you not understand?" His voice explodes across the manicured front lawn. A bird that was hiding in a tree takes flight.

"What?" I jolt upright, forced backward by the unexpected rage.

"I've asked you to leave, and I think it's time that you do." Terry's eyes narrow. "I think your family has done enough."

"What's that supposed to mean?"

"Ask Darren." He spits the words at me, and I feel whiplashed by the stark turn in the conversation.

"What does Darren have to do with this?"

His glare is an accusation. "I said leave."

He storms up the porch steps, yanks the door open, and lets it slam shut behind him.

For too many seconds, I'm frozen in place, gaze locked on the closed door. I need to get moving—police will probably be here to escort me off the property—but . . . what just happened?

The incoming call on my phone pulls me out of my stunned state.

"Will, it's Lacey." Her voice is a whisper. "We need to talk."

The rehab center reminds me of the ICU. For a heartbeat, I consider running. My car is packed, ready for the long drive back West, and I could just go.

But I don't want to run. I'm done with that for good.

Inside the rehab center, a receptionist asks me to fill out a form. While I do, she calls Darren's room to announce my arrival. Her mouth turns down as she listens to the answer on the other end of the phone.

She hangs up. "I'm so sorry, but he's not—"

"Tell him I know about Lacey," I say and brace myself against the desk. "Call him back and tell him that."

The receptionist's eyes widen. She slides a gaze left and right. I remove my hands from her desk. "Please. He's my brother, and I need to apologize for . . . a lot of things."

She swallows audibly and lifts the receiver to her ear. She dials again, and this time, when she uses Lacey's name, her brows draw together. She hangs up and regards me more curiously. "Room 214."

I head the way she pointed, passing a living room–type area with a number of residents sitting in a circle and another with tables set up for eating. A part of me half hopes to see Darren among them so we don't have to do this in a real way. Just a pleasant surface way.

I find him in his room. The TV is on but muted. Two beds are neatly made, but Darren's alone in the room, sitting on the windowsill and peering out at the parking lot.

"All packed to run again?" His voice sounds like gravel, but there's a clarity to his words I haven't heard in too long.

"Not run this time, but yeah, I'm all packed. Heading back to LA for a job."

"The prodigal son exits." Darren turns to face me. The bruises have mostly healed, and his pupils are a normal size. His skin is dry and weathered, making him seem closer to fifty than forty, but mostly, he looks like Darren.

"I'm sorry I've been MIA these last ten years," I say, addressing the elephant in the room. "That was shitty of me."

"Yeah, it was."

Silence thumps between us. A bluebird lands on a tree branch outside Darren's window.

"That bluebird is taunting me. I fought its friend at the Inn a few weeks ago. The bird won."

Darren's stony expression cuts the words from my throat. My attempt at levity failed miserably. I can't remember the last time Darren listened to one of my stories, let alone laughed.

Darren and I aren't close, and we know nothing about each other's lives.

"How did you find out about Lacey," he says, his voice crackling with barely restrained emotion.

"I went to visit Terry. To beg him to come back and help Mom."

"Aah." Darren turns to look out the window, at the bluebird watching us with a steady gaze.

"Lacey was worried about you. She . . . uh . . . didn't know you were in rehab."

Slowly, he turns back to face me. "So you know?"

"Why didn't you tell me about her and the baby? I would have—" That night long ago flashes through my mind. Darren even said, "We can stay in Mom's spare room." The word caught my attention, but I chalked it up to an alcohol-induced error. "You did. I didn't give you a chance."

Darren's silence is my answer.

"I'm sorry, Darren." Guilt makes my voice rasp. An apology isn't enough. The truth might be. "I should have done . . . everything different. Including believing you when you told me you didn't steal from Mom or the Inn."

Darren turns his gaze back to me. "If I were you, I'd be my first suspect too."

"Turns out, it was Terry. Lacey admitted that too. He'd been falsifying records and payments for a while."

The corners of his mouth turn down. "I'm guessing that means he won't be available to help Mom."

I shake my head.

"And you're still leaving?"

"Mom will be okay. She's already hired a great staff, and Mike will be there. I'll call more and do what I can from LA."

Darren regards me with a withering expression, and in his silence I feel like I've shrunk to half my size.

"So I heard you're doing well?" I want to pull back the words the moment they're out. I don't want to be the kind of brother that has to hear from someone else that his only sibling is doing well. Obviously, though, I am.

"'Well' is relative." The tone of his voice shifts, grows thoughtful.

"What's that mean?"

"You and I aren't all that different. We both have a strong flight instinct. The difference is your flight is actual flight and mine is more like getting so messed up I forget where and what I was running from. But with Lacey and the baby—I don't want to be that guy. I don't want to run anymore. I want to be the guy who starts a memorial garden and actually finishes it. I want to be the guy who shows up. A dad like we had."

It feels like an olive branch, and I venture a seat on the corner of the bed closest to the door. "You will be. I know you."

His answering shrug feels like a surrender.

I sigh. "Why do we do that, anyway? The flight instead of fight."

Darren shakes his head. "We haven't gotten to that part in therapy, but I'll be sure to email you the answer when we do."

Once upon a time, we were as close as two brothers can be, and now I'm leaving with nothing but a promise to email.

"Darren, I'm sorry. Not just for the night when you came to me for help and I didn't, but for all the other nights I could have reached out to help you and all the days you were in here and I didn't break down the door to be with you. I know 'I'm sorry' isn't enough. But I hope you'll see it as a start. Maybe even an invitation to come visit me when you're better."

Eyes that have always been able to see through to the very core of me lift to mine. "I'd like that." He pauses. "If Hope is there, I'd love to spend time with her outside of here too. Lacey would like her too."

"Hope?" The question sputters out of me before I can control my surprise. "The woman who came with me to the hospital that night?"

Darren reaches for a bottle of water on the nightstand. He drinks deeply, and time slows to a crawl. I can't tell if he's purposefully stalling or just incredibly thirsty. Either way, I'm about to combust from the impatience. Finally, he puts down the water bottle. "Yes, that woman. She's kind. She's been coming a few days a week and bringing me lunch, says she knows the food here is barely more edible than hospital food. She's right, you know."

"Hope's been visiting you?"

My brother's mouth lifts with traces of a smile. "She didn't tell you?"

"No." She mentioned that she'd visit and do what she could to help, but she didn't say anything again, and I just assumed that meant she'd forgotten. Or, really, I assumed she'd said it because it was a thing people say and never had any intention of following through on. I should have known better.

"She's awesome. Don't mess that one up." Darren sounds more like my big brother than he has in decades.

I grimace. "You're too late with that advice."

Darren sucks his teeth. "And you're still running?"

"I ran after her," I say, my voice rising with protest, though I'm not sure I even convince myself this time. "She's not interested. I have to respect that."

Darren looks out the window, at the bluebird still sitting there watching us. "You ran after her, but did you really try to catch her, or were you just going through the motions?"

39
HOPE

An ache swells in my chest as I crest the trail and take in Maeve's cottage and the empty space where Maeve's tree once stood. The grass over that patch of land is smooth, unblemished. As if a tree with gnarled roots and carved branches were never more than my imagination. A trick of the light.

With a steadying breath, I get to work. Maeve has only been gone a few weeks, and despite my best efforts, the flowers have lost some of their brightness and the stalks have a limpness that wasn't there before.

Or maybe the drought, which has decimated most gardens in Kingsette, has finally struck Maeve's garden too. When she left, she took whatever magic had protected them with her.

After I've finished watering, pruning, and harvesting a few flowers and plants to brew some of Maeve's most popular teas—specifically her sleep aid and heartbreak tea—I set to work searching for the final plant I need to brew the tea Maeve left for me.

The more I think about nursing school and that apartment in Newport, the more unsure I am about any of it. It's moving—real moving—forward, but is it the forward I want?

But if not Newport and not Greece, then what?

A breeze bends the flowers, and I imagine Maeve laughing somewhere with a tree strapped to her back.

For an hour, I pick through Maeve's garden, studying each stem and petal. The final flower I need for Maeve's tea isn't in her garden. The blanchefleur, the hundred-leaved rose, is not growing anywhere around the cottage either.

Maeve never mentioned this flower to me, but Google filled me in. The blanchefleur is not native to Rhode Island and probably would do terrible here, but Maeve has a way of making things grow, even things that should be impossible.

Still, I don't see the flower.

Sweat beads on my forehead, and I wipe it with the back of my arm, which feels gritty.

Why would Maeve leave me a tea recipe that contained a flower she doesn't have in her garden?

Even as the question enters my mind, the answer has already formed. Because she wants to encourage me to leave the garden. To travel and find the flower and make the tea. Maybe because what I need isn't here, in this plot of land. Maybe it's heading to LA with a man whose suitcases were never unpacked.

I think of Will, and a weight drops onto my shoulders. He didn't say goodbye.

Maybe it wasn't fair to hope for it.

A small chirp startles me out of my thoughts. A moment later, a flurry of blue appears in the corner of my vision.

"You're still here?" Tears in the backs of my eyes feel ridiculous—Icarus is just a bird.

He stops fluttering long enough for me to see the way he's holding his wing.

As if it's broken again.

It couldn't be. Maeve fixed him.

In response to my disbelief, Icarus tries and fails to take flight. His left wing doesn't match the movements of the right.

"I can't. It's not—I'm just keeping the garden, and not even doing that well."

The bird makes a small sound. It echoes in the empty space surrounding us.

I'm this bird's only hope. Either I do nothing, and Icarus will never soar. Or I try something. It might not work. I might fail. But it's worth the risk.

I scoop him up the way Maeve did that first day and carry him inside.

In the kitchen, I craft the recipe Maeve taught me, using calendula and jasmine. It's not long before the kitchen smells as it did that day I arrived with an emergency bird kit. It feels like forever ago.

While I work, the bluebird attempts flight a few dozen times.

A dozen tries and a dozen fails.

My heart breaks at each attempt because I don't know that I would have kept trying.

When Maeve's recipe is ready, I pipe it into the bluebird's mouth and wait. His breathing evens, but tension remains in his injured wing.

"I'm sorry." My breath flutters his feathers. Something in my chest unlocks. "I'm so sorry."

A moment passes, and the bird goes still.

My pulse tracks the seconds ticking by, and my breath becomes edged with the same raw sob that left me without a voice in the days after Brandon's funeral.

Then, a movement. It's so small, it has to be my imagination.

It happens again.

Then again.

Then a slow wing beat.

I hold my breath as the bird flaps his wings and, in a burst of energy, takes flight. He swoops around the kitchen, circling twice. In the time it takes me to blink, he disappears through the open window, where he melts into the clear blue sky.

I brace myself against the windowsill to find the bluebird.

Another figure, in a blue T-shirt, stands at the top of the hill.

He looks as stunned as I feel.

"What are you doing here?"

"I'm . . ." He holds out a planter with a tiny stalk, a sad little thing with barely a nub pushing through the dirt. Somehow it's already wilting. "Maeve's plant. I figured I'd replant it. Try to save it."

His gaze drinks me in, revealing more than I want to see.

"It needs water."

He glances at the plant, then lifts his eyes to me. "The whole town needs water."

"I heard . . . I mean, I thought you left."

"Leaving. Had a couple loose ends to take care of. I'm trying this thing where I don't just run from my problems and leave other people to deal with them."

His brown eyes fix on me, revealing something that takes my breath away, and . . . Maeve was right. Will's on a journey. He stumbled, but he's righting himself.

My gaze lifts to the sky. "I'm glad you've found your way."

"Hope," he says, so quietly that my heart shatters. "I'm so sorry. For lying to you. For asking you to trust me and then not trusting you to know what was best for you. I—you trusted me with your heart, and I ruined that. If you can find a way to give me another chance, I won't ruin it again."

"Will . . ."

"Come to LA with me. We'll figure it out there. Away from all of this." He gestures toward the woods, where Kingsette waits on the other side. "It's this place. This fucking town."

His eyes lock on mine, willing me to give the answer he wants, the answer I can't give him because it's trapped beneath a tidal wave of emotion that's rising up.

"I can't," I say, the words escaping on a breath, and then gaining momentum. He pulls away from me.

The need to close this new distance is almost primal, but somehow, impossibly, I hold myself in place. Our story needs to end here, before we hurt each other more. "We can't keep doing this to each other. You run, then I run. We're just—we're not good for each other. You have to see that too."

He needs to know it's true.

Will shakes his head. "Yes, we run. It's what we both do. But we've only ever run toward each other. Don't you see that?"

We. Will and I are *we.*

In the distance, a crow caws.

"It's not supposed to be this hard," I say.

He closes his eyes. Silence vibrates between us. The space between us widens, though we both seem to have become rooted in place.

"Say something," I say, when the quiet becomes too loud.

He looks up at me through lowered lashes. The heartbreak I expected to see is only there in the corner of his eyes. The rest is a storm. His features have gone hard. "What should I say? Should I say that we both know you can, but you don't want to because you're afraid? Should I say that we both know you're panicking because—yeah, I made a huge mistake, and I'm sorry—but if you forgive me, and you let me in all the way, you might lose me? No matter what promises I make for you here today, no matter how much I mean them, I can't guarantee you anything. That terrifies you."

His words hit too close to a truth that's too ingrained into every fiber of my being.

"I did let you in. I trusted you. You broke this. Not me." Barbs in the back of my throat make my voice sound thick and scratchy.

"You're looking for an excuse to walk away." Will's gaze cuts into me like diamond against glass. Every part of me shatters. He squeezes his eyes shut, and I think he's shattering too.

"Don't do this," he says. "My whole life I've run away from people. You're the only person I keep running toward. I can't keep chasing you."

"Then don't." My voice is barely audible. I take a step back; the rush of wind cools the sweat on the back of my neck.

"You're scared." He sounds uncertain, which fuels the heat charging through my bones. "That's all this is. You're scared and still just going through the motions."

"No, Will. I'm finally moving forward. I have an apartment and nursing school and—"

"It wasn't supposed to be like this," he says.

I shake my head. "We both know it never goes the way it's supposed to go."

Will walks away. For too long, I stare at the space between the trees where he disappeared. As I turn back toward the cottage, my gaze snags on the planter Will left. The flower bloomed.

A blanchefleur.

40
WILL

Pale moonlight illuminates the way to the ticket stand where my father's makeshift memorial lives on. Even with the light, when it's this dark, Adventure Land is more creepy than adventure-y, but I don't want to leave town without at least one more visit. Besides, I can't think of another use for the rock Maeve gave me, and it seems pointless to carry it around now that I've abandoned the blanchefleur.

Along with Kingsette, my mother. And Hope.

Our last conversation drifts through my mind, and for the hundredth time, I play over what I said and what I should have said. It may have changed nothing, but at least I would have unequivocally run toward something, rather than away.

Too little, too late. Again.

Movement on the ticket stand makes me stop in my tracks.

Something is balanced on top of the pile of rocks. A white flower that I've only ever seen once before, and it's slowly unfurling beneath the moonlight.

Maeve's midnight blooms.

My heart crashes against my rib cage. "Maeve?"

The moment I hear my trembling voice, I know I'm being paranoid. The park is empty, and even if she were here, Maeve isn't the evil villain I wanted to believe she was. She was always only trying to help.

I step closer. The flower dips open, exposing its powdery soft inside to the moonlight. An invitation. A promise of something impossible.

Even though I know better, I lift my gaze to the moon and repeat one of Maeve's affirmations under my breath. Echoes of my whispers drift through the park.

Silence greets me when I'm done.

Of course, what else did I think would greet me? My father's voice? Some sign from the universe? Maeve was a lot of things, and magical wasn't one of them. She was just a sad woman with a sad—

A crackle of electricity breaks the silence.

My ears perk up.

Nothing follows. Seconds tick by.

A high-pitched sound whines from somewhere up ahead.

A heartbeat later, half the sign near the Ferris wheel lights up.

The words: **ADVENTURE STARTS WITH HOPE** glow brighter than the stars against the night sky.

41
HOPE

It's Tessa's big night. Well, technically Noah's big night, but no one can take their eyes off Tessa. Her joy is infectious and has been ever since Noah walked into the ballroom and his jaw dropped as he took in the Ian Summers Band and the dessert table and every inch of the ballroom.

I sweep my gaze over the twinkling lights, gauzy tablecloths, and red velvet cupcakes—the baker came through on what he'd promised and more, thanks to Will.

My gaze travels to the bar. Three young bartenders work in graceful synchronicity to fill drink orders. The line for a drink has never gotten more than three deep. I wouldn't be surprised if the efficiency was due as much to the enthusiasm of the Inn's new hires as to the difference between wedding drinking and fortieth-birthday-party drinking. Or retirement-party drinking, for that matter.

"Are you having fun?" Tessa glides off the dance floor and takes a hold of my wrist. Her eyes twinkle.

"It's an amazing night." I giggle at the sight of my two nieces holding court on the dance floor in front of the band—also Will's doing.

"You're never getting those girls to bed," I tell Tessa.

Tessa raises an eyebrow. "You're not dancing."

I show her my half-empty glass. "Just taking a breather."

"Uh-huh. There's no other reason you're parked in the corner with a clear view of the bar?"

We both glance toward the bar. Will's mother and her new boyfriend have appeared and are in a heated discussion with Annette Martina, who managed to guilt Tessa into a last-minute invitation thanks to their garden-club connection.

I turn to face Tessa. "No other reason."

She grins. "You really are a terrible liar."

"There are worse things to be," I say and gesture toward the bar. "What's happening over there?"

"Aah, I bet Will's mom just told Annette that they're not backing down on the new coffee shop."

I raise an eyebrow, waiting for Tessa to fill me in on the part of the story I'm missing.

Tessa rolls her eyes. "Come on, Hope. Seriously? Everyone's been talking about it."

I shrug. "I've been busy packing. I don't have time for rumors."

Tessa hesitates for less than a microsecond. "Well, I heard Will's mom and her new boyfriend bought a space at the edge of town. They're turning it into some fancy new coffee place. Rumor has it Darren and Lacey are helping. They're going to be opening a public memorial garden on the Inn's roof-deck and taking over Maeve's garden too. Annette's obviously pissed about the competition. She's trying to get a committee together to stop them—something about poison flowers from the garden contaminating the coffee—but I think people are beginning to see the real Annette. Or at the very least, they're excited to try a new coffee and breakfast menu."

"I kind of feel sorry for Annette," I confess. "Imagine being so afraid of change that any little shift in the wind makes you panic to the point of igniting a town-wide hysteria."

Tessa flashes me a rueful smile. "Mm-hmm. And you're so wise and unafraid of change now, huh?"

"Unafraid? No. Prepared to accept that things are going to change whether I want them to or not? Yes. Life won't stand still for anyone. I think when I saw the blanchefleur transform into this impressive, full flower I just realized . . . I didn't want to settle for good enough, or happy enough, or existing as a wilted flower in a plain pot. I want to bloom, and the only way I can do that is to do the thing my heart wants to do but is too afraid."

Tessa gives me a dubious look I probably deserve. My sudden change of heart must be causing her whiplash. But it feels right. It feels like living.

"How did Lydia take the news that you withdrew your application from school?"

I inhale. "She was disappointed, but she gets it. I actually think she's talked Rosalie into applying."

"Rosalie? I-take-advantage-of-my-kind-lonely-coworkers Rosalie? That one?"

"People can change."

Tessa narrows her eyes. "Are you sure Maeve didn't use some mind-control trick on you? Is that what's really behind this decision to move to LA?"

"First of all, no. Second of all, I'm not moving there. I just want to tell Will how I feel. Face to face." A familiar alarm begins to wail, urging caution. It's saying that if I fly too high, risk too much, I'll fall and lose it all. Instead of surrendering to the noise, I touch the locket around my throat and take a breath. "We don't always get a second chance."

"Eh. I'm not convinced. Mind control is cooler," Tessa says, bringing my thoughts back to the present.

"I'll be sure to pass that message on to Maeve." If I ever see her again, that is. She doesn't seem like the kind of woman to double back, and it's a big world out there—a lot of adventure to find if you choose to seek it.

Annette makes a frustrated sound that lifts above the party din. Tessa and I turn and watch her storm away from the PTA soccer moms, who surrounded her while Tessa and I were talking.

When my sister turns back to me, a sly smile is ghosting her lips. "While you're passing on messages to Maeve, maybe you can ask her who spread a rumor to the soccer moms about what a great kisser Will Reynard is. It somehow got back to Natalie, and . . . let's just say Annette seems to be taking that as well as she's taking the coffee shop news."

My cheeks hurt from suppressing my smile, but I'm saved from answering.

The band kicks off a fast-paced song. Tessa glances over her shoulder and beams as Noah crooks his finger, summoning her to the dance floor. "I'll be right back."

"Go. Dance. Enjoy."

She hoots and shimmies onto the dance floor. She pauses and peeks over her shoulder. "Oh, there's a surprise for you on the roof-deck. A thank-you."

I watch her and Noah dance through another song before I decide that what I need is not a new drink, but some air.

I head toward the roof-deck—the only place I'm guaranteed to be alone.

I'm not alone. The door slams closed behind me, and a man spins around.

He grins that familiar grin, and my heart backflips and somersaults and goes through a series of moves that haven't even been named yet.

I blink a few thousand times to be sure I'm seeing straight. The white button-down makes his golden-brown skin glow, and he's clean shaven. Usually I'm a sucker for stubble, but the hard cut of his jawline isn't terrible to look at. "Will?"

Thunder rumbles in the distance. A flash of lightning on the horizon.

"I had a feeling I'd catch you up here. Although . . ." He makes a show of looking at my empty hands. "No wine? At least when I interrupted your quiet time, I brought wine." The familiar deep voice sends a thousand chills down my spine.

"The finest bottle of twist-off red wine blend you can find on this side of the Atlantic coast, if I remember correctly," I say, suddenly standing within inches of him. As if I floated.

He closes the distance. "You do remember correctly."

"What are you doing here?" My hand reaches to touch his tie. It's soft and real. He's here.

Will trails a finger down my bare arm. "You look great."

"Tessa's dress. She's always squeezing me into something two sizes too small."

My blood heats as Will's gaze travels the length of my body. "Remind me to thank Tessa if I make it downstairs."

"If?" I raise an eyebrow.

He answers my question with a grin that makes me think of the last night we were on the roof-deck together.

A long moment passes. A million words pass through my mind, but none are right.

"So," he says.

"So," I say.

The air is thick with the promise of desperately needed rain. Thunder cracks in the distance.

"I heard you applied to nursing school. Congratulations. That's . . . great."

"Thank you, but—"

"Hope, wait. I just have to say this before I lose my nerve. I know you don't want to be with me anymore. I messed it up. I just couldn't leave without saying goodbye." He runs a hand through his hair. "And telling you one more thing."

"What's that?"

"I love you, Hope. And I will love you for the rest of my life. Even from a distance."

A swell of warmth settles in the space behind my eyes. I want to tell him that I love him too. That loving him feels like an adventure and a piece of home all at once.

The words catch in my throat. Once I tell Will, there's no going back. There's no safety net.

"Maeve left me one final tea recipe," I start, my voice thick.

He looses an awkward laugh. "Okay, not what I was hoping you'd say."

I put a finger to his lips. "She didn't tell me what it was for. Just said, 'You'll find out.' I tried to make it, but I was missing one ingredient. I thought Maeve did that on purpose, because she wanted me to go out and see the world."

"I'll go with you. We can flower hunt—"

"No, Will. I found the flower. You brought it to me."

"The blanchefleur?" His brows draw together. Air, thick with the promise of rain, weaves between us. "It was half-dead, though."

"It just needed to find a place where it belonged—and maybe a bigger pot and a steady watering schedule."

Will laughs, a genuine laugh now, which fills long-darkened parts of my heart with light. "That sounds like Maeve. Did you brew the tea?"

I shake my head. "I'm not going to. I've been thinking that Maeve's magic was never really about the teas or the plants. I think her magic, or intuition or whatever, was people. She knew what we all needed and helped us give it to ourselves."

I think of Bailey, who left for art school and has posted every moment of her joy on Facebook. I think of Ashley and Vicky, who last I heard were backpacking through Europe. Of all the others.

And my brain-tumor patient. They needed hope. And Maeve gave it to them.

And me. Maeve talked to me about forgiveness so often, and I thought she meant Brandon's forgiveness. She knew all along that it's not his forgiveness I needed.

I needed only my voice—my forgiveness, my permission, my ability to believe in myself.

For two years, I buried my head in the sand—hid from life and played it safe—built a world where I had as little to lose as possible.

I still lost.

Because maybe it was never about building a life safe from loss. Maybe that's impossible, regardless of how small you make your life. The universe isn't safe. Bad things happen to good people. And none of that is a reason to stop living.

Maybe the real work is in finding a way to be brave enough to live every bit of the life that's left.

Will's expression grows thoughtful, and his eyes search mine. "She certainly understood what I needed long before I understood."

"What was that?" I ask, my words edged by the unsettled rumble in the sky.

"The courage to stay and find home."

My throat tightens. "She knew I needed the courage to live and lose. I'm leaving for LA tomorrow—to see you."

For too many heartbeats, for a lifetime, neither of us says anything. There are so many words I want to say, so many more things I want to admit, but I don't know how to start. There's no tea for that.

Behind my ribs, a thousand little butterflies begin to flutter their wings. "Say something."

"What about the garden?"

It's my turn to breathe an awkward laugh. "Not what I was hoping you'd say either."

His hands take mine. "I just mean—you loved the garden. You lit up when you were in that garden. I couldn't ask you to leave it for me."

The smell of rain fills my lungs. "I'm not leaving the garden for good. I'm—my whole life I thought I had to go from point A to point B. That didn't work out. Then, I thought if I just stayed on point C, I'd be safe. Now, I don't think I want a point. I want—nursing school and the garden to help people and Greece and LA. I want to live all of it with all that I have."

His gaze anchors me in place. "More than one dream. I understand the feeling."

Thunder cracks, and this time a bolt of lightning streaks through the sky.

"How did you make the Ferris wheel work that day?"

He laughs. "What?"

"The Ferris wheel. It shouldn't have worked, but you made it work. You said it was magic."

"Magic," he says, a slow smile spreading on his face, "with a little help from a friend of Darren's who trained as an electrician. About ten years ago, he—"

"You know what?" My hand reaches for his. "Maybe magic is all the answer I need."

Heavy, drenching rain pours down.

Within seconds we're soaked. Will looks stunned, and I start to laugh. A moment later, he's laughing too and shaking the water off his hair. It's Maeve's last bit of magic.

A heartbeat later, Will's hand slides across my waist.

Rain pours down around us, and he holds me closer.

"I love you, Hope," he whispers. "I have for as long as I've known you. Whenever you're ready for me, if ever, I'll be here."

I owe him the truth.

I owe myself the truth.

I owe myself the chance to do more than survive. To live. To love. To thrive.

"I love you too." I lean forward and kiss him, and it feels like fate and promise and home.

THE END

ACKNOWLEDGMENTS

Writing a story is a solitary endeavor, but I've learned that creating a book takes a village. I am forever grateful to the village that has helped bring this book to the world (and I still can't believe it's in the world!).

My first thank-you, and my most impossible thank-you, goes to my husband, Matt—who will never get to read or hear my gratitude, but hopefully somehow still feels it anyway. (Maeve would say he does—and I would believe her.) Thank you for being the first person to step into my writing village. Thank you for believing in me when I told you I wanted to write a book. You were ready to move mountains to make my dream come true simply because it was my dream and you loved me. That kind of love is rare, and I'm deeply grateful to have known it. Really grateful to still know it. You are the reason I believe in magic, the reason I see magic in bluebirds and rainbows. The reason I hold on to a little hope.

A huge thank-you to my agent, Kim Lionetti at BookEnds. From the moment I received your email in the earliest, scariest days of the pandemic, when I was losing hope in everything, I knew our partnership would be magic—the kind of magic that's threaded throughout this book. Thank you for your guidance, your mentorship, and your belief in me. Thank you also to the BookEnds team, especially Maggie Nambot, for working to make this dream a reality.

A just as huge thank-you to my editor Erin Adair-Hodges. I can never thank you enough for seeing the heart of this story so perfectly and believing in the magic. From our very first conversation, I knew you understood Hope, Will, and Maeve on a soul level, and I am deeply grateful to you for that. A big thank-you also to everyone on the Lake Union and Amazon Publishing team for caring about this book and giving it your time and attention.

Thank you to my developmental editor Dee Hudson. Thank you for pushing me—in the kindest way—to elevate this story and these characters. Your insight, spark, and vision truly brought this book to another level, and I'm so grateful I got to work with you.

Thank you to my children, Gabrielle and Henry, who so generously (well, most of the time) shared their mom's time with Hope and Will. You two are my heart and soul and inspire me every day to be a better version of myself.

Thank you to my first readers who read this book (and the five that came before) and offered feedback and encouragement. Gemina Klein and Stephanie Roth-Goldberg—I lost count of how many times you both read this book and offered your honest thoughts. I'm endlessly grateful for the way you set time aside in your busy lives to read my writing. That's a gift I'll never take for granted. To Faith Matlin, Ali Wise, Felice Yudkin, Elle Marr, Kathleen Petrones, Robyn Roth, and so many others who read and offered insight, who listened and gave encouragement, who showed up for a young widow with a big dream, thank you a million times over.

An endless thank-you to my family, especially my mom, who showed me exactly what a solo mom can do when she puts her mind to it, and my brother, Eli Mekhlin. Susan and Rob, your support—in all areas—has meant the world to me. Becka Livesay, Jake Klein, Dan Goldberg, and Glenda Bryson, thank you for being part of this journey.

And last but not least, one huge thank-you to all my friends—near and far—and my Pilates family. I am lucky to be surrounded by so many brilliant and talented women who stepped in during the hardest days, who stepped in when it would have been so much easier to step away. I am forever grateful.

ABOUT THE AUTHOR

Elaine Roth is a New Jersey–based writer, parent, young widow, and comprehensively certified Pilates instructor. Her written work has appeared on Refinery29, Well+Good, Insider, HuffPost, and Scary Mommy, among others.

At the tender age of fourteen, Elaine had the chance to model in *YM* magazine. She was paired with a seventeen-year-old male model for a photo shoot about kissing. The article was titled "Kissing A–Z," and she was the photo underneath "O, orthodontics." In true fourteen-year-old-girl fashion, Elaine told all her friends about her modeling debut. Months later, the issue was published. The caption accompanying the photo was "Brace yourself, metal mouth. Don't lose your kissing cool."

Life has been throwing her curveballs ever since. She's grateful for the chance to share her writing with others and for the chance to make a little light out of things that are often too dark.

You can visit her online at www.elaineroth.com or on Instagram @theelaineroth.